THE
ARK

THE ARK

HARUO YUKI

TRANSLATED FROM THE JAPANESE BY JIM RION

PUSHKIN
VERTIGO

Pushkin Press
Somerset House, Strand
London WC2R 1LA

Hakobune © 2022 Haruo Yuki. All rights reserved.
First published in 2022 in Japan by Kodansha Ltd., Tokyo.
Publication rights for this English edition arranged through Kodansha Ltd.
English translation © Jim Rion, 2026

First published by Pushkin Press in 2026

ISBN 13: 978-1-80533-189-6

All rights reserved. No part of this publication may be reproduced, stored in a retrieval system or transmitted in any form or by any means, electronic, mechanical, photocopying, recording or otherwise, or for the purpose of training artificial intelligence technologies or systems without prior permission in writing from Pushkin Press

A CIP catalogue record for this title is available from the British Library

The authorised representative in the EEA is eucomply OÜ, Pärnu mnt. 139b-14, 11317, Tallinn, Estonia, hello@eucompliancepartner.com, +33757690241

Designed and typeset by Tetragon, London
Printed and bound in the United Kingdom by Clays Ltd, Elcograf S.p.A.

Pushkin Press is committed to a sustainable future for our business, our readers and our planet. This book is made from paper from forests that support responsible forestry.

www.pushkinpress.com

1 3 5 7 9 8 6 4 2

CONTENTS

Prologue   9

1 The Ark   11
2 Disaster and Murder   52
3 Severed Head   118
4 Knife and Nail Clippers   199
5 Choice   240

Epilogue   277

And behold, I Myself am bringing floodwaters on the earth, to destroy from under heaven all flesh in which is the breath of life; everything that is on the earth shall die.

But I will establish My covenant with you...

GENESIS 6: 17–18

PROLOGUE

The fluorescent lights on the hallway ceiling flickered dizzyingly.

The floor at our feet had an industrial feel, made of steel plates welded to a metal frame and covered with plastic sheeting. The walls, too, were steel plates, giving way in sections to protrusions of bare rock.

We were on the highest floor of three in this underground building. Even so, it was nearly ten metres below the surface.

Nine of us stood in the corridor, as solemn as a congregation preparing for service.

The door to room 120 stood open. A corpse, rope tied around its neck, lay in the narrow storage room.

The murderer had to be one of the nine people standing there. And no one knew who it could be except the murderer themselves.

No one spoke. Our ears were filled with the far-off hum of the generator.

It seemed, too, as if we could hear the sound of water filling the floor below. But that steady flow made no sound. It must have been our imagination.

We wanted to call for help, but our phones got no reception. Not just because we were below ground. Even if we could get out to the surface, we were deep in the mountains, far from any towns. There was no signal.

Someone had been murdered. Strangled to death.

For almost anyone, being faced with such a crime would be the shock of a lifetime.

But at that moment, it was not the murder that weighed most heavily on us.

The threat we faced was far greater than any single murderer. In fact, some of us were likely thinking that this murder might be the key that allowed us to break free of the trap we were caught in.

To escape this underground building, shaped like some kind of cargo ship buried in the mountains, one person among the nine of us would have to be sacrificed.

We would have to choose one person to die. Otherwise, we all would.

How to make that choice? Who among these nine people could… or *should* be sacrificed?

It had to be the one who killed our friend.

Every one of us except the murderer was thinking the same thing.

We had one week. We had to find the murderer before our time ran out.

ONE
The Ark

I

The seven of us left the path running alongside the highway and entered the woods. We stepped over fallen logs and waded through dead leaves along the way until we broke through to a secluded clearing overgrown with dead weeds.

Before us was an ancient-looking wooden bridge spanning a ravine about ten metres deep. The sun was already sinking out of sight behind the mountain peaks.

Ryuhei reached out one thickly muscled arm to grasp the railing of bundled staves and gave it a shake.

The bridge creaked, and at the sound, his chiselled wrestler's face crinkled. He turned to Yuya, standing beside him, and asked, 'Are we seriously going to cross that? You never said anything about this. It'll collapse!'

'Nah, it's fine. I went over before. It wasn't that bad. It's all right, see?'

Yuya stepped out onto the bridge and spread both arms wide as he rocked his body back and forth, showing off the bridge's stability.

Of course, it was not like there was any other choice. The rest of us followed him.

After we crossed the bridge, I took my smartphone out of the pocket of my jacket to check the time. It was 4.48 p.m.

When she saw me holding my phone, Hana, in her neon-coloured hiking outfit, sped up to walk next to me. She was holding her own phone in her right hand.

She asked, 'Shuichi, are you getting a signal?'

'No. Mine's been at zero bars for almost an hour.'

'Right. Mine, too. What do you think? We're not getting back to the house today, are we?'

No one answered. It was obvious there was no way we'd be making it back.

The terrain on the other side of the bridge was a rough meadow surrounded by steep mountainside. A few hundred paces on, Yuya suddenly shouted.

'There it is! I can see it! Just a little further. It's right there!'

Yuya, who must have been feeling our dissatisfied and doubtful glares burning into his back for some time, sounded relieved. But none of the rest of us saw anything like the entrance to a building.

This little adventure had started that morning. After we had all gone out for a boat ride on the lake, Yuya told us a story.

'There's this mad place within walking distance of here. Want to go and see? It's out in the woods, right, and there's this massive underground building. And, like, way back I bet they did messed-up shit there, but now no one even knows about it. No way.'

The day before, we had come to stay at a vacation house in Nagano Prefecture that belonged to Yuya's old man.

Yuya was a friend from our university days, and he'd invited us to all come out. There were six of us who had hung out together back then, so it was also a bit of a reunion.

It had been two years since we had last seen each other. Yuya, who had been known for his bleached hair and piercings, had let his hair go natural and taken the metal out, so he was almost a stranger in my eyes.

A certain sense of foreboding had driven me to bring my cousin along, making it seven of us in total.

An underground building in the mountains. It sounded like pure fantasy.

It's incredibly difficult to build anything underground, and Yuya made the place sound huge, so who would be able to construct something like that so far out in the mountains? And for what? It was hard to believe, but Yuya said he had actually been there about six months before.

It started to sound interesting, so we all agreed to go see it if it wasn't that far.

But now the reality was not living up to the promise. We walked and walked and never seemed to reach this 'underground building'. Yuya had made it sound like it would be maybe twenty or thirty minutes, but he had spent the past few hours staring uneasily at his map app.

This place was, of course, not listed on the map. Yuya said he'd dropped a pin in his app when he'd come here on his own, but it turned out the pin had actually been quite a bit off the mark. After wandering lost for a while, it was already nearing sundown by the time he figured out where we were.

'Well, Yuya? What's your plan? Are you seriously thinking we should spend the night in this underground building of yours? Cause there's no time to get back now. Is it safe? You did say it was really messed up, didn't you?'

'No, no, I said they got up to some messed-up shit there way back, is all. It'll be fine. There's no way anyone's there now. We can try out some abandoned building exploration.'

Ryuhei and Yuya had gone on about ten metres ahead of the rest of the group.

That was the way it had been the whole trip. Ryuhei acted like he spoke for all the rest of us and kept telling Yuya how unhappy we were.

Mai, walking beside me, shot me a strained grin. She seemed embarrassed by Ryuhei's bluster. In the gloom of nightfall, her long-lashed eyes seemed to float against her pale face.

I wanted to talk to her but kept my mouth shut, worrying that Ryuhei would notice. Mai didn't seem to want that either, since she quickly looked away before he could see us.

I looked behind me and saw Sayaka rushing to catch up. Her thick brown hair was up in a bun and her brow was running with sweat.

She asked something that seemed to have been worrying her for some time.

'Um, what is the toilet situation in this underground building of yours? And it looks like we'll be sleeping on the floor with our backpacks as pillows. Are you all OK with that?'

Yuya hadn't shared any details of the amenities with us before we left. We hadn't been planning on spending the night, anyway.

Shotaro, my cousin, who was walking nearby, answered her. 'You shouldn't get your hopes up. I imagine it's not going to be too pleasant. It'll surely be better than sleeping rough, though. And if it's underground, it shouldn't be too cold, at least.'

'Ah. You're right. And it does get cold out at night.' Sayaka accepted Shotaro's opinion easily enough.

The day before had been the first time my university friends ever met my cousin. He had fit in even better than I'd imagined.

Shotaro had inherited a fortune from his mother five years before, and ever since he'd avoided working. Instead, he went on trips, studied geology, just bounced around from here to there. At first it had seemed like he was planning on just burning through his inheritance, but then he would sometimes go overseas with a few million yen and come home with several times that.

As his cousin, I had known him much longer than any of my friends, of course. While I was closer to him than anyone else in my life, there was still a lot about him I didn't really understand.

The reason I'd invited him along was that I'd had a feeling this little gathering would end up stirring up some old conflict with another member of the group, and I'd wanted someone on my side. It had been easy to convince him to come. He said he wanted to check out the local rock formations.

The trouble I'd been fearing hadn't happened yet, but instead, now we had this surprise trip to some mysterious underground building. I was glad to have him there, since I was sure he could handle whatever happened, if anything did.

II

Yuya stopped short in the middle of a withered meadow. He pointed at the ground.

'Here! It's right here! The entrance!' he shouted.

He crouched down and pushed his hand though clumped dead weeds. He flipped up a round metal hatch, like a manhole cover, about eighty centimetres across.

We looked inside. The hole went straight into the ground. The sides were lined with concrete and steel bars embedded in the side formed a ladder.

'This is how we get in—'

'What?! No way. No. Look at how tight that is!' Hana interrupted him. She shone her smartphone light into the darkness. It was not bright enough to illuminate the floor.

I felt the same way. Of course we shouldn't have expected anything more comfortable than an old coal mine all the way out here, but from the way Yuya had been talking I'd expected something a bit more civilized.

'Yeah, sure, the entrance is a bit scary, but once we're inside it'll be fine. It's huge in there, I'm telling you. There are three floors. One night will be no problem.'

Hana and the others were clearly not convinced. I wasn't particularly keen on it, either.

Ryuhei was the first to break.

'Right, fine. I'm going to go see it. I just go through here, right?'

Ryuhei climbed down the ladder, trying not to let his backpack scrape against the concrete sides. Yuya glanced at the three women as if to gauge their reactions, then hurried after Ryuhei as if to keep him from claiming all the glory of being out in front.

Hana, Sayaka and Mai stood quietly whispering 'What are you going to do?' and 'Who's going to go first?' back and forth until, finally, they took it in turn to climb down the ladder. Shotaro and I brought up the rear.

After climbing down seven or eight metres, we touched ground.

A cave-like tunnel stretched out in front of us. It was quite high, so we could all pass through without so much as stooping.

It went down in a gentle slope. We all walked along it, shining our phone lights ahead.

A little way in, a massive boulder almost closed off the tunnel completely.

It looked too heavy for anyone to move by hand. And, for some reason, it was wrapped tightly in thick chains.

'What the hell? Were they trying to drag it out and gave up halfway or something?' I asked.

'I wonder,' Shotaro answered. His tone hinted at some deeper meaning.

We squeezed past the boulder and saw an iron door.

In front of it, the raw stone floor gave way to dirty wooden planking. Clearly, we were entering the main structure.

Yuya opened the door and shone his light inside.

'Whoa, it's true. Look at that!' Ryuhei said. It was hard to tell if he was impressed or intimidated.

The door had opened onto a wide corridor with a low ceiling. It twisted to one side up ahead, so we couldn't see very far along it, but from the way the sound of the door opening echoed, we could tell it must stretch out for a long way.

'Ugh. It reeks of mould,' Mai muttered.

The air was filled with a spoiled, stagnant odour. It was like the mouldy depths of a damp forest where the sun never reached, mixed with an almost chemical smell.

'How did they light this place? There's no way the mains reach out here.'

'They don't. There's a massive generator, though. It looked like it might actually run. If it doesn't, well, we'll just have to make do with our phones. I've got a power bank.'

Ryuhei and Yuya stepped through the doorway and into the dark corridor. Everyone filed fearfully after, holding up their lights like a parade of fireflies in the dark.

The floor was covered with a deteriorating layer of cheap-looking plastic, and the walls to either side were lined with doors like a hotel.

Just before the corridor turned left, Yuya pointed to the room door on the right. It had a plate reading 107.

'This is where the generator is. It didn't look broken, but still…' He turned the doorknob and shone his light into the room.

It looked like a general machinery room. The walls were lined with black cables which were bundled together and connected to a generator at the far end.

It was a fairly standard commercial power generator, about the size of a bathtub. I'd seen the same type once when working part-time at a hospital. An exhaust pipe ran up the wall and out through the ceiling. It looked older than I was, but the many liquid propane tanks fuelling it all looked relatively new.

We checked the tank gauges and saw they still had fuel left. Yuya and Ryuhei walked around the generator, trying to figure out how to start it up.

When he realized they had no idea what they were doing, Shotaro quietly said, 'First, make sure the tanks are hooked up properly. After that, I think we can get it going by turning on the engine switch and pulling the starter cord.'

Yuya did as he said, and the engine started up with a sound like a motorcycle.

A moment later, the fluorescent lights hanging from the ceiling began to flicker. Their blue-white light soon filled the facility.

'Oh, lovely. It would have been a real pain without any lights,' Sayaka said, glancing at the others' faces as she did.

With relief in the air, we left the machinery room.

The underground facility was filled with mystery. Now that the lights were on, we wanted to explore, but exhaustion won out over curiosity.

Yuya led everyone a few steps back up the corridor. He opened the door to room 106, on the opposite side.

'This used to be the dining room, it looks like. Might be nice to take a rest, yeah?' he said.

It was a large, rectangular room filled with long tables, which were all lined with decrepit old chairs. It looked like it could seat dozens of people at once.

Hana pulled out the nearest chair.

'Ugh, filthy. You think they'll hold?' she said.

The chairs were all simple things like you'd see in a school dining room. But they'd been in this dank underground room so long, they'd sprouted black mould and started to rot.

Hana gave the seat a wipe and gingerly sat down. The chair did not break.

On close inspection, I saw the long tables were covered with a cheap veneer. They were all rotting, and it looked like it would be dangerous to put much of your weight on one.

There was a sink in the back of the dining room. When I turned the tap, there was an airy coughing sound, then dirty water came sputtering out. I let it run for a bit. Soon it started to clear.

'Huh. There's still running water,' I muttered to myself.

There was a shelf for dishes above the basin. It was lined with heavy, old-fashioned plates and glasses.

Sayaka knelt down beside the wall, fussing with something.

'Oh, yes! The sockets are working. Look!'

She had plugged her smartphone charger into an electric socket hanging from a mess of exposed wires.

We all slowly gathered in the dining room, stretching and yawning.

There was little conversation. We all collapsed in exhaustion, like we used to do on arriving at a mountain hut to spend the night after a long hike. It was the first time during this gathering it truly felt like the old days.

But behind everyone's conspicuous stretching and relaxing, a heavy, uneasy mood filled the room. After a while, Shotaro tapped me on the shoulder.

'Shuichi, do you want to look around with me? This really is an interesting place.'

I had just been thinking about eating something, but I was also curious about this underground structure.

Just then, though, Yuya broke in, an eager look on his face. 'Um, if you're going to go exploring, Shotaro, I can show you around, right? I saw all kinds of stuff when I came the last time.'

We agreed, so the three of us left the dining room and started our exploration.

The low ceilings, dim fluorescent lights, filthy floors and walls made of cheap, drab materials, the exposed cabling running this way and that... It all gave the feel of a battered old cargo ship.

To add to the illusion, the space and layout felt like a ship's, too. The whole facility was built of steel plates welded to a latticed frame of steel braces. It was long and narrow, with three decks, and consisted of long corridors lined on both sides with what looked like storage rooms and bedrooms with simple bunk beds made from steel pipes.

Each door had a nameplate with a room number, like in a hotel. Going back to the entrance and standing with our backs to it, room 101 was on the right and room 102 on the left. As we went down the corridor, the numbers went up, 103, 104, and so on. Every room had a number, both storage and bedroom alike. There were crooked gaps between the doors and the surrounding wall, with no proper doorframes. The whole structure was similarly crude.

Room 104, next to the dining room, was the lavatory. It had four toilets in stalls, like you'd see in a public restroom. It also had a shower stall, though none of us felt like using it.

The air stank, but not enough to truly bother us. It seemed the building had been out of use so long that all traces of human waste had decayed past that point.

'The sewer pipes don't reach here, do they? I wonder where all the waste went,' I thought aloud.

'They probably gathered it in septic tanks then pumped it up above ground. Same with the rest of their wastewater,' Shotaro answered, staring into an old-fashioned squat toilet.

The toilets soon lost their fascination, and we returned to the corridor.

We went past room 107 and the machinery room, after which the corridor took a ninety-degree turn to the left. At the bend, there were metal stairs leading down to the middle floor.

We ignored them for the moment and continued along the corridor. Five metres further on, it turned back ninety degrees to the right. From there, the corridor was once more lined with doors. They started at 108, and the final room was numbered 120.

The walls outside the rooms showed bare, black stone poking through in places. It felt a lot like the stone walls of the tunnel back at the entrance. They were damp, and it looked like water was seeping out in spots.

It seemed that whoever built this underground facility had followed the shape of a naturally occurring cave. They built multiple floors, partitioned them with walls and furnished the whole like a building. That odd bend in the corridor was the result of a natural curve in the surrounding cave.

When we reached the end of the path, Shotaro spoke with the gravity of someone at the end of a museum tour.

'Twenty rooms. It must have cost a pretty penny. Overall, I'd say they did well. Although it was obviously totally illegal.'

'And you haven't seen everything yet. There are still two more floors,' said Yuya. He took the lead and guided us back to the stairs.

The next floor down was the same as the upper: a lightning bolt-shaped corridor lined on both sides with doors. It didn't have a large space, like the dining room above, and the area below the toilets above was occupied by the septic tanks. Still, there were twenty rooms, numbered 201 to 220, as Yuya explained.

The lower corridor was lit with fluorescents as well. However, just to the left of the stairs after coming down, the end of the corridor with lower-numbered rooms was dark. Lights were installed, but they weren't on. Perhaps a wire was cut somewhere, but since the other end was lit, it must be on another circuit.

Before we started looking into the rooms, Shotaro asked, 'How did you find this place, Yuya?'

'Oh, well, it was about six months ago, yeah? I got really into solo camping, and so I wanted to find some spot that absolutely no other arsehole knew about. So, I just kept going deeper into the hills, and I found that lid thing. I came inside, and it was just wild in here,' Yuya said. He stood in the middle of the corridor and spread his arms wide. 'What the hell is this place? Who built it? And what for? I got to tell you, they surely did some messed-up stuff in here. I can feel it.'

Shotaro thought for a moment, then said, 'I think this was probably a base for some kind of militant group. About fifty years ago or so.'

'Seriously? Militants? Like, back in the seventies?'

'I haven't examined it very closely, but the structure looks like something from those days. And there was that big boulder in the middle of the entrance tunnel, right? The only explanation I can think of for that is, it's an emergency barricade. They'd use it to block that metal door if anyone tried to get in. But it looks like some other criminal group used it after them. Recently, I imagine. The wiring was installed twenty years ago, at the earliest. I don't think any of the old militant groups lasted that long.'

A similar, if less concrete, suspicion had been forming in my mind. There really wasn't any other explanation for why someone would build something like this underground in the mountains. They didn't want to be found. But speaking the words aloud like that only made the place feel creepier.

Shotaro went on, his voice cheerful. 'Well, anyway, I think I'd need to look closer to get a better idea.'

He walked into room 208, which was right in front of us. It appeared to be storage for refuse.

We poked through it looking for anything useful, but there as only a pile of rubbish: used work gloves, rusted sickles, old speakers, copper pipes and scraps of wood. Some of it was practically ancient, while some was relatively new. It was like a mounded rubbish tip.

'Huh! It looks like even denizens of the criminal underground sometimes wear straw hats,' Shotaro said. He was grinning as he showed me a wide-brimmed straw hat with a crumpled crown.

I grinned back. 'Guess so. I was wondering if we might turn up an old pistol or little bags of white powder, if you get me. But not here.'

'They'd have taken the really bad stuff with them when they pegged it. If whoever hid out here even messed with that stuff. Maybe if we combed the place, we might find something interesting.' Shotaro placed the hat on top of a battered wooden box.

We moved on to room 209, across the corridor at an angle from 208.

At first glance, it appeared to be dedicated to another pile of junk. It was smaller than the first one, but there was a pile of rubbish in one corner.

When we turned on the lights, though, we saw that the things inside were not nearly as mundane as those in 208. With all that talk about criminal organizations using this place, I'd imagined things like weapons and drugs, but what we actually found was somehow more unpleasant.

The first thing my eye fell on was a restraint with four hand and ankle cuffs attached to long chains. In the back of the room was a blackened chair of steel pipes with a seat that rose to an unpleasant point.

There were other things, too. A thick wooden rod wrapped in leather, and a mystifying contraption made of a metal frame just big enough for a person's head to fit inside with vice-like devices attached. There were piles of rusted spikes and concrete blocks, as well.

Yuya, Shotaro and I exchanged looks. We were almost embarrassed, as if we'd accidentally glimpsed a stranger's intimate secrets.

Yuya walked over to a corner of the room and crouched down. He pointedly did not touch anything.

'No way. Bloody hell. These are for torturing people, right?' he said. His voice was thick with emotion.

'Obviously,' Shotaro replied.

It seemed Yuya hadn't seen this room the last time he'd come. 'You think they actually used this shit?'

'I don't really know, but it looks like it, right? I've only seen stuff like this in museums. I always doubted they were real, though.'

The torture devices were old and rusted. It's not like they were covered in blood, but they were far too worn just to be tasteless decorations. I looked around at the floor. There were long furrows in the plastic lining, as if someone had been scratching at the floor, writhing in pain.

I'd read about incidents where internal conflict in the militant extremist groups of the 1970s had sometimes exploded into infighting, even murder. If we were right about the history of this building, then it probably shouldn't be so shocking to find implements of torture here.

The dead metallic structure suddenly seemed to take on an aura of bloody violence.

'But, you know, there's no proof they were used, right?' Yuya pressed him.

'No. And even if they were, it would have been ages ago. These are all just relics of history.'

Yuya seemed relieved at Shotaro's calm pronouncement.

I decided to let his words convince me not to let whatever had happened here in the past bother me too much. Naturally,

I'd never had any contact with torture devices in my life before, and no matter how twisted things might get in my future, I surely never would again.

We went and had a look around the other rooms nearby, but there wasn't anything else even half as troubling.

'Oh, hey, Yuya, you said there were three floors, right? How do we get down to the bottom one?' Shotaro asked. We couldn't see any stairs going down from where we were.

'Right, the way down is at the very end of the corridor, but you don't really want to go down there. For all kinds of reasons. Well, let's go over and see. You'll understand.'

Yuya led us onward.

The numbers on the doors got lower as we walked. The lights were off in this part of the corridor. It wasn't so dark we couldn't see our way, but I turned my phone light on all the same.

We saw a heavy steel door at the very end. It was similar to the door at the entrance to the building, but smaller scale.

He pointed at it.

'I think the way into this place is right above us, see?'

Thinking back on the way we'd come, I guessed he was right.

Yuya slowly opened the door.

This was a space totally unlike the other rooms. Inside, there was a narrow opening in the rock, like the mouth of a bottle, and beyond that, all the walls were exposed black stone. The ceiling was lined with metal plates only at the very entrance, and it was lower here than anywhere else. Beyond that lining was a lip of stone. This room alone remained an unfinished cave.

On the wall at the very back of the room was a device like a winch off some sunken ship.

'What the hell is that? It's covered in rust.' The winch was wound with thick chain. The chain ran round a pulley, then up through the ceiling to the upper floor.

'Ah! I bet that's the chain wrapped around that huge boulder!' I said.

'It must be. I told you it was a barricade,' Shotaro replied.

Turning the winch would drag that rock down the tunnel to block the metal door above.

'Right. Just like you said, isn't it? A barricade. I didn't really give it much thought. That's why this is the only room without any lining on the ceiling, so they can run the chain through more easily.'

'I suppose. There might be more to it than that, though,' Shotaro said, sounding intrigued.

'Oh, and then the stairs down to the bottom floor are over here. But we can't use them. See?'

Yuya pointed toward the back right of the room.

There was a large square hole cut in the floor, and stairs leading down.

We went over close to look down and immediately understood what Yuya meant.

The stairs to the bottom floor were underwater from the fourth step down. It looked like the water almost came up to the ceiling of the floor below. I crouched down and stretched my hand as far as I could. I could just barely touch the surface.

'It's cold!' I exclaimed. 'Are you serious? The place is flooded?'

'It's underground. And it was built by amateurs. Since it's surrounded by natural rock, of course it's flooding. Nature is just taking its course. I imagine the pump that would normally take the water out is broken. That might even be why they abandoned the place,' Shotaro explained.

The bare rock on the walls of the floor above had, in fact, felt like they were seeping water.

'Yeah, I doubt they were hoping for some kind of holiday home with a pool. Honestly, I'm a bit scared now. This is going to eventually flood the whole building, isn't it? If it doesn't stop, I mean,' I said.

Yuya laughed out loud.

'Yeah, eventually, if you want to speak theoretically or whatever. But it's going to take a while. It doesn't look like the water level has changed at all since I was here six months ago. It might have come up a bit. So, maybe in five years or something.'

That was a relief, at least.

I shone my light down into the water and could see that the bottom floor looked like it had been left mostly unfinished, with exposed girders and bars held in place with concrete.

There wasn't much else to see, so we went back out into the corridor and returned the way we came.

As we approached the stairs, we saw Sayaka walking down the other end of the corridor with her smartphone held out. It looked like she was taking pictures of everything.

'Yuya, is that tunnel we came through the only way in? It seems odd that they'd only have one entrance or exit,' Shotaro asked.

'No, actually, there is one more, but we can't use it. You know that bottom level? There's a narrow tunnel from there leading up to the surface, almost like a rubbish chute or something. But we can't get there because it's flooded.'

'I see.'

'Oh, right! There's kind of a map in the machinery room. You could see for yourself,' Yuya offered.

The three of us went back there together.

Yuya went over to a desk and opened the drawer. It was packed with random things. Old sticking plasters, nail clippers, biros and stationery.

He pulled it all out and put it on the desktop. Finally, he dug out a piece of A2 sized paper folded into fourths. It had a diagram printed on it.

'Here it is. I stuffed it way in the back last time.'

It wasn't exactly what I would have called a map, more of a building plan for the whole facility. It was yellowed and tattered and looked like it was made when the place was first built.

At the top, someone had later written in biro, 'The Ark'. That must be the name they'd used for this place.

The Ark was, as we had already seen, a long, narrow three-level structure with a bend in the middle like a backwards zed. The diagram showed that the bottom floor was not divided into many smaller rooms like the upper two, but a few large ones. The tunnel we'd taken was at the western end, and at the east end of the lowest floor there was another tunnel leading up to the surface.

'You see. The tunnel that opens near the bridge must have been an emergency exit. It has the same kind of flip-up hatch

THE ARK: FLOOR PLAN

THE ARK: CROSS-SECTION

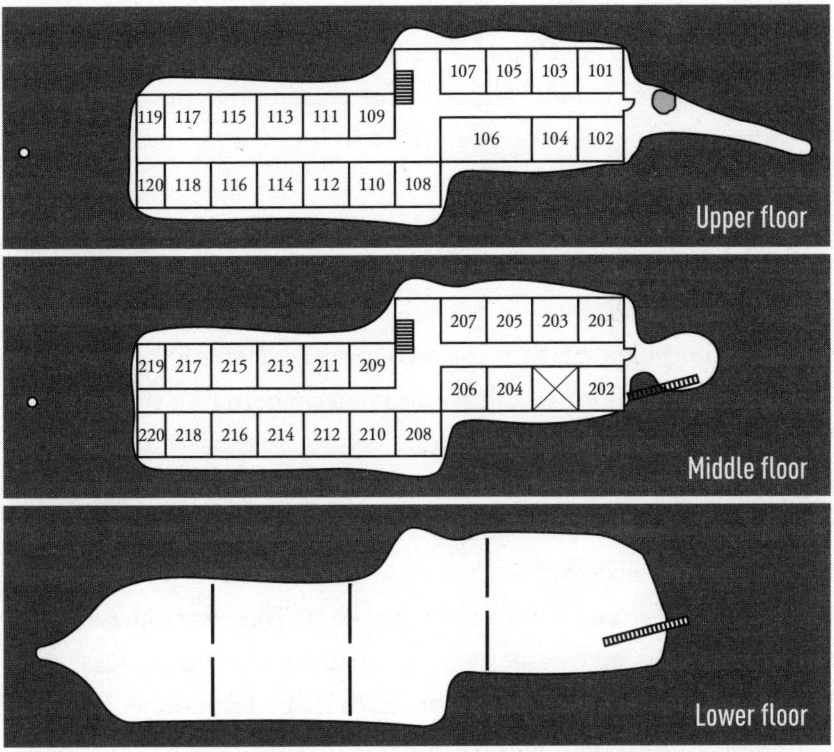

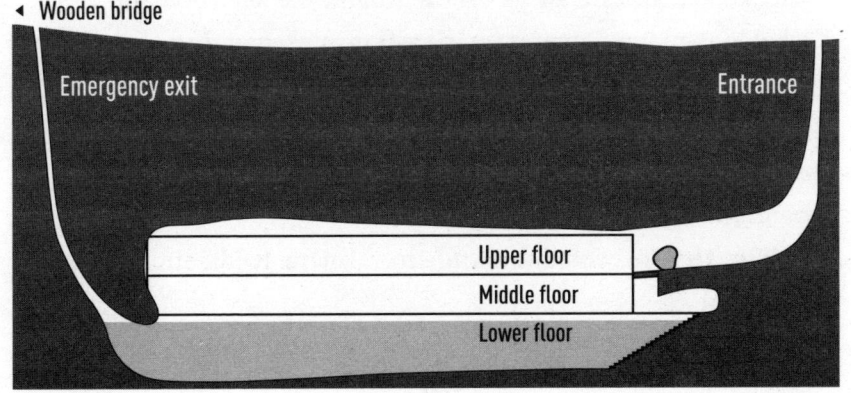

as the one we came through. We passed it on the way here, actually. And I bet no one even noticed it,' Yuya said.

So, the other hatch had been just by that terrifying bridge we'd crossed. I hadn't noticed, of course, but neither had Shotaro. It had already been dusk by that time, so that was no surprise.

'Did you look inside, Yuya? Is it just like the layout shows?' I asked.

'Oh, yeah, I did. I even tried climbing down into it. There's a ladder, and I got all the way down to around where the ceiling of the bottom floor would be, and that's where I hit the water. So, I came back up.'

'Not much of an emergency exit, then, is it?' Something else caught my attention. 'What are those?' I said, pointing at the wall above the desk.

There were two CRT monitors there. They were the kind of old fifteen-inch screens we used to have in our library at school to watch video cassettes. Each had a label on its bezel. One read 'Entrance' and the other 'Emergency Exit'.

'Right, those! I noticed them when I was here before. I think they're monitors for surveillance cameras. See the labels? I checked at the entrances on my way home last time and saw what looked like cameras up in trees near each of those hatches. One by each. So, I figure the video must feed to here, right? But last time the power wasn't on so I couldn't check.'

While he rattled on, Yuya reached out and switched the two monitors on.

'Oh, they're working! And the camera feeds are coming through!'

The two monitors came to life with a quiet electric buzz and displayed the video from the two surveillance cameras.

The sun had already set, so the images were as murky and blurry as an old woodcut. The cameras were certainly as old as the monitors, so the image likely never got very clear.

Even so, we could make out the withered grass of the meadows above. The moonlight showed a peculiar hump in the middle of each: the entrance hatches. The video feeds would show if anyone came near either one.

Yuya traced the shape of each hatch with a finger as he went on.

'Look, here, this is the entrance we came in through. And this one is the emergency exit, near the bridge.'

'So that would put them about a hundred metres apart from each other.'

'That's right. About that much. East and west. If anyone stumbled on either one, whoever was in here could escape through the other one,' Yuya answered.

Setting up and running the wiring for cameras must have been a real effort. I was astonished.

'This is some tight security. What did they get up to in here?' I wondered aloud.

'This place might actually have been used by some kind of cult for special discipline or the like. The way they set up the cameras is a bit weird if they were just worried about people sneaking in. It looks to me more like they were worried about people escaping,' Shotaro said.

It was a convincing argument.

'You think they really did name it after Noah's ark, like in the Old Testament?' I asked.

'I can't think of any other place they could have got the name from.'

I thought back on my limited experience with the Bible. I'd flipped through it for a cultural anthropology lecture in my university days. The famous story of Noah and his ark was just a short section at the beginning of the Old Testament.

The Lord found that the world was overcome with wickedness. He then came to Noah, the only righteous man, and told him that he had decided to destroy humanity. Noah was to build an ark to survive the coming flood. When the ark was complete, Noah and his family and two of every animal on the earth, male and female, went into the ark, and waters covered the surface of the earth. Or, that was how I remembered the story going. The original text was relatively direct, just talking about Noah building the ark and riding out the flood. Many of the stories based on it, though, both novels and films, showed people mocking the pious Noah and his family as they built the ark on a mountaintop.

A facility built deep in the mountains in the shape of a ship… The 'Ark' name might have been a later addition, but it certainly seemed to fit.

It seemed a pretty poor joke to me. I could see no signs of piety in this weird old building underground. All we'd found of note was a pile of torture devices.

None of our group were particularly religious or political. Rather than being part of Noah's pious clan, we would surely have ended up on the other side with the mocking bystanders.

'Hey, what are you lads up to?' Sayaka stood looking in through the open door. The sound of our voices must have leaked from the machinery room.

She was soon followed by Hana, who'd apparently been looking for Sayaka.

'There you are, Sayaka. Were you out taking pictures?'

'Oh, yeah. I wanted to record it all, since I doubt I'll ever come back.'

She explained how she'd looked into quite a few of the rooms and taken pictures of what was inside.

'That's fine and all, just don't be posting them online anywhere. If any of the old owners saw, it could be a pain.'

'Oh, right. That makes sense. I'll keep them to myself.'

While Sayaka and Hana stood talking, Mai and Ryuhei came up together.

All the others had been as curious about the inside of the building as we had been and gone on their own explorations. Now, all seven of us were gathered in the machinery room.

The others were surprised to see the monitors switched on.

Yuya started filling them in on what he'd already shared with Shotaro and me: the flooded bottom floor, the emergency exit and the cameras.

'Yeah, all right. I think we get it,' Hana interrupted him. 'But right now, I want to go outside for a bit. I got a message from my boyfriend around noon. If I don't answer today, he might end up dropping by the house while I'm out.' She tapped the smartphone in her hand as she spoke.

Yuya's face wrinkled in a frown. 'Oh, but listen, the reception out here is really bad.'

'I know. I just want to go out and try it out. If it doesn't work, I'll give up. Anyone want to come with me?'

Anyone would be nervous walking around alone in pitch dark mountain woods.

'Well then, I'll come along, shall I?' Yuya offered.

Hana, though, seemed less than pleased at the idea of going out alone with Yuya.

Sayaka threw her a lifesaver.

'I suppose I should try, too. I've probably got some work emails waiting. Is that all right?'

'Oh, really? Great! Thank you!'

And it was settled. Hana, Sayaka and Yuya would be going outside for a bit.

When the three of them left, Ryuhei came up behind me and stood staring at the monitors.

'Are those really live?'

From a distance, the poor quality meant the screens almost looked dead.

But before I could answer, there was movement on the monitors.

'Oh, there they are.'

The camera looking over the entrance hatch caught the three signal seekers arising from the tunnel.

The silhouette in the lead waved a hand at the camera. That must have been Yuya. Then came Hana in her gaudy jumper, followed by Sayaka. Their faces were hidden in the dark.

A little while later, three figures holding glowing smartphones appeared in the emergency exit feed. They crossed the bridge, probably heading for higher, open ground in search of a signal.

'I guess they are working,' Ryuhei muttered, apparently convinced.

Then he and Mai went over to the desk and started rifling through the stuff Yuya had piled there. Eventually, they got tired of it. Ryuhei took Mai's hand, and they left.

Shotaro and I stood silently in the machinery room, staring at the monitors.

With nothing better to do, I asked my cousin a question that had just popped into my head.

'Do you think the others have eaten?'

'No idea.'

We'd all been so caught up in exploring the place, I doubted any of us had eaten anything yet.

Yuya, Hana and Sayaka came back about thirty minutes later. We spotted them through the monitors easily enough.

But something was different.

'Wait… There's more of them now? How could that be?'

The three figures on the monitor had doubled. There were six people out there now.

It was like something out of a horror film. Shotaro and I headed to the entrance to see what was going on.

Yuya was the first through the door. He was followed by Hana. Her jumper was muddy now. She must have fallen somewhere.

Then came Sayaka.

And behind her, a family of three, clearly nervous about the whole situation.

The father looked to be in his fifties, with trimmed salt-and-pepper hair and glasses with thick black frames. Mother was a bit chubby and had short-cut hair. Their heavy-lipped son looked in his early teens.

Sayaka started explaining as soon as she saw our faces.

'So, apparently these folks got lost in the woods, right? And we ran into them and brought them with us. Just, you know, for shelter and all. What was it, you were mushroom hunting, I think you said?'

The father answered.

'That's right. Sorry to barge in like this.'

It was mushroom season, in fact, but they certainly had come deep into the mountains for it.

It wasn't as if this was our house, but we still invited them to the dining room.

As we walked down the corridor, I whispered to Hana as she brushed pine needles from her shoulders, 'Did you find any reception?'

'Nothing. It's like a dead zone or something. I bet the people who used this place abandoned it because they couldn't get a proper internet connection.'

It was as good a reason as any, I supposed.

III

The seven of us and the new trio sat across a long dining room table from each other.

The wife and son kept glancing nervously between us and the strange building, like people who'd accidentally stumbled into a stranger's wedding.

'We're sorry to intrude on you all like this. We're the Yazakis. I'm Kotaro Yazaki,' the father started the introductions. 'I'm an electrician. I grew up around here, but I just didn't pay any attention on the walk and got us all lost. On one of our rare family trips, even! This is my wife—'

'Hiroko Yazaki. Pleased to meet you.' Hiroko spoke nervously, a grim expression on her face.

'And this is our son. Just started high school. Come on, introduce yourself, then.'

'I'm Hayato,' the boy said, staring downward.

I was surprised to hear he was as old as that.

Spending the night in some unknown building with his parents, thrown together with a bunch of older men and women he'd never met… He must have been utterly miserable. I recalled once when I went out to karaoke with some friends in middle school and we ran into a classmate out with his family. The look on his face stuck with me still.

'And what about you all?'

Sayaka explained that we had been in a hiking club together back in our university days, that Yuya had invited us to come stay at his father's vacation house the day before, that we'd come to this building on his word, and that it had got too late for us to go back.

'Oh, so, you're all students?' Kotaro asked.

'No, we've graduated. Um. My name's Sayaka Nouchi. I'm a yoga teacher in Tokyo.'

'Oh, yes, you certainly look it,' Yazaki said, probably noting her dyed hair and suntanned skin. His wife and son grimaced at the unneeded commentary.

'I guess we'll just take turns, then. Come on, you next!' Sayaka poked Hana, sitting next to her, in the thigh.

'Oh. Um. I'm Hana Takatsu. I'm just a regular office worker.'

The three Yazakis bowed their heads briefly. They seemed somehow comforted by petite Hana, with her bobbed hair and round face.

'Next!'

'What is this, speed dating? Anyway, I'm Yuya Nishimura. I work in fashion. Nice to meet you.'

Yuya scratched his cheek nervously, as if trying to hide embarrassment.

'Ryuhei Itoyama. I'm a gym instructor. A pleasure.'

Ryuhei had the physique to match the job, certainly, and the Yazakis nodded in understanding. The next introduction, though, seemed to surprise them.

'I'm Mai Itoyama. I'm a nursery school teacher.'

'Another Itoyama?' Yazaki could be rather blunt, it seemed. 'Are you married, then?'

'Yes, that's right.'

'Imagine that! Oh, beg your pardon, it's just you're so young. So, you met in a university club! How nice.'

The last comment felt rather forced.

Young as they were, they'd already been married for two years. And still, it was hard for anyone to see Ryuhei and Mai as a couple. Or it was for me, anyway.

My turn came, and so I followed the others' leads and introduced myself. 'Shuichi Koshino. I'm a systems engineer.'

And as we came to the last person, Sayaka rushed to interject, 'Oh, sorry, I just told you that we were all in the hiking club together, but he's different. He's related to Shuichi—'

'Yes, I'm Shotaro Shinoda. Shuichi's cousin. He asked me to come along because I had some interest in the local area. Nice to meet you.'

I imagined that the Yazaki family had already noticed something a bit different about Shotaro. While everyone else was dressed in practical outdoor gear, he alone was done up in a striped getup totally unfit for the mountains. He was also three years older than the rest of us, and taller than anyone else present.

For a moment, Kotaro looked at Shotaro with open suspicion. He quickly hid it with a smile, though, and said,

'Pleasure to make your acquaintances. How did you all find out about this place? Did you have anything to do with it before?'

Yuya was the one who answered.

'No, no, it's not like this is our place or anything.'

He went on to explain how he had discovered the building on his lone camping adventures. He then added Shotaro's speculation about how it might have been built by an extremist group, then used by some kind of criminal organization or cult. Naturally, he left out our discovery of the torture tools.

Even so, the family members kept exchanging nervous glances, clearly worried they might have stumbled into somewhere genuinely dangerous.

Shotaro tried to comfort them.

'Anyway, we should be fine for just an evening. Think of it like one of those prison-themed hotels or something. It clearly hasn't been used in a while, so I wouldn't worry too much.'

Yuya piped in, 'Oh, right! You really don't need to worry about anyone coming in. Nothing has been touched in the six months since my first time. I took lots of pictures then, and everything is exactly the same. Honestly, I wasn't planning for any of us to spend the night or anything, but we ended up taking a bit of a detour on the way. I really thought it was closer than it was. Sorry, everyone.'

He bowed in mild chagrin.

If all had gone to plan, right now we should have been in the much more comfortable surroundings of his family holiday home, playing cards and having some drinks.

As the same dissatisfaction was likely roiling up inside all of us, Sayaka blurted out, as if to cut off any budding arguments, 'Well, it's not like we can help it now. But the Yazakis were in trouble, so it might actually be for the best, right? It's no season to be sleeping rough out there. Mr Yazaki, I know how you feel, but can I ask you to consider staying here for the night? It might be hard if any of you have claustrophobia, though.'

'Well, it is just for the evening. Right?' Kotaro said and looked at his family.

'But, how do you all feel about us being here? It almost feels like we're intruding. I hope you don't mind us also being here for the evening,' Sayaka said, and the family finally seemed to accept we weren't some gang of lunatics they needed to worry about.

She went on in a more cheerful voice, 'Hey! Would you like something to eat? I'm starving, myself. Did you bring any food with you, Mr Yazaki?'

Which reminded everyone of our hunger, forgotten in all

the introductions and explanations. Everyone started rummaging through their packs.

Our group had stopped at a convenience store that afternoon and bought our own snack buns and such, as well as a load of nibbles we'd been planning on taking back to the house for the evening drinks. The facility shelves also had tins and other preserved food, but no one was of a mind to try anything of unknown age or provenance.

Hiroko Yazaki opened her backpack and took out two homemade rice balls, probably left over from lunch, to divide between the three of them.

'Is that enough for you all? Here, take some of this.'

Hana handed over three packs of sweet bean jelly. Hayato mumbled a barely audible 'Thank you' as he took one.

After that, the rest of us divvied up our packets of fish sausage, chocolates and whatnot until the Yazakis had as much of a dinner as the rest of us.

When we'd finished eating, Ryuhei said, 'What about beds, then?'

'When I was looking around, I found a bunch of mattresses and sleeping bags lying around. They're a bit dusty, of course,' Sayaka said.

Some of the rooms had been outfitted with bedding, like dormitories. We would be better set up for sleeping than most mountain huts, in fact.

'All right then. Mr Yazaki, when you all are ready for bed, just take whatever room you like. If you don't mind, would you put something in front of the door? That way, the rest of us will know it's taken.'

'We'll do that, sure,' he answered after glancing at his family to see if they minded. 'Well, thank you all. I think we'll be turning in now.'

'Of course. Goodnight,' Sayaka said in her clear, piercing voice. The family went off in search of a place to sleep.

IV

It was after eight o'clock in the evening.

The seven of us were still in the dining room. We couldn't lie in our sleeping bags looking at the internet on our phones, so none of us was in any hurry to go to bed.

The atmosphere in the dining hall was dull as death. We were all a bit reserved with the Yazakis there. It felt like we had decided that their presence meant the gathering couldn't be any fun at all.

Sayaka had tried her best to smooth things over, but I was still on the verge of blowing up at Yuya for getting us into this.

I'm sure the others felt the same. But it wouldn't do any good to make the mood any darker.

When Hana finally broke the silence, it was obvious she was trying to keep the depth of her dissatisfaction under wraps.

'Well, there's no chance I'm actually getting any sleep tonight. Come on, you just know somebody has died here.'

Yuya's face was twisted in a nasty grin when he answered, 'Oh, yeah. And that's not all, you can bet. The people who used this place were some bad bastards, I just know it.'

Apparently the three of us had been the only ones to stumble on the torture room down below, and we hadn't told anyone about it yet. Even so, Hana had sensed the disquieting aura that filled the Ark.

'Like, you know this place wasn't designed by any experts or anything, right? And there's no way they had proper builders in to do the work. Somebody surely died in the middle of all that. Working in a cave like this has to be deadly dangerous. And the shady people behind this would have known how to get rid of the bodies so no one could find them, for sure. Like, they could be buried all around here.'

Shotaro interrupted.

'That's certainly plausible. There are stories about people dying during legitimate, even famous construction projects.'

At that point, it started to feel like we'd locked ourselves in a house of death as some kind of test of courage.

Hana yawned as she continued insisting she wouldn't sleep.

'It'd be the worst to die underground like this. No way I could deal,' she muttered.

'Where would be a good place to die?' Ryuhei asked.

'Nowhere at all. But I couldn't bear any place where I can't see the sky. When I die, I want it to be outside in a tulip field and feel like going to sleep. What about the rest of you, then? What do you reckon is the worst way to die?'

Hana had found a conversation topic befitting this dark subterranean space.

With nothing else to do, everyone gave the question their full consideration.

Yuya was first to answer.

'I think it's that one way with the horses, you know. Like, back in the Middle Ages, when they'd tie your arms and legs to four horses and tear you apart.'

'Ugh, for real. That sounds horrible.'

Next was Sayaka.

'I hear when there's a fire, it's supposed to be best to inhale smoke and pass out, but if you don't and you just burn to death it must be excruciating. What do you all think?'

'Burning to death! Ugh! A long, slow death would be terrifying.'

Then Ryuhei decided to add his opinion.

'No one wants a slow death. Like, being buried alive.'

'Oh, totally. How about you, Shuichi?'

I answered, 'Death by overwork.'

Then it was Shotaro's turn, and he said, 'Lingering death from illness.'

Mai was the last one left. She thought for a long time, then answered,

'I would hate to drown. Death by drowning would definitely be the worst.'

She had been quiet since we'd all gathered yesterday, and her voice was still low.

'I was thinking, if there was any kind of Unpleasant Death Ranking, things like being strangled or stabbed would barely rank at all, right? There are so many worse ways to die,' said Hana, ending the discussion with this disturbing pronouncement.

I wasn't deliberately trying to stoke up the haunted house mood, but it seemed like something everyone should know. So, I told them what we'd found down below.

The general reaction was pretty much the same as mine when I saw the things. Surprise, but more than that, a reluctance to really consider the possibility that people had been tortured here. It was like watching a news story about a foreign country. It felt like it had nothing to do with us.

But everyone did seem to withdraw a bit after that. They talked less. It seemed we had all come to clearly understand something we'd only vaguely sensed before: this Ark was no proper place for us to be.

V

It was after nine.

Hana was the first to stand up.

'I'm going to bed. Not much else to do, is there?'

'Oh, then, I will, too,' Sayaka said and followed her out. The two had stayed in the same room at the vacation house, too.

Yuya followed suit and stood up. He had been feeling the silent pressure of everyone's discomfort.

'I think I'll go to bed, too.'

And just like that, there were only four of us left in the dining room. I was suddenly very uncomfortable.

Ryuhei glared at me, like there was something he wanted to say. But when he did finally speak, it wasn't what I'd been expecting.

'So, where are you bedding down tonight, Shuichi?'

'Oh, uh, I haven't given it much thought. I'll just look for something later. I'll go wherever Shotaro goes, I guess.'

'Right. Well, we're off, then.'

Ryuhei and Mai stood and left together. And then it was just Shotaro and me.

We sat in silence for a while. I'm sure Shotaro noticed how uncharacteristically curt I'd been talking to Ryuhei just now.

Shotaro and I decided to take room 112.

It was almost completely empty, with only a set of bare steel shelves. We dragged in some mattresses and sleeping bags from a nearby storeroom. At the very least, we wouldn't freeze in our sleep.

'I'm not very keen on these sleeping bags.' I inspected everything carefully, hoping not to find any dodgy stains. I even sniffed them.

'Before you start whinging about the bags, try giving your own socks a sniff. This lot isn't that bad. It's no worse than any mountain hut.'

'Maybe, but still, some criminal type probably used them.'

Shotaro had already crawled into bed and was resting his head on his laced fingers. He watched my inspection with indifference.

I eventually satisfied myself that there was no visible proof that my bag had been used to wrap a corpse, so I spread it on my mattress. I'd brought a change of clothes, since we'd started the day at the lake, but I decided to sleep in my sweaty hiking clothes.

I was about to switch the lights off when my smartphone suddenly buzzed. I had a call notification.

How could I be getting a call without any network connection? I checked the screen, and saw it was coming through an offline walkie-talkie app we used. It let phones within a few dozen metres of each other communicate directly even where there was no network access.

I saw that it was Mai calling.

'Hello?'

'Oh, it worked. Shuichi? Is that you? Sorry, I just wanted to give the app a try. I was wondering if everyone else had already uninstalled it.'

Everyone in our hiking club had installed the app back in university days. We thought it would come in handy out in the mountains. But in the end, we'd hardly ever ended up using it. I guess the only ones who hadn't deleted it were Mai and me.

'Is Ryuhei there?'

'He went off to the toilet. He's not feeling well, he said. Anyway. See you tomorrow.'

She sounded about to hang up but added one more rushed comment before she did.

'This must be really tense for you. We shouldn't have come. Sorry.'

'No, not at all. I think we're over all that at this point. But what about Ryuhei? How's he doing with it?'

'He's fine now. Right, then.'

She hung up.

When I turned around, I was faced with Shotaro grinning nastily at me, like he'd seen through everything.

'So, Shuichi, don't you think it's about time you told me just what's up with you and the Itoyamas?'

'It's not nearly as interesting as you probably think.'

But he was right, it was time to stop trying to keep things under wraps. I lowered my voice and told him the story.

'This was maybe a year ago. Mai came to me in secret to talk about how Ryuhei was acting. Things like, when he was in a bad mood he'd start complaining about how her cooking wasn't healthy enough, or how she spent too much money. And there were other things, like how he'd not wear his seatbelt when driving out in the country. It feels like those two got married before they even started going out.'

'Is that so? Huh…'

Even though we'd all known each other in university, I still didn't really understand how they had ended up married. They started dating just after graduation, and since I'd been busy looking for work, I never even noticed. All I knew was that Ryuhei had been the one to approach her.

Then, just a few months later, they got married. The way Mai put it, she'd got tired of the whole dating thing, so she just went along with the idea.

'I've known Ryuhei since middle school, so I know what kind of guy he is. But that doesn't mean I know how to deal with all his nonsense. All I could say was, I wasn't surprised. He's always been a difficult guy. But I guess he figured out somehow that Mai came to ask me about that stuff. Since then, I haven't heard a word from her. Then came Yuya's invitation, and when I found out the two of them were coming, I started to get a little worried.'

'I see. And? Did you invite me along to aid in your nefarious plan to steal another man's wife?'

'Nothing so grandiose as all that. It really isn't like that, either. I was just really scared. I don't know what Ryuhei actually thinks about anything. I had this idea he'd go off on me. Not physically hurt me, or anything, just humiliate me. I was more worried about emotional pain than physical.'

If I got into it with Ryuhei, the real damage would be to my self-esteem. That really was my biggest worry, and so I'd brought my cousin as a kind of buffer in case things did start to go sideways.

Shotaro was still grinning.

'It looks like I didn't need to be so worried, anyway. Now I'm sorry I dragged you into all this.'

'Don't worry about it. It gave me a chance to see this fascinating building, after all.'

'Seriously? Well, I'm glad of that. Now that I see them together, Mai and Ryuhei seem much more normal than I expected. I do think Ryuhei's got his eye on me, but that's nothing. And now we just get up and go home tomorrow.'

'If that's good enough for you, it's good enough for me. Of course, it's not over yet.'

Shotaro might have secretly wanted to stoke the flames of hope, but somehow his tone struck me as ominous.

The conversation ended. I switched off the lights and crept into my sleeping bag.

The fluorescents in the corridor were still on. The door was framed in a bright rectangle of leaking light.

It would probably be best if we all got up as soon as the sun rose and left first thing in the morning.

We would hike back to the holiday house, get in our cars and go back to Tokyo. I imagined we would all be in a hurry to get home.

TWO
Disaster and Murder

I

The sound of metal rattling against metal woke me up.

It was a sound that shouldn't have been, a sound of terrible portent. I sat up and looked around, trying to figure out where it was coming from. I saw that the steel shelves lining the walls were moving.

When I saw that, it finally broke through that it was actually the room that was moving.

'Earthquake? Shit!'

My brain was still half asleep, so it took a while for me to remember exactly where we were. We were not in a typical building. We were underground, deep in the mountains.

'Hey! Watch out, there! Best get away.'

Shotaro was already up. He grabbed my arm as I sat blinking blearily around and pulled me away from the shelves.

I rolled off the mattress onto the floor.

Shotaro grabbed the doorknob to keep his balance. The steel shelves toppled over as the shaking grew fiercer. The sound of things falling and breaking echoed through the building. There was a short scream. It sounded like Hana.

The building itself was beginning to give off a metallic shriek, like a rusted saw cutting though hardwood. I could not help picturing the whole place collapsing into a chasm opening up below us.

The shaking went on and on. It had to have been nearly five minutes now, hadn't it?

And then it got even stronger.

A bizarre sound rang out, like someone had struck an enormous gong. It reverberated through the whole Ark.

'What was that sound? What's happening?'

'That was bad. Very bad.'

Shotaro had been calm to that point, but now he was starting to show signs of panic.

The shaking trailed off. The building had not collapsed, but Shotaro did not seem to calm down at all. He jerked open the door, now barely fitting in its frame, and rushed toward the entrance.

Everyone else was milling around in the corridor. Seven of us were gathered near the stairs.

'Hana! Are you all right?' Yuya asked. Sayaka was supporting her.

'I really banged my head. It hurts. A lot.'

It seemed everyone had been asleep when the shaking struck. From the look on their faces, being down in this bizarre structure seemed to make it hard to accept the reality of what had happened.

The Yazaki family came out of room 103, across from the dining room.

'What was that sound just now? Is everything all right?

Don't you think it would be better to go outside?' Mr Yazaki said to everyone in general, his voice loud. His wife and son were already wearing their packs, as if the whole family was ready to bolt.

Shotaro answered, 'You're right. We should leave immediately. If we can.'

If we can?

When he said that, my muddled brain finally figured out what that massive gonging sound must have been.

There had been a huge boulder in the tunnel-like passage leading to the metal entrance door. It had apparently been put there as some kind of emergency barricade. So, what if the earthquake had set it rolling? Wouldn't it make a sound a lot like that when it hit the metal door?

Shotaro rushed to the steel door. Everyone followed him, wanting to find out for themselves.

He turned the handle and pushed at the door. When it didn't open, he threw his whole body against it.

The door opened a mere fraction of an inch. The boulder was up against the other side of it, with only the tiniest gap.

'Here, let me try,' Ryuhei said. He grabbed the door handle and pushed with a deep groan.

I joined him, and the three of us all pushed and shoved at it, even running into it like rugby tackling practice.

It didn't budge. We could feel it ourselves. After all that, there was no way this door was going to be opened by sheer strength alone. We let our arms dangle, powerless, and turned to the others. They stared at us in desperation.

The ten of us were trapped underground.

'What are we going to do? Are you saying there's no way out? How can that be?!' Hana said. Her voice was thick with panic and anger.

'Um. Let's go downstairs first. There might be something we can do,' Shotaro said. He took the lead as we all went down to the middle floor.

II

First came the understanding of our situation. Then came the fear.

We were trapped underground in the mountains. No one on the surface knew where we were. Our phones had no reception.

What if we couldn't move that boulder? We would die trapped here in the Ark.

I recalled how once I had caught a mantis and put it in a cage, then left the cage in a desk drawer until it died. When I'd discovered the body, I had found myself overcome with dread as I thought about how it had died, alone in the dark. I took its corpse to the park for a proper burial, but even after that, and even though it was just an insect, the feeling haunted me for days afterward.

Now, as we all walked through this underground building, each of us was surely replaying our own lives in our minds.

We stopped before the metal door on the middle floor.

It was directly below the main entrance and opened onto a room more like a cave.

The space was too narrow for everyone to enter. Shotaro led the way, then I went in, followed by Ryuhei, and finally Kotaro Yazaki, who stood at the threshold.

Inside, we saw that there was a change in the ceiling.

The low ceiling around the door was crossed by thin steel rods with metal plates welded to them, but the boulder above had broken through the plates and bent the bars. It was visible from below.

'Whoa! It's really wedged in there!'

Ryuhei grabbed a bar and gave it a shake as he looked up.

We could see the blocked door above through the broken plates. The chain-wrapped boulder was tight against it.

Yazaki examined the state of the ceiling with care. 'I wonder if we could remove some of these bars and bring the boulder down here. That would let us through above.'

He was checking to see if it would be possible to pull the boulder down through the ceiling to this floor below. The bolts holding the bars were all exposed below, so it did look like we could remove them.

Shotaro answered, 'We'd have to do more than just remove the bars. The boulder is lodged between the door and the cave floor. After we removed the bars, we'd have to pull it through that gap. It would take a lot of power.'

A lot of power to pull the boulder down? Didn't we have the equipment to do exactly that? The chains wrapped around the boulder were connected to a winch, after all. We'd just have to turn the handle.

But as soon as I thought of that, I realized there was one major problem with using the winch like that.

I glanced at Shotaro in the back of the room, and he nodded.

'So, you're suggesting that we remove the braces above and use the winch to pull the rock down here, right? But, if we do that, whoever is using the winch is going to be trapped in here.'

If we pulled the boulder down into the winch room, then it would end up blocking the door to the little room on the middle level. The stone mouth just inside the door was quite narrow, so the boulder would be held tight.

And of course, the winch could only be operated inside this room.

That meant that for us to get out of this underground building, someone would have to be left behind in this cramped room.

Shotaro grimaced as he spoke.

'That's how it looks. I imagine that the original builders planned it so that pulling the boulder down to the middle floor would seal this room's entrance. The boulder really is huge.'

So, if someone did manage to pull the boulder down to the middle level, it would become a barricade blocking passage between the middle and bottom floors.

The boulder blocking the door to the upper floor could, with enough time, be broken down from the outside. So, the people inside could temporarily block off entrance to the upper floor while they all evacuated to the bottom floor. Then, they could pull the boulder down to the middle floor, which would make it even harder to get through. It was a trick that seemed somehow fitting for this place, built so clearly in service to some master plan beyond normal concerns.

This little room led to the only stairs down to the bottom floor. Under the original plan, the person who pulled the boulder down could escape through the bottom floor to the emergency exit, but now, it was flooded with water. Which meant that anyone who operated the winch would be sealing themselves in this tiny cave-like chamber.

Once we'd grasped the situation, we all went out into the corridor.

Ryuhei groaned.

'So, what the hell are we going to do? Someone has to use the winch, right? Then the rest of us get out, hurry up and get help, then come back to save them!' Ryuhei practically shouted.

Whoever got that job would be trapped in a tiny dark room, alone, waiting for rescue. The thought sent a shiver through every one of us. Who would ever accept such a task?

Yuya forced a cheerful tone, saying, 'Let's not get ahead of ourselves, OK? We have an idea, now, so let's just sit back and think the details through.'

The Ark had plenty of tinned food and, of course, all the water we could want. We wouldn't have to worry about starving for a good two or three weeks.

'So, why don't we look through the place a bit more? There might be some bad-ass tools we could use to bring the boulder down without using the winch. It would be best if all of us could get out together, right? And anyway, we'll definitely need a hex key at least. We've got to get those bars off. Let's start by looking for one of those.'

He was right, of course. Without a hex key, the whole plan was for nothing.

Everyone agreed to start searching. We could deal with the problem of who would stay behind later.

The steel shelves in storeroom 207 were lined with saws, hammers and other tools, so it seemed a promising place to begin. Working together, we tidied up the mess left by the earthquake before starting our search.

But in the end, there were no suitable hex keys to be found in 207.

There were other storerooms scattered about the Ark. And given how disordered the place seemed, the key we needed could have been in any one of them.

We decided to split up. The ten of us scattered and started combing the building. Only Hana, who said her head was still hurting, stayed out of the search. Her room was still a mess from the quake, so she decided to rest in the dining room.

Shotaro and I started looking through room 205, next to the tool room. It seemed to have been used for storing materials. Leftover insulation and bits of metal were strewn across the floor.

'If we don't find a hex key, we're screwed, right? There's no way we can get those bolts off by hand,' I said, half to myself.

'Not likely. But there's sure to be one here. They must have had tons when they built the place.'

But we still didn't see any. Some builder had probably just dropped the key they'd been using wherever they were when they were done putting the last bit of the structure together.

'What do you suppose Yuya meant by "bad-ass tools"? What could possibly move that enormous boulder without a winch?'

'No idea.'

'The only thing I can think of is dynamite. Which I wouldn't be surprised to find in a place like this.'

'Dynamite's no good. It'd bring the whole place down and kill us all.'

He had a point.

'So, then, someone really is going to have to stay behind. How do we choose?' I asked.

I couldn't imagine anyone volunteering for it. Would we end up drawing straws? I doubted the Yazakis would go for that. Would the boy have to draw, too?

Shotaro looked irritated.

'We all decided to leave that problem for later, so why are you worrying about it now? We'll just have to deal with it when the time comes.'

He closed a box he'd been rummaging through. It looked like it was full of different kinds of tape: electrician's tape, duct tape and the like.

'I doubt there's anything in this room. Shuichi, there's no reason for us to search together, is there? There are still loads of places left to check. It'd be more efficient to split up.'

'Oh, right. Yeah, I'll do that.'

I'd been hung up on how to choose who was going to stay behind and wanted to talk to someone about it, but Shotaro brushed me off and left.

I spent a while puttering around in a residential room with a bunch of beds and mattresses.

The most likely rooms were already being searched, but I still had a hunch there might be a hex key somewhere unexpected. So, feeling a bit like I was playing hooky while everyone else was working, I set about checking under the beds. All I found was an old, empty cigarette packet.

I stepped out into the corridor and went up the stairs, idly wondering which room to try next.

A thought suddenly struck me, and I rushed to the machinery room.

What was going on above ground? If the cameras weren't busted, they should show everything.

I checked the time on my phone. It was 6.13 a.m. The sun should be up already.

I turned on the monitors. They took an irritatingly long time to warm up.

'Oh, would you look at that…'

The cameras were both fine.

The monitor for the main entrance showed very little sign of the earthquake apart from a few new rocks around the hatch.

The emergency exit, though, was utterly changed.

The image on the screen showed the meadow covered in earth and debris, with boulders and fallen trees protruding from the mound of soil. It was more than anyone could move by hand.

The emergency exit hatch was now completely buried. Of course, we couldn't have got out that way anyway, because of the flooding, but now there was another problem.

We'd come through that meadow on the way here. Now it was completely buried under a landslide. Even if we made it out of the main entrance, would we be able to get past this new obstacle? The wooden bridge over the ravine might have collapsed, too. There was no way off the mountain without crossing that ravine, and, without any reception, there was no way of calling for help from this side.

Which meant that, if we did get out, the person left behind in that tiny cave-like room would surely have to wait there for a very long time. It was becoming less and less likely that anyone would want to draw that straw.

This is something everyone needs to know, and they need to know now. At the thought, I went back out into the corridor, but then a voice rang out, something between a shriek and a bellow.

'Hey! You all had better come! It's really bad! Oh shit!'

It was Ryuhei. It sounded like his voice was coming from below, near the winch room.

Everyone came out of the rooms they'd been searching and started heading toward the winch room.

Shotaro was in front of me. I followed him down the stairs, along the corridor and through the narrow metal door.

Ryuhei was crouched at the very back of the tiny room, holding a hex key in his right hand, looking down the stairs leading to the bottom floor. I couldn't see what he was shouting about and craned my neck to get a better look.

He stood up at the sound of our footsteps, then pointed down below with the hex key.

'The water's rising. It's higher than yesterday. It's obvious.'

'What? No way…'

The water filling the lowest floor had built up slowly over years and years. Or so we thought, anyway.

But now it had risen visibly since the day before. Shotaro and I knelt down beside the stairs and looked with him.

'It's really rising? You're sure?' I asked.

'Yeah, it really is,' Shotaro answered.

There was no denying it. Yesterday, the water had been up over the fourth step down. Now, the third step was totally underwater.

We turned around to see the rest of the group lined up in the corridor, watching what was going on. Everyone was there except for Yuya, for some reason.

Sayaka stepped forward.

'Are you sure it's the water that's rising? Maybe the earthquake made the stairs start sinking or something?' she said. Her voice was pleading.

'No, that's not what it looks like. The surface of the water is moving. There's a current, meaning the water has to be flowing in.'

The earthquake had shifted the rock around the Ark. It had turned what was once slow, gentle seeping into a steady flow of water.

Shotaro stepped out of the room and came back with a builder's square. He aligned it with the top of the third step.

Everyone stood waiting silently. After about five minutes, Ryuhei turned on his phone light so the marks would be easier to see.

Finally, Shotaro checked the marks and stood up.

'The water is rising. It's for sure. At this rate, it will completely flood the whole building before too long,' he announced.

Ryuhei's phone slipped from his hand into the water.

III

We all stood outside the winch room, staring at each other in silence.

Ryuhei's phone was apparently waterproof. He'd retrieved it from the submerged stairs and was busy wiping it dry on his clothes.

'And I'd just found the hex key we need, too,' he groaned. He'd gone to the winch room to check if the hex key fitted the bolts on the beams, glanced down at the water without even thinking about it and noticed it looked higher.

'So, did anyone think of a way to bring the boulder down without trapping someone behind it? Find any tools we could use?' he asked, but there was no reply. No one had found anything.

'So, I guess someone's going to have to stay behind, aren't they?'

It appeared so.

'Listen, I don't know what we're going to do, but whatever it is, shouldn't we be quick about it? If someone's going to have to stay behind, the others have to get down the mountain fast to bring help. Before the water gets too high,' Hana said.

'But we still might not make it,' Mai said darkly.

There was something I still had to tell everyone. I led them back to the machinery room.

There was a chorus of groans at the sight of the camera feeds.

The landslide had buried the area around the emergency exit, so Shotaro spread the Ark diagram out on the desk and compared the location of the emergency exit it showed with the scene on the monitor.

'From what I can see here, there's a very good chance the bridge was caught in the landslide and collapsed.'

Even if the bridge was still intact, the path had been narrow and difficult in places, so there was a good chance the earthquake had blocked it completely in several spots. In which case, even if we managed to get out, getting down the mountain would be much more difficult than coming up.

'That means if we get out, it's going to take forever to bring back help, right? And even if help does come right away, I think it's going to be hard to rescue the trapped person. That boulder won't be easy to move, and if the emergency exit is buried, they can't get in through there,' Hana said. She was nearly weeping.

That earthquake hadn't just set the boulder rolling. It had caught us in a truly fiendish trap.

Earthquakes often generate chains of following disasters. After the tremors can come tsunamis or even volcanic eruptions. The Ark had been become a secondary disaster in miniature.

'Basically, it all comes down to this: for the rest of us to get out of here, one person has to stay trapped in this slowly flooding underground building. And, even if the rest of us manage to get out, it's going to take a lot of time to bring help. In the meantime, there's nothing anyone can do about the flooding. So… In other words, for the rest of us to survive, one person is going to have to sacrifice themselves. Now, we have to think about who will stay behind,' Shotaro said.

The worry we had been feeling suddenly weighed much heavier on our hearts.

One of us in this building was going to have to be willing to die! And if they did, it would not be an easy death. They would be alone in a dark, narrow cave, waiting for it to slowly fill with water.

I looked at the people around me, my eyes going from face to face. Shotaro looked gloomy and Ryuhei tense, like he was getting ready to hit someone. Mai was staring at the floor, biting her lip in despair. Sayaka was on the verge of tears. Hana was wearing an expression of shock, like she was still struggling to accept reality.

And then there was the Yazaki family… Kotaro seemed angry. His wife, Hiroko, looked frightened, while Hayato alone appeared unfazed, like it was all happening to someone else.

No one said a word. It was as if they were afraid that the first person to speak would be the one left behind.

They were afraid… But what about me? Would I be the one left behind?

'Hey, where's Yuya? Where'd that wanker run off to?' Ryuhei said, as if he'd just noticed the absence.

And he was right. I hadn't realized with all the tension, but Yuya still wasn't with us. He hadn't shown up after the search for the hex key. Had he not heard Ryuhei shouting?

'We should go and look for him. We can't make any decisions without everyone here,' Shotaro said, and led the way as we filed out of the machinery room.

Everyone was eager to join the search.

It was a relief to have something to do before we faced the choice of who would be the sacrificial lamb to save us all, but we were also all pretty annoyed with Yuya.

His leading us astray on the way here was the reason we were trapped in the Ark. If he'd found the place more quickly, we never would have had to stay the night. I think we all had a few choice words for him now.

And he surely knew it himself. He might even be too ashamed to show his face for the moment. Would we end up having to drag him bodily out of some room where he was holed up sulking?

We split up to search the building, just like when we had looked for the hex key. But this time, we were looking for something much bigger, so surely it wouldn't take very long.

The building was soon echoing with the sound of rushing footsteps. I could also hear angry voices calling Yuya's name. Our group scattered through the Ark like the crew of a ship rushing to stations to ride out a storm.

I went to check room 209. The torture implements stacked in one corner had scattered across the floor in the earthquake. But Yuya was not there.

Why go straight to that room? I wondered to myself. Somehow, I had felt that I should check the least pleasant place first.

We did eventually find Yuya.

It was Hayato Yazaki, the boy, who stumbled on him. His screams filled the building.

'He's here! I found him! He's dead! Dead! Someone killed him!'

IV

It was in room 120, a narrow room at the very eastern end of the top floor.

Since the building was inside a natural cave, the end rooms like 120 were irregular, like the odd bits trimmed off the end of a rolled cake. This one was used as a storeroom.

Yuya's corpse was lying face down at the back of the room. There was a dirty length of rope wrapped around his neck and knotted at the back.

Shotaro laboured to turn the body over, like rolling a log.

'It really is Yuya, and he is dead.'

Yuya looked ghastly. His mouth and eyes gaped unnaturally. His face was a blue-black colour.

Everyone entered the room, one by one, to see the truth for themselves, to convince themselves Yuya was dead. No one came in for a close look, though, as though out of respect for the deceased.

Afterwards, we all stood in the corridor, stunned.

'Why? Why is everything going so crazy right now?!' Hana shouted. She was in a near panic.

But she was right. So much had happened in this last couple of hours. The earthquake had trapped us here, and the water was rising, and just as we'd realized one of us would have to be sacrificed for the rest to escape, someone had murdered Yuya.

'When did they get him?' Ryuhei asked.

Shotaro answered him, saying, 'It had to be while we were all looking for a hex key. There was no other opportunity.'

'And who did it?'

There was no answer that time.

It was one of us, of course. But we'd all been scattered throughout the building, searching alone, making it the perfect opportunity for a murder. The killer had found a bit of rope, sneaked up behind Yuya as he searched and strangled him.

Although murder is an inherently abhorrent act, the killing itself was not the most shocking part of it all. We have all seen how trouble between friends can sometimes lead to murder, at least on the news, if not in our own lives.

But right then? Under such circumstances? It was beyond comprehension.

We were going to have to decide which of us would be sacrificed so the rest could live. And someone had sought Yuya out to kill him.

'Who was it? Who hated Yuya that much?' Sayaka asked.

Mai answered, saying the words that had started to vaguely take shape in my head. 'If they'd just hated him, they wouldn't have done it now, would they? Like, we're going to have to choose someone to stay behind, right? How were we going to do that, do you think?'

It was a frightening question.

If Yuya had still been alive, and the ten of us had met to decide who to sacrifice, how would we have made the decision? Would we all have drawn straws, accepting the fact that we were essentially risking our lives on a one in ten chance?

Maybe, or we might have had an anonymous vote, for example.

Each of us would write on a slip of paper who we thought should stay behind, and the person with the most votes would be forced to stay. And if it had gone that way, who would have been chosen?

Yuya would have been a likely candidate. It was his fault we were trapped. Surely everyone felt the same thing.

Or maybe it wouldn't have been anything as complicated as an anonymous vote. We might have just ganged up on him instead, saying it was his fault we were all trapped, and pressuring him into that room to pull down the boulder. If he resisted, it might even have come to violence, to inflicting so much pain that he agreed to give up his life for ours.

I struggled to picture my cousin, my university friends, the Yazakis who we'd just met yesterday, and even myself, doing something so brutal. But what if it was the only way out? The water was rising. If we didn't choose someone, we were all going to die.

Shotaro summed up Mai's doubts like this:

'What you're saying is, even if someone hated Yuya enough to murder him, it would have been senseless to do it now. If they'd just let him be, there was a good chance he'd end up dying a much worse death than strangulation.

'Even if the murderer didn't hate Yuya, their actions still don't make sense. If we decide to draw straws, then killing him has reduced the number of participants and therefore increased everyone's chances of getting chosen.'

'Shotaro, do you think the murderer actually understood just how bad a mess we're in?' I asked. 'When we were looking for the hex key, we all just thought the rock had us trapped. Maybe they didn't know that the emergency exit was blocked, and that water was pouring in?'

'I can't really say,' he replied. 'It seems unlikely they knew everything, but from the timing, I can't rule out that the murderer grasped the situation before any of us and still went through with it. Both possibilities seem equally likely.'

So, the murderer could have checked the cameras before I did and also noticed that the water was rising from the bottom floor before Ryuhei.

'Whatever the case, I still can't figure out what the murderer was trying to gain by killing someone now, with things like this. But I think you'll all agree that whoever did it, they did it calmly, right?'

He was talking about how the murder had not been committed in a room where rope was stored, so the killer must have brought the murder weapon from somewhere else. That indicated they hadn't done it in the heat of the moment with whatever came to hand.

'So, the murderer must have been shockingly cool-headed. I mean, they're standing here right now, in a situation where all our lives are on the line, and they're still calm enough that we can't tell them apart from all the innocent people here.'

He made an extremely good point.

Each of us was reacting to this impossibly stressful situation in our own way, but no one looked guilty, or like they were worried about their crime being discovered.

Ryuhei burst out, 'I don't really think it matters why they killed him, does it? Not at a time like this.'

'I guess not. The motive is irrelevant. Understanding it won't make any difference, I imagine. What we all need to figure out as soon as possible is, who did it? That's the one thing we have to know before the building floods. That's what you're getting at, right, Ryuhei?'

Ryuhei, just like everyone except the murderer, must have felt that we had no other choice.

If we didn't find someone to sacrifice, no one would get out of the Ark. So, who to sacrifice? It was obvious. We would sacrifice whoever it was that had decided to become a murderer.

V

Shotaro told us we probably had just over a week.

He'd made a quick calculation of the rate at which the water was rising, based on the measurements he'd just taken, and concluded that in little more than seven days' time, the water would be up to the ceiling of the middle floor. If it rose any higher than that, it would make it impossible to run the winch. The generator would also run out of fuel in about the same amount of time. It would be hard not to panic after that, trapped in the pitch black darkness of the Ark.

And so, before that happened, we would have to unmask the murderer lurking among us. Then, they would be the one left behind to turn the winch.

'But there's no way the murderer will just do what we say,' Hana grumbled to no one in particular.

She had a point. Even if we did catch the murderer, we couldn't expect him or her to calmly accept being sacrificed.

'We'll just have to talk all that over once we've figured it out, won't we? Like, we could all promise to support their family if they agreed to run the winch, or something,' Sayaka said, but her voice trailed off at the end as if she couldn't endure the cruelty and hypocrisy of her own idea.

Ryuhei, though, seemed to want to make clear what no one else seemed to have the courage to say.

'So, what, this murderer is just supposed to help the rest of us because they're going to get arrested if they escape, anyway? And if they don't listen to us, what then? Do we all just give up and die? Or do we force them?'

And that was the big question. Could we really make someone operate the winch against their will? It had occurred to me when I was thinking that we might have to force Yuya to stay behind. Now the same issue had arisen again. The only difference was that this time we would be sacrificing a murderer.

I didn't really think we'd have been able to force Yuya to run the winch, but what about a killer? Could we suppress our feelings of guilt and torture them until they gave in? Luckily, or unluckily, we had the equipment for it.

Mai glared angrily at her husband.

'Why'd you have to say that now? It's like you're trying to start a fight!'

'She's right. Because the murderer is here, listening to us right now. We shouldn't be talking about forcing people,' Hana added.

It sounded like a perfectly reasonable attempt to avoid conflict. At the same time, she was also essentially accepting the possibility that we would have to use violence later, which was why she thought we should avoid discussing it now.

Don't get me wrong, I agreed with both Hana and Mai. We had no idea who the murderer could be, so what good was there in talking about how we were going to treat them? And didn't my own thinking indicate that, when the time came, I'd be ready to use violence?

Shotaro listened to everyone with the look of a teacher standing in front of a class, then added his own comment.

'There's no point in thinking about what we're going to do to the murderer at the moment. That will depend on who it is. The only thing that's clear right now is, we can't decide who we're going to leave behind without knowing who the killer is. I think we're all in agreement on that.'

Everyone nodded meekly. We simply had to find the murderer. That was all.

The most frightening thought was, what if we couldn't do that before the time limit ran out? If we had to choose someone to stay behind without knowing who among us was the murderer?

Could we force someone to pull down the boulder and trap themselves in that room, knowing that they might be innocent? And what if we found out that the murderer was among us after we escaped? The moment we forced an innocent person to die miserably, trapped below ground, we would all be murderers. Of course, I might very well be the one to die.

And what of the possibility that, unable to uncover the murderer, we couldn't choose anyone to sacrifice? Would we have the strength to force someone to take that burden with the knowledge that they might be innocent? If we didn't, we would all die here.

'So, anyway, for now let's just all show each other our hands,' Shotaro said. 'Maybe the rope left burn marks on the killer's palms. Well?'

The first people he turned to were the Yazakis.

The three of them had kept silent this whole time, presumably watching events progress in hope that, as outsiders, they could keep out of this whole thing.

'What?!' Kotaro snapped. 'On top of being trapped in here, now we've got to be treated like murder suspects along with the rest of you? We only met that guy who died yesterday. We barely even talked to him.'

'That's certainly true. But in this situation, I'd say it would be just as odd for his old friends from university to have killed Yuya as some total strangers who happened to spend the night in the same place. I'm genuinely sorry if you didn't have anything to do with it, and for you getting trapped. For now, though, we are all suspects.'

'And we're all going to be treated the same?'

'That's right. There is only one way for everyone to escape without any lingering resentments or doubts. We all have to agree on who the murderer is. The police could probably clear it all up easily with forensics. I doubt the murderer had time to worry about leaving physical traces. But we have to find the murderer before we can even get out to call the police. And all we have to do it are slow, old-fashioned methods.'

And that summed up the trap we were in. We had to find the murderer on our own before we could even try to get help from the police.

Kotaro looked Shotaro up and down.

'And I suppose you're the one who's going to play detective in this murder mystery?'

'There's no reason for me to be the only one. Those of you who aren't murderers could investigate it yourselves, too. But you would have to come up with a logical explanation that convinces everyone. For now, though, please just show me your hands. It might not mean much, but it's better than not looking at anything at all.'

The three Yazakis shuffled forward and held out their palms. All three of them had dirty hands. Of course they did; they had been searching for a hex key. There was no trace of rope burn or anything like it, though.

The rest of us did the same. All had the same dirty hands, except for Hana, who hadn't been searching because of her aching head.

No one stood out as suspicious. Perhaps the murderer had worn gloves, or maybe the marks had simply faded by now.

'Let's ask, for what it's worth. Can anyone prove that they aren't the murd—'

'The three of us were together the whole time. We were searching for the hex key,' Kotaro interrupted. Ryuhei's face clouded.

'Hold on just a second. You three are a family. You can't give each other alibis. And you know what? I saw you on your own! You were walking down on the middle floor! Why are you lying?'

Kotaro clammed up. Everyone turned suspicious eyes on the family, and the three of them seemed to shrink in on themselves. Finally, Hiroko spoke in a dead voice.

'There was just one time when we split up during the search. It was only for about five minutes, though.'

'Yeah, and I'd say those five minutes are the problem, wouldn't you? Five minutes would have been plenty for this, right?' Ryuhei growled and pointed at the corpse. 'I'm not trying to say one of you is the murderer. I don't know anything. What I'm saying is, stupid lies and comments like that are just going to waste all our time.'

With that, the Yazaki family finally seemed to accept that no matter how much they resisted being drawn into this, they wouldn't be able to just watch from outside as innocent bystanders.

We went round the group, and no one had a watertight alibi. I had split off from Shotaro, so I'd had an opportunity to kill Yuya. Hana had stayed in the dining room alone, and she hadn't been so badly injured that she couldn't have committed the murder.

'Right, sure, I get it. I'm a suspect, too. My head really hurt, but it's not like just saying that means anything,' she said, like she was trying to get out in front of the inevitable suspicion.

'Excellent, that's the spirit. We're all suspects! We should all be happy that no one's getting left out of the game,' Shotaro said brightly. His lame attempt at lightening the mood fell flat.

Not knowing the murderer's identity was frightening enough, but we were also in danger of seeing our already fragile relationships fracture and of losing all grip on calm reason.

No one could predict what kind of trouble might arise if one person was proved innocent while the rest remained as suspects. Which meant that, for now, it would be better for all to be in the same position.

'What do you think the murderer is hoping will happen? Are they just waiting for time to pass until we have to choose? If we end up having to draw straws and someone else draws the short straw, are they really going to let that person die? Then they'll be guilty of another murder, too, not just Yuya's.'

'Mai, come on, you just told us that we shouldn't be talking about stuff like that!' Ryuhei muttered at her, but Sayaka took up the thread.

'How could any of us be such a monster? I don't know why whoever it is killed Yuya, but you could just tell us, all right? Then, maybe we can do something to help,' Sayaka said, her voice frantic.

We were not really prepared to get friendly with a murderer, of course. But we could not abandon the hope that they would confess, and that we would solve the murder and escape this underground trap.

For a moment I thought someone might step forward.

But the nine of us just stood in silence, looking from face to face, as if hoping a change in the murderer's expression would give them away.

VI

We were still gathered in the upper floor corridor, but soon we moved to the stairs leading down to the middle floor.

We all understood that the murderer would not be announcing themselves on the spot. We had to prepare ourselves to spend the rest of our one-week time limit here in this underground building. And to do that, there were some things we had to take care of besides finding the murderer.

It was Shotaro who set the plan.

'Mr Yazaki, I'd like to ask you to check the wiring. We'll be in trouble if anything short circuits.'

The walls of the middle floor had electrical wires strung in the open. They were set low on the wall, so they would probably be submerged within three or four days.

The big concern was the sockets. We would have to cut their connecting wires entirely.

As an electrician, Kotaro Yazaki was the natural choice to take the lead on that issue.

'I'll need a set of large wire cutters and some insulating tape.'

Shotaro and I went off to get what he needed.

There had been a carton of rubber tape in room 205, next to the tool room. That should serve as insulation. We grabbed a wide roll of the black tape and went to the tool room next door to get a pair of wire cutters.

But when we got back to Yazaki, he already had what he'd asked for.

He was holding a blue toolbox filled with pliers, cutters, and other electrician's tools. It even had insulating tape.

'I found this while we were looking around before,' Sayaka said. She'd brought the toolbox from room 215, on the east side of the corridor.

The equipment in the box looked much more reliable that the junk we'd found.

Yazaki headed to the machinery room. He studied the fuse box, then flipped the circuit breakers for the places he would be working on down below before he got to work. Most of the wires leading to the sockets were out in the open, making them quite easy to handle. Yazaki used the cutters to sever the wires, then covered the exposed ends with insulating tape. His wife and son, along with Shotaro, Sayaka and me, stood by to light the area with our phones while he worked.

There were about twenty sockets. When the adjustments were done, he flipped the circuit breakers back on. With the job all finished, the Yazaki family conscientiously put the toolbox back in room 215.

We also needed to move essential supplies up from the middle floor, away from the rising water. Hana, Mai and Ryuhei got started on that while the rest of us were working on the wiring.

The priorities were tinned food and water, and then things like enough pairs of wellingtons for everyone. It was easier to move all of it now, before the water got any higher.

The tins of fish, vegetables and fruit had all reached their best-before dates four or five years earlier. We opened a few to try, and none of them seemed spoiled. For the time being, we were in no danger of starving.

I found a pair of fishing waders in storage. There was only the one set, but they would help us to stay dry if we had to go down to the middle floor even once the water rose above waist height.

Once we'd moved all the essentials, we scoured the rest of the floor for anything else that might come in handy. Sayaka happened to look into room 204 and let out a cry of surprise.

'Hey, look at this!' Shotaro and I were in the corridor outside, so we peeked in to see what she'd found.

It was a set of scuba tanks. The building was so sprawling that Shotaro and I hadn't stumbled across it yet.

There were two ten-litre tanks. We poked around some more and turned up a plastic box with two regulators for breathing, masks, and more. But there was no sign of a harness to hold the tanks or any weights to hold you down in the water.

There was also a submersible pressure gauge, and when we used it, we saw that each tank was about one-third full.

'Do you think we could use these?' Sayaka's excitement was understandable, what with the water slowly rising toward us. The air tanks seemed somehow reassuring.

'They don't look broken or anything, but...'

After a bit of thought, I realized that that diving equipment wouldn't be much help in our current situation.

Without a harness, there was no way to strap the tanks on and dive underwater. Even if there were, we'd only be able to swim down to the bottom floor. And since the emergency exit was blocked by the landslide, we couldn't get out that way, either.

So, the tanks would serve only to put off the inevitable drowning by a few minutes when the end came.

'Why do you think they had diving stuff out here in the mountains, anyway?'

'Don't be so dense, Shuichi. The bottom floor is flooded, so they needed it to bring things up from there.'

'Oh, right. Yeah, that makes sense.'

Shotaro had a good point. Now that I thought about it, some of the tools we'd found lying around were oddly rusted, much more so than the rest. They had probably been brought up from the flooded floor down below.

'I don't know why there's no harness for the tanks, though. Maybe someone used it to carry other stuff when they abandoned this place.'

In a pinch, I supposed a harness might serve as a replacement for a backpack. It wasn't that strange a thought.

We left the diving equipment where we found it.

We went up to the top floor. There, stacked up in a corner like someone had hoped to keep them from being noticed, we found the torture tools from room 209.

They might end up being useful, I supposed.

Once everything had been carried up, we all gathered in the dining room.

The food we'd brought up was piled at the end of one long table. Everyone was free to take what they wanted, but no one seemed hungry at the moment.

'Would it be all right with everyone if I looked through Yuya's personal effects?' Shotaro asked, and no one objected.

Since the murder was apparently tied to the earthquake, an unpredictable event, it was hard to imagine anyone had planned it far in advance. Which meant there wasn't much chance of us finding any clues in Yuya's belongings. But there wasn't anything better to do, and there was a small chance we might turn up something useful.

Yuya had been using a golden yellow daypack. He hadn't been planning on spending the night, so it didn't hold much. I fetched it from room 109, where he'd stayed the night, and spread the contents out on the dining room floor.

There was the same billfold wallet he had used since his first year of university. A mobile battery pack decorated with music group stickers. A bundle of tangled cables. A digital SLR camera he'd just bought for 200,000 yen, or so he'd said. Beneath those was a set of underwear. Sundries like nail clippers and cotton buds all packed in individual resealable plastic bags. A few plastic shopping bags folded into triangles. And finally, an unopened bag of crisps he'd bought at the convenience store the day before.

My chest grew tighter with each item I took out.

I hadn't been this upset when I'd seen Yuya dead. But these things from his pack seemed to evoke the life he had left behind so much more poignantly than his corpse ever could. Together, they spoke of the decades he had believed stretched out before him.

I could feel my breathing grow ragged, but it was not from grief over his death. It was a very simple reason. I was suddenly facing fear of my own death.

I might soon meet my own fate, just as he had. Yesterday, being trapped underground like this was beyond imagining. That was the same for me as it had been for Yuya.

Those of us who had known Yuya well struggled with the inspection. The Yazakis, though, watched in cold, if somewhat respectful, silence as we went through his things.

Shotaro patted the pockets of the pack to make sure nothing was left inside, then said, 'I expected as much. Nothing that tells us anything. Well, I think we should take this, at least. I doubt Yuya would have minded.'

He added the crisps to the pile of tins. Then, he returned the rest to the daypack.

'I'll just keep this with me, shall I? Is that all right?' he asked.

No one objected.

VII

After we finished checking the daypack, we decided we would all go our separate ways for some free time, to relax or do anything else we wanted.

Part of me wondered how we could even think of relaxing at a time like this. But no one seemed to be able to come up with a better idea.

We could stand in the dining room glaring at each other for the rest of our time, but it wouldn't change anything. So, why not try and act as normally as we could, pretending we were at a nice country inn rather than trapped under the ground in the middle of the mountains? Perhaps it would get the murderer to lower their guard and make a mistake.

At least, that's what Shotaro said, and no one disagreed. It might not help us catch the criminal, but we were all tired of desperately scrutinizing each other's expressions for signs of guilt.

'Let's just try to relax. As much as possible, anyway,' he recommended.

As soon as he'd finished, the Yazakis quickly slipped out of the room and retreated to room 103, where they'd spent the night.

We watched them go like wary students watching a teacher prone to fits of temper leaving the classroom.

I half wanted to talk about the evident Yazaki problem with the others and half wanted to ignore it completely, but Shotaro clapped me on the shoulder before I could decide one way or another. He drew me along with him as he followed the family out of the dining room.

'What are we doing?' I asked.

'I want to take another look at the crime scene. It wouldn't be any fun on my own, so you're coming with me.'

We walked down the corridor to room 120, the storeroom at the very end of the upper floor.

It was not a scene I wanted to revisit, but I hoped we might spot some piece of evidence we'd missed before.

We opened the storeroom door, which was slightly narrower than any of the others.

The crime scene was exactly as it had been when it was discovered. It had been hard to look Yuya in the face after Ryuhei had turned him over, so someone had rolled him back face down. No one had thought to lay his body out properly or move it somewhere else.

'What do you think Yuya was doing in here? It doesn't seem like a place he would have come to look for the hex key, does it?' Shotaro asked.

The storeroom was stacked with lengths of PVC pipe. There was nothing that looked like a tool anywhere to be seen.

'Not really, no. But he was probably in a panic. Knowing him, he'd have been really upset by the idea that all this was his fault. And remember, he was talking about finding some kind of tool that would mean no one would have to stay behind, but nothing turned up. I bet he was just getting more and more freaked out, pretending to look for a hex key but actually just trying to hide his panic,' I said. 'Which meant it was a perfect opportunity for the murderer, right? The one person they wanted to kill had run off from all the others on his own.'

'I wonder about that. I mean, sure, Yuya being alone was certainly a good opportunity if he was the target. But he might just have been the easiest one to kill.'

That brought me up short. It sounded like he was implying that Yuya could have been a target of opportunity.

'You think the murderer might not have minded who they killed? That anyone would have done?'

Which meant it could have been me.

'That could be the case. But, if we're just thinking he was easier to kill because he was alone, then what about everyone else who was looking for the hex key? One of them could easily have come to check this storeroom and caught the killer in the act. Given that, then we must assume there was a reason Yuya had to be killed when he was. Which all means that this murder must have a very, very interesting motive. But I wonder if there's any value in thinking about motive at all. I'm kind of torn.'

'How so?' I asked.

'Even if we thought we knew the motive, we could never be really sure. It would just be an assumption that best fits the situation, right? Isn't that all we could do at a time like this? It might feel satisfying but wouldn't help us find the killer. No matter how many likely explanations we come up with, we won't be able to pin anyone down and say, "You're the only one with the motive to do this!" or anything.'

He paused before going on. 'What we need now is a clear chain of logic that would definitively prove who the murderer is. We can ask them about the motive once we've figured that out. And listen, Shuichi, you should be careful what you say. Baseless speculation could kill us all.'

'I know. Really, I do.'

I could imagine how easily things might spiral out of control if we started hurling around wild accusations. If we turned on each other, it might even lead to more killing.

I couldn't bring myself to think about it. Perhaps because the threat of the rising water still didn't feel real. We still had a week, so I couldn't quite shake the optimistic feeling that things would work out, somehow.

'It certainly would be nice if we could find the murderer quickly,' I mused.

'It certainly would. As quickly as possible. But, well… How?'

We searched the murder scene once more but, try as we might, we found no clues left behind: no button dropped by the murderer, no strands of hair, and, of course, no dying message. There was only the corpse, the rope still around its neck.

'Do you think we could figure out if the murderer is left handed by the knot in the rope?' I asked.

'Maybe, but all nine of us are right handed anyway.'

'All right, then, what about calculating the murderer's height based on the marks on Yuya's neck or something?'

'Probably someone could do it. The police maybe.'

'Do you think a woman could have killed him?'

'Whoever it was took him by surprise from behind and strangled him. You said yourself how Yuya might have been in a panic over the guilt of having got us into this mess, so it's easy to imagine he could have been distracted and easy to sneak up on. He wasn't particularly well built either, so… Yeah, I think a woman could have killed him. I wouldn't swear to it, though.'

Has there ever been such a useless crime scene investigation?

Neither of us was any kind of expert, so of course we didn't know what we were doing. But this was no way to start building the logical chain that would lead to our murderer.

The murderer had brought a rope from somewhere, sneaked up behind Yuya and slipped it around his neck. His breath stopped forever, they had tied the rope tight then left the scene, a look of innocence on their face. That's more or less what must have happened. The problem was, however, that there wasn't any real puzzle as such in that whole chain of events.

Apart from the murder itself, nothing that the murderer had done was particularly odd. The room had not been locked from the inside, no article of clothing was missing for unexplained reasons, nothing in the room had been inexplicably turned upside down, or the like. If the killer had left some bizarre puzzle behind, they might have given us something to work with that would result in a clue, but without any mysterious elements like that, there was nothing to solve.

In the end, the only puzzle in front of us was the question of why one of us would choose to kill someone in the middle of this crisis. A puzzle to which the answer, even if we managed to work it out, could not possibly be of any use.

'Nothing to be done, I suppose. We've still got a week. I'm sure something will come along in the meantime.'

I wondered what 'thing' might 'come along', and how. Much like the night before, I couldn't tell from his tone whether he was expressing a hope or predicting further calamity.

We decided to abandon our fruitless crime scene investigation. I bowed goodbye to Yuya, silent on the floor, and we left the storeroom.

VIII

The clock ticked past five in the afternoon.

On the surface, the sun would soon be setting, but down here the light remained unchanged. Still, the breaths of outside air wafting in through the ventilation seemed to get cooler.

I sat in the dining room, staring vacantly into space.

There were two other people in the room. Hana was sitting across the table to one side, and Sayaka was sitting at a distance from us both.

Both of them had propped their elbows on the tattered veneer of the table and were intent on their phones. Hana was playing some kind of puzzle game on hers, and Sayaka was going through old photos.

'Where's Shotaro?' Hana suddenly asked.

'He said something about going back to see how much the water had risen. He's trying to get a more accurate idea of how much time we have until the water rises too high,' I said.

'Huh.' She didn't seem all that interested in the answer.

Ryuhei and Mai were talking about something in room 117. The Yazakis were holed up in their own room.

The sound of the two women's nails tapping every time they touched their phone screens seemed to echo in the quiet. Normally, it would not be nearly so irritating.

'You think this is really OK? I don't. This is all wrong,' Hana grumbled, still staring at the screen.

On the surface, I supposed the dining room would seem peaceful. Like we were lounging around in the hotel lobby on the last night of a group holiday.

We hadn't forgotten the seriousness of our situation. But it seemed that the rising water and the murder had somehow cancelled each other out. We couldn't get out until we solved the murder, so we felt we had no choice but to wait for that to happen. And while we waited, there was really nothing we could do but try to hide from the reality of the situation we were in.

I understood Hana's dissatisfaction. Shouldn't we be out there trying to find the killer? Didn't we have to get out as quickly as possible?

I knew, of course, there was no way to get out onto the surface without sacrificing someone. Which meant we couldn't just ignore the murder.

But there was no reason to think that we were anywhere near solving it. I could feel that, deep inside, Hana and Sayaka were nearly ready to scream with the need to get out, the desire to just go home.

The same thought had to be bouncing around in all our heads. *This is no time to be sitting around doing nothing.*

But it would have taken some courage to say that we should prioritize escaping over finding the murderer. That was just what the murderer would say.

Hana had kept her feelings to herself when everyone was here. Now, with just me and Sayaka present, she must have wanted to open up a bit.

'What do you think we should be doing, then?' I asked.

'No idea. But, like, having nothing to do is really bad, isn't it?'

She let out a sigh of irritation and slammed the phone she'd been fiddling with down on the table.

Hana cocked her head toward the corridor, as if listening for footsteps, then lowered her voice and went on.

'Don't you think there's something weird about that family?'

'The Yazakis?'

'Right.'

'Such as?'

Hana glared at me in annoyance, as if she'd been hoping I'd share her suspicions.

'Just the whole thing, about them being out hunting mushrooms and getting lost, you know? This is really high up in the mountains. If they did get lost, why'd they keep climbing?

Most people start going downhill if they lose their way in the mountains.'

'Maybe, but who can say for sure? Perhaps they looked at a map and thought they'd find a trail if they came this way. It happens, you know.'

'Well, what kind of high school boy goes mushroom hunting with his parents then?'

'Why wouldn't he? I mean, it's not something I'd have done when I was that age. Or now, even. But maybe they're just a close family?'

I could tell from Hana's expression that she was still unconvinced and losing patience with me.

I went on, though. 'No, listen, I get it. I do feel like there's something off about their story. Like, how could it be simply a coincidence that we just happened to run into them out here, in a place like this?'

'Right! That! That's it. It was such a shock running into them last night in the woods. But then they seemed totally calm about this crazy old building being underground. I think they were more surprised about running into us than finding this place, don't you?' she said, nodding.

Sayaka joined in, saying, 'Well, yeah. I mean, of course I think it was only natural to be surprised running into us. All of us out wandering in the woods at night like that.'

To be honest, I had sensed something off when the Yazakis came back with Hana and the others the night before. The path here had been long and treacherous—not one you would choose to follow if you were lost. And there was something odd about how calm the family were. It was like they knew this place.

'Let me get this straight, then. Hana, you don't think those three just happened to stumble on this place, but came here intentionally? To this building?'

'Don't you, Shuichi?'

I had to admit it was possible. But even if we were right, the problem was what, if anything, that had to do with the murder.

'So, let's say they did come here on purpose. They still couldn't have planned the earthquake this morning and us all getting trapped here. Which means them getting mixed up in this has to be a pure accident.'

In other words, could there be any possible connection between the Yazakis' reason for coming here and Yuya's murder?

'Who knows what's really going on? I'm just saying, they're suspicious, is all.'

I was sure Hana thought one of them was the murderer. It must have been easier to believe that than to accept that one of us, who had been friends for so many years, could have killed Yuya.

But with a little thought it was clear that, if one of the Yazaki family really had killed him, the situation would become much more difficult.

It was hard to judge the how the Yazakis got on with each other, but if one of them was the murderer, it was a safe bet the others would try to cover for them. And once we'd named the murderer, forcing whoever it was to accept death wouldn't be a matter of laws and courts, but something much more brutal.

It might even be that all of them had worked together to commit the murder. Whatever the case, it would pit the rest of us against the three of them.

That would be something close to war. Shotaro said we'd have to prove the murderer's identity in a way no one could dispute, but all his logic would probably vanish like smoke in the wind. This underground building slowly filling with water could quickly become a battleground.

'So, Hana, if one of the Yazakis did kill Yuya, what do you think their motive was?'

'Hmmm… I wonder.' She sat and thought for a moment. 'So, maybe they thought if they killed one of our group, we'd assume it was one of us, then that person would become the sacrifice and they'd all be sure to get out? Something like that?'

Her tone was nonchalant, despite the incredible things she was saying.

Would anyone actually think that far ahead? And the idea that we would automatically believe that if one of us was killed, it must have been one of us that did it… Had they really thought they could survive this ordeal through such ridiculous logic?

It was absurd, and if it had been their plan, clearly it hadn't worked, since the Yazakis were in fact being treated as suspects. Still, the father had suggested himself that the killer must be one of our group as proof that his family had nothing to do with it.

Hana paused for a moment. 'So, have they been in their room this whole time?'

'Huh? Probably, yeah. All three of them, I think. Or, I haven't seen them outside it, at least.'

Then, Sayaka closed the blue denim case over the smartphone she'd been poking at and said, 'Didn't they come out and go to the dining room a little while ago? I thought I heard their voices, anyway.'

'They did? I didn't notice. Are you sure?' Hana said.

I hadn't noticed, either. But, so what if they had gone to the dining room?

The two women had been together in room 115 at the time, so Sayaka said she hadn't actually seen the family.

'You had your earphones in, Hana. I just barely heard them myself. But I reckon they're avoiding us.' Sayaka sounded like this last thought had just occurred to her.

'Never mind whether one of them is the murderer or not, we can't let things go on like this, can we? They're probably planning on staying in their room as much as they can until the very last minute. So, are we supposed to just figure everything out until then? That's rather…' She didn't finish the thought, but I could imagine what she felt. It was rather irresponsible. Rather sneaky.

'We might need to ask for their help finding the murderer. And don't you think it's weird that we still don't know anything about them?'

Apart from their names, all we knew about the Yazakis was that they were local and that the husband was an electrician. Of course, they didn't know much about us, either.

'Shouldn't we set up some kind of regular time for everyone to meet up and get to know each other? Otherwise,

I get the feeling things are just going to get worse and worse be—'

We heard footsteps in the corridor and Sayaka's mouth snapped shut.

Kotaro Yazaki opened the door and came into the dining room.

'Um. Sorry to interrupt. I came to get something for dinner. Do you mind?'

He was alone. His wife and son were still hiding out in their room. His tone, his expression, and the way he kept sneaking glances at us all were thick with suspicion. He walked over to the pile of cans at the end of the table. He hurriedly grabbed enough food for three and stuffed it into a nylon supermarket bag.

As he was rushing back to his room, Sayaka called out to him.

'Wait, Mr Yazaki. Would you like to have dinner with us this evening? You and your family. With everything the way it is, I think it would be best if we all got together and talked things over. What do you think?'

'Oh… Uh…' Yazaki's face twisted in discomfort. 'At the moment, you see, my wife and son are in a bit of a panic. Another time.'

He left without waiting for an answer.

It was easy to believe that his wife and child were in a panic. I also felt like Sayaka's invitation had seemed to gloss over the true gravity of the situation, but I couldn't come up with anything better myself.

For whatever reason, Yazaki had seemed more distant than earlier, when he'd been helping with the wiring. The realization of this discouraged us, and we sat in silence, slowly eating our canned dinner.

IX

It was ten o'clock at night.

Hana and Sayaka were still chatting in the dining room. Everyone else had gone back to their rooms.

The underground building was silent apart from the generator's hum. The more courageous were probably sleeping; the less so were probably curled up, hugging their knees, holding back the mounting anxiety.

I walked through the corridor of the upper floor. There was something bothering me that I just couldn't get off my mind.

I hadn't seen Ryuhei or Mai since we'd all gone through Yuya's daypack.

The two had been shut up in their room this whole time. I had the feeling they were talking something over, but it had been so long, I was starting to think they must be having a fight.

I hadn't seen them come to get any food, either. They could well have been arguing without a bite to eat all day.

They were in room 117. I took care to make sure my trainers didn't make a sound on the floor as I crept up to their door and pressed my ear to it.

I could hear them clearly through the door.

'Why do you keep saying the same thing, Ryuhei? I truly do not understand. What's the point?'

'What?! Is that what you're on about? Not a word about what's bothering me? Even though it's obviously not me that's acting weird?'

'No one's acting weird! There's nothing going on, and the fact that you don't see that is just... Enough. I've had enough!'

I had no idea what they were talking about, but the fact that they were arguing even with everything else going on implied this wasn't just some lovers' spat.

They'd only been married for a couple of years, so when they were with the rest of us it still felt just like a club get-together, back in university. Which was probably why I couldn't recall ever seeing them act like a proper couple before.

But their fighting like this seemed proof that they truly were a married couple. I was surprised at how deeply it shook me. Distracted by the general sense of emergency, I hadn't steeled myself against all the complicated feelings I still had for Mai.

The conversation broke off. I could hear footsteps.

I had the sudden premonition that the door was about to open. I leapt back guiltily.

'Shuichi?' Mai said, holding the door open. She had her pack hooked over one shoulder and stared at me in surprise and confusion.

I was far too close to the door to say I'd just been walking past. While I was wondering how to respond, Ryuhei came up behind her.

'What? Shuichi? You were you eavesdropping?!'

He stepped in front of Mai and stared me down.

Which, oddly, helped me decide exactly what to say.

'I'm not sure I'd call it eavesdropping. And normally, I'd not intrude. But with the way things are, I think it's natural to take an interest when people start arguing. In fact, I think it's almost a duty to listen. You never know what you might hear, you know?'

'Right, that's true. Sorry,' Mai said, and her support encouraged me. I wasn't worried about Ryuhei's reaction, but I was terrified Mai would tell me to mind my own business and accuse me of spying.

'So, can I ask what happened?'

'Well, it's nothing, really—' Mai actually seemed anxious to explain.

To sum up, it was all about the crisps from Yuya's pack. The ones we'd put with the rest of the food in the dining room.

It must have been while Shotaro and I were going over the crime scene the second time. Hana and Sayaka went off somewhere, and the dining room was empty. It seems Hayato Yazaki, the son, went in to get the crisps for himself.

But just then, Mai and Ryuhei showed up. Ryuhei started shouting at the boy.

'He was all, "What do you think you're doing? Put them back!" but they were no one's in particular, you know? And then Ryuhei grabbed him by his shoulder.'

'But it's absolutely unacceptable, though! We should all get to eat them together! It's obvious! The boy's crazy, just taking them for himself like that.'

Mai seemed disgusted by her husband's reaction. 'That is not the problem! Why don't you just let the boy eat the crisps? Are you really that desperate for them yourself?!'

'I said I wasn't...'

'Well then! Poor kid. No one else was dying for the crisps either. Hayato's the youngest. You could have just let him have them.'

'What happened after that?' I asked.

'Hayato started crying. He put the crisps back and ran to his room. Then his parents came to see what had happened. They were worried, of course. I explained, and Mr Yazaki apologized, then they left.'

So, Mr Yazaki had been on his guard when he came to get dinner because one of us had gone off at his son. That was certainly understandable.

'Look, all he had to do was say something. "Is it OK if I take these crisps?" or whatever. Am I wrong?'

Well, I could see how taking something left by a person you'd just met the day before without a word was a bit thoughtless.

But the story actually lessened the growing suspicion of the Yazaki family I'd been feeling. They'd been hiding because of the slightly immature selfishness of a boy, which was a far more mundane thing than murder. In a stressful situation like this, some people found it hard to eat, while others started to crave junk like crisps.

'I was just saying that, sure, maybe Hayato lacks a little common sense, but what's the harm? You were wrong to blow up at him like that. I'd say your reaction was a hundred times crazier than what he did. What was the point in yelling at him when we still have a murderer to catch? When we might need to ask for their help?'

'Um. Well. Yeah, there is that.'

I saw something more worrying about what Ryuhei was up to, and said, 'We're going have to talk to the Yazakis a lot more during the investigation, so going out of your way to worsen our relationship with them is a bit out of line. But I guess you aren't all that sure we're going to find the murderer, are you, Ryuhei?'

'That's right!' Mai added. It seemed I'd struck upon the essence of what she had been trying to get at with Ryuhei.

'You're thinking it makes more sense to just run wild, aren't you? You're going to threaten and bully everyone so if we don't find the murderer, no one will have the guts to try and force you to be the sacrifice, or something? If that's the path you choose, it's all over for everyone.'

Mai and I stared at Ryuhei reproachfully.

The fact that Mai had taken my side right away seemed to have hurt Ryuhei deeply. He fell back a step, a stunned look on his face.

'So, what are you going to do, Mai?'

'Me? I told you, I'm spending the night somewhere else. You told me to leave, didn't you? I agree, it's better that way.'

'Where? With Shuichi, I guess?'

'What? What are you talking about?' For the first time, Mai sounded truly angry.

'What is going on between you two? Talking behind my back like you do. It's disgusting.'

'See, that is what I mean. I've had enough! This is no time for your pathetic "he saw this, she said that" rubbish! Bye. See you tomorrow.'

Mai reached out to close the door, but Ryuhei beat her to it.

'Have you been arguing this whole time?' I asked.

'Yeah. But we spent more time just ignoring each other.'

'All because of Hayato?'

'Not just that. There's just been a lot, you know. Like I told you before. And I just realized I couldn't take it anymore.'

The two of us walked slowly down the quiet corridor.

Mai didn't seem embarrassed by my seeing her arguing with Ryuhei. She might have already grown numb to that kind of feeling.

'Ryuhei likes to talk about logic and reason, but when the slightest problem arises, all he knows how to do is bully his way through it. He's always been that way, but now that we're in a real emergency, it's only got worse. I just wish he would let me help him.'

'That sounds hard.'

I expressed sympathy but left it there. I felt it might be dangerous to go any further down that road.

We walked up and down the corridor looking for a decent room, and finally Mai settled on 116.

'I suppose I'll sleep here.'

It was across the corridor at an angle from Ryuhei. It wasn't far at all, in fact, but there wasn't much choice—most of the rooms on the upper floor were still a mess from the earthquake, so would have to be cleared out before anyone could use them.

'Are you all right on your own?'

'Yeah. I'd prefer it that way, honestly. I might call you if I need something. You're right there, after all.'

I helped her drag a mattress from another room.

'Right, I think that'll do for now. I can clear up the rest tomorrow,' she said.

'Right.'

Was going to sleep really the only choice we had? While I stood and wondered, Mai stared at me in silence. She was surely feeling just as worried about being trapped down here as the rest of us.

As we stood staring at each other, the fear and emotional confusion grew and mixed until it felt like the Ark was shrinking, crushing me. But finally Mai said, simply, 'Goodnight.'

She quietly closed the door to her room.

When was the last time I had been alone with Mai? We'd talked on the phone since her marriage, but we'd never even brought up the idea of meeting on our own.

Back in our hiking club days, we'd sometimes end up waiting for the same train or stepping into a cheap restaurant for dinner. And one time, we'd gone shopping for hiking gear together so she could help me choose. Back then, it almost felt like we were on the verge of dating.

Compared to all those times, the few moments we'd just spent together had been so short. But at the same time, we had never so clearly shared the same feelings. The fact that those feelings had been directed at her husband was not a particularly healthy sign.

As I walked toward the room I shared with Shotaro, troubled thoughts kept running through my fevered mind.

Even then, in a situation as extreme as that, all I could think about was Mai.

I wasn't ignoring the reality of our predicament, though. Quite the opposite. The more I thought about her, the deeper my fear of death became.

X

The rest of the first day of our confinement passed without any further incident.

I didn't sleep. I lay listening to music until morning. Shotaro, it seemed, slept peacefully all night, without any apparent worries.

After he woke up, we went to the winch room to check the water level and found that the second step was now submerged.

The water would probably rise above the floor by noon of the next day.

We went to the dining room around eight o'clock. Shotaro opened three cans, but I was in no mood to eat. I just sat beside him, silent.

Soon, Hana and Sayaka came in.

Hana seemed grumpy. She stifled a yawn and said, 'So, what was going on with Mai and Ryuhei last night?'

I told them what had happened between Hayato and Ryuhei. The two of them nodded in understanding. Sayaka, in particular, was concerned about the fallout.

'So, we really do need to get everyone together and talk it out, don't we? Before things get any worse,' she said.

'I suppose. If we can. It's just, I don't think Mai and Ryuhei are at a point where we can ask them to "Try to get along," or anything.' I was talking about it like it had nothing to do with me, for some reason.

'But surely the two of them can make an effort as long as we're trapped in here, can't they? They can be adults about it.'

'You'd think, but…'

I trailed off. I could tell that Sayaka thought everyone getting along and playing nice would somehow get us out of this mess. And maybe we did need to do that, but it would still only treat the symptoms. Our underlying problems were not the kind that would simply be fixed by everyone pulling together.

The Yazakis did not emerge from their room, but maybe they'd had their breakfast earlier.

I left the dining room. It would be awkward running into Mai this early in the morning, and I didn't want to see Ryuhei at all just yet.

Shotaro and I went back to our room. I was finally sleepy, and Shotaro didn't seem to have anything else to do. He sat on his mattress and rifled through the paperbacks he'd brought.

'It sounds like Sayaka wants to plan some kind of friendship rally where we all get together and hug it out or something. What do you think? Should we give it a try?'

'Why not? It's better to get along than not, at least until the final decision.' Shotaro didn't seem all that interested one way or another.

I'd talked to him about Ryuhei the night before. I'd framed it like I was just an onlooker, but there was no way he believed that, or that I had no feelings for Mai.

The friendship rally ended up happening much sooner than I'd imagined.

That noon, the nine of us who were still alive gathered in the dining room. Sayaka had talked to the Yazakis and convinced them to join us.

They must have been scared. It would be natural for them to worry that, as the pressure grew, we might band together and turn on them.

I sat at the end of the long table nearest the door. Shotaro was next to me, then Mai, Sayaka, Hana, and finally Ryuhei at the far end. We had been avoiding each other since the night before.

At the other end of the table sat Hayato, with Hiroko and Kotaro at his side. Everyone had one tin of chilli con carne and one of fruit in front of them, along with a cup of water. We were dressing it up as a group lunch.

Sayaka kicked things off.

'Mr Yazaki, I want to apologize for what happened to Hayato yesterday. It truly is unacceptable that, on top of being trapped in here, he was made so miserable.'

'Well, you know. With the crisps put alongside the tins like that, it seems he thought whoever wanted them could take them. He never considered that they had belonged to your late friend. We're sorry about that.'

Kotaro seemed confused as to why we were wasting our energy on crisps at such a time.

Our conversation seemed at odds with the gravity of the situation. But looking at Hayato, his shoulders slumped, his body trembling, I could tell that we needed to comfort him.

'Yes, and on our side, Ryuhei got a little overheated. He didn't mean to threaten anyone.'

I'm sure that Sayaka actually wanted Ryuhei to apologize and smooth things over himself.

But Ryuhei was radiating such ill will at Mai and me that he didn't seem interested in even an empty apology. His jaw was clenched as he sat, glaring into empty space, which for Hayato—who couldn't know what else had happened—must have been even more frightening.

Still, Sayaka went on, her voice kind, and Hayato soon raised his eyes.

We started to eat, and the conversation slowly began to feel more natural.

We learned some things about the Yazakis, like how Kotaro and Hiroko were the same age, and had married at thirty-two. How they had a Shiba Inu at home, and they were worried if their neighbours would take proper care of him. How Hayato was going to a prefectural secondary school where he was in the drama club.

I couldn't help thinking about the suspicions Hana had voiced the day before. About how the three of them might have had some prior connection to this underground building.

But before any of us could bring it up, Yazaki broached the topic of the Ark himself.

'So, did you really all come out here for no particular reason? It was some kind of test of courage or something?'

'Huh? Well, I suppose you could put it that way. Well, not really a test of courage so much as we heard it was an interesting place.' Sayaka was taken by surprise when they brought up the exact topic we wanted to ask them about.

'And the one who led you here was this Yuya Nishimura? The boy who died?'

'Right.'

'And only him?' Kotaro seemed oddly persistent.

'I think so. Did any of you know about this place before then?' Sayaka asked the rest of us, but of course, apart from Yuya, none of us had ever even imagined anywhere like this existed.

Or, so I thought, until Sayaka herself seemed to recall something.

'Oh, wait. Now that I think about it, Yuya sent me some pictures about six months ago. So, I guess I did know about it, in a way.'

'What? You never told me that!' Hana interjected.

The rest of us were equally surprised. Sayaka realized she might have just invited suspicion and rushed to defend herself.

'It really was nothing much. Yuya texted me and asked how I'd been, you know, and I answered the usual. Then he told me he'd found this weird place in the woods and sent me pictures of the entrances.' She brought out her phone to show us. 'It didn't really strike me as all that important, so I just said something like "Cool" and that was it. I never really paid it much mind, but now that I think about it, those pictures must have been taken here.'

It really wasn't much, now that she'd told us. All the photos but those of the hatches were dark and hard to make out, and they'd come along with pretty pictures of the scenery outside, so it really wasn't the kind of thing anyone would pay much attention to. But it was odd that she hadn't remembered them after coming here herself.

Sayaka was the only one he'd sent them to. Maybe Yuya had chosen her because he knew she was into photography. There probably wasn't much thought behind it.

But what was Kotaro's interest in all this?

'So, Mr Yazaki, could it be that you have some connection here?' Sayaka asked.

'Oh, not at all! We just lost our way.' His denial was immediate.

I wondered if we should press him further. He didn't seem to be entirely sure of himself. No one seemed to have the heart to set off more conflict, though, so we sat awkwardly avoiding the topic for a bit.

Finally, Kotaro worked up the nerve to ask, 'Actually, I was wondering about the… incident. Have you found out anything else?'

Everyone fell utterly silent.

Finally, Shotaro said, 'Nothing significant.'

Kotaro shook his head in disappointment.

Our lunch party broke up.

As the Yazakis began to head back to their room, Sayaka called out:

'Hayato! If you'd like, you can have the crisps.'

But Hayato shook his head. 'No, thanks.' He probably didn't want to reawaken that particular conflict.

The couple led their son from the room, making apologies for his abruptness.

When it was clear the conversation was well and truly over, Ryuhei stood and stomped out of the room, practically kicking chairs out of his way.

'That didn't go very well, did it?' Sayaka said. She sounded exhausted.

In the end, we'd made no progress toward solving our real problem by finding the murderer. As things stood, the Yazakis had probably decided that the best policy was to say nothing rather than risk raising more suspicion by admitting to any connection to the Ark, if in fact they had one.

'There's something going on with them. I know it. Why was he so interested in why we came here? It's not like we want to be stuck in this place,' Hana grumbled, but no one joined in.

Our friendship rally had lasted just under an hour.

I was starting to think it was dangerous for us to spend too much time together. As long as we met in small groups, we could get along OK, but when we were all in the same place, I felt like people might get worked up and start yelling at each other at any moment. *Who's the murderer? Come on, out with it! Show yourself!* And I wasn't the only one to feel that way. I'm sure that everyone else, except the murderer of course, would be fighting the urge to start throwing accusations through all the chitchat and empty pleasantries. Our fears multiplied when we were together, like figures in a hall of mirrors.

In fact, I thought Sayaka's plan had gone pretty well, since our little gathering hadn't broken into a screaming brawl.

XI

It was around three o'clock in the afternoon.

Once again, everyone was off doing their own thing. I was on my way back to my room after using the toilet when I ran into Sayaka coming out of room 115.

For some reason, she had her backpack on. It almost looked like she was running away from home. She stopped short when she noticed me.

'Hey, Sayaka. What's going on?'

'Oh, um, hi, Shuichi. Yeah, uh…' No one else was in the corridor. Sayaka kept glancing back at the room she'd just left while she talked. 'I talked it over with Hana and we decided it would be better to have separate rooms. She said she wasn't able to relax at all last night, so, you know, I thought maybe I should leave.'

'Ah, I see. Well then.'

The two friends had stayed together at the holiday house and here the night before, but I guessed there was nothing odd about people changing their minds at such a time.

Sayaka looked sad. Not that she and Hana would be in separate rooms, but more that we weren't all going to get along in this situation, no matter how hard she tried.

'So, do you need any help? Can I carry your mattress for you?'

'Huh? Oh, no, I'm fine. I can do it.'

She had seemed half lost in thought but snapped back to herself when I made my offer. She chose room 108, near the stairs, as her new room, and moved right in.

108 was a mess. I could hear her tidying up down the hall for some time.

Just before eight in the evening, Shotaro and I went to get dinner from the dining room.

Once more, it was tinned food. We were all growing tired of eating cold dinners. There was a gas hob in the dining room, but the igniter was broken. I poked around at it, but it didn't look like anything we could mend. None of us were smokers, either, so there was no way to light a fire.

As we were finishing up, Sayaka came in.

'Oh, hi. I just thought I'd come and get dinner.'

She looked for something she wanted to eat in the pile of tins. She picked out a tin of chilli con carne and held it toward us.

'Do you think it's all right to take this? It's the last one.'

'Oh, is it? It's fine, I'm sure. No one's going to get angry or anything.'

Now Sayaka was so hesitant to take the last can of chilli con carne. With the whole crisps incident, she must have been nervous about the idea of laying claim to anything potentially valuable.

'I'll take it then. This chilli is pretty good.'

'Is it? Well, I'm glad for you, then.'

I got the idea that Sayaka was trying to make friendly conversation, but I wasn't in the mood to get excited over tinned food, so my responses were anything but enthusiastic.

She looked disappointed and must have decided to go and eat alone. She picked up her tin and water and left the dining room to go back to her new room in 108.

Then, Shotaro and I spent a little more time trying to see if we could repair the hob.

I had no idea what anyone else was doing. The Yazakis had picked up their tins around seven and then remained in their room, as had become their habit.

Around nine in the evening, we gave up on our fruitless attempts at repair and headed back to room 112.

When we stepped out into the corridor, we saw Sayaka and

Hana standing in front of 108. Sayaka was handing something small and black to Hana.

I wondered what it could be. Some kind of folded cloth? The two split up before we got close.

It didn't seem that important, so I didn't dwell on it too much. I assumed I could just ask the next day.

Back in our room, I put one earphone in and sat listening to music and spacing out. Next to me, Shotaro sat on his bed reading a book, just like that morning. It looked like some kind of overseas travelogue.

The second day since the murder was passing us by. We only had five more days.

The water was rising, but we just sat with our smartphones and books, killing time.

Never in my life had I felt time pass in such a bizarre way. I was sure I never would again.

I asked, as I had more times than I could recall, 'You seriously don't have any idea who the murderer might be?'

'I don't have any idea who the murderer might be,' Shotaro answered in a monotone, the same as always.

There was just no evidence to go on. No matter how hard he thought, he just couldn't make any progress.

So, what were we waiting for, sitting here doing nothing at all like on a typical boring Sunday night?

Shotaro went on, as if to calm my anxiety. 'The way things stand, there's really nothing we can do. In which case, I think it's better to relax than rush around in a panic.'

'Do you think time could run out without us ever finding the murderer?'

'It could. And if it does, we'll just have to think about what to do when the time comes. For the time being, though, there's no point worrying about it. I mean, I doubt we could convince everyone even if we thought of something.'

He put his book down on the mattress, stood up and stretched. Then he sat down again.

'Hey, you said Hana and Sayaka are in separate rooms now, right?' he asked.

'Oh, yeah. I did.'

I'd told him before we saw them in the corridor.

Mai and Ryuhei were still split up after their argument, so everyone except us and the three Yazakis were in individual rooms.

'Those two aren't fighting or anything, are they?'

'I don't think so. Sayaka said something about Hana not being able to relax the night before. I get it. Sometimes other people can get on your nerves.'

'Do you think one of them might have started suspecting the other? Begun to worry they were rooming with a murderer?'

'I guess it's possible, but it's probably nothing so concrete. More like, just a feeling.'

I thought Hana and Sayaka both suspected those among us they were least familiar with, the Yazakis, if they suspected anyone. Which suggested the last people they'd suspect would be each other. That's why they had been able to stay close, even in the same room, for so long after the murder.

And it wasn't that much of a risk, anyway. In the very unlikely case that one of them was the murderer and killed the other in the room they shared, the rest of us would figure out who the culprit was pretty quickly. The murderer's life was on the line, too, so they wouldn't be taking such risks.

Despite that, Sayaka and Hana probably couldn't avoid feeling a bit uneasy around each other. I could understand waking up in the morning and realizing maybe it would be better to sleep apart.

When I told Shotaro what I'd been thinking, he nodded.

But it seemed that he hadn't been harbouring any suspicions of his own.

'What they're doing makes sense. And I think your reasoning is right. But, there's something more to it. Let's imagine we weren't trapped in this underground building, but snowed in at a mountain cabin. It's going to be a week before rescue reaches us. Then, one of us is strangled to death. What would you do in that situation, Shuichi?'

'Huh? Well, I'd say we should gather everyone in one place so we could all keep an eye on each other.'

'Exactly,' he agreed. 'That's the best idea. We could sleep in shifts, and anytime people had to leave, like going to the toilet, they'd have to go alone. No one could complain about a system like that, and if we followed the rules strictly, everyone would be safe. But now, we're doing the exact opposite. We're spending almost no time gathered together in one place, and the groups that did exist are gradually splitting up and moving rooms.' Shotaro sighed and went on. 'I suppose what I'm getting at is… If the murderer is planning to kill again, you could call this an ideal situation for them.'

I had thought of the possibility myself, but I was taken aback by how dispassionately he was talking about something so serious.

'Shotaro, do you really think the murderer wasn't finished after Yuya?'

'That's not what I'm saying. I have no idea. To be honest, it would be crazy for the murderer to kill again.'

I saw his point.

If the murderer were discovered, their fate would be condemnation to a horrible death, perhaps after actual torture. The first murder ended without a single piece of useful evidence. So, then, why go to all the risk of doing it again, when they were safe? It was exactly this thought that kept Shotaro and me from being overly wary of each other.

'Then, what's the problem?'

'There is a murderer among us. And yet, we don't seem at all concerned about preventing any more killing. It almost feels like we're intentionally making it easy for the murderer to strike again.'

Had Mai and Ryuhei, and Hana and Sayaka, decided to split up to tempt the murderer into another crime?

He was reading too much into things. I doubted very much that anyone was acting so deliberatively.

Still, I couldn't deny that, deep inside, we felt a certain amount of impatience, a yearning for something, anything, to happen soon.

'People might be thinking that another victim is an acceptable price to pay if it helps us identify the criminal. I can't say whether this is a good or proper way to think, but if we don't identify the murderer, we're going to have to choose a sacrifice somehow.'

There was a fate more terrible than being strangled to death awaiting us in the Ark. Strangulation would be nothing compared to being trapped underground, in the dark, with water slowly rising until it swallowed you.

'So, what should we do?'

'Nothing. There's nothing to do. Even if we set our consciences aside and began praying, "Oh murderer, please kill again to leave us a clue," I don't see it happening.'

I could only agree.

But then, I couldn't see why anyone would have killed Yuya in the first place, either. So, how could we be so sure there wouldn't be a second murder?

I was growing to hate even thinking about it all. I could actually feel myself starting to hope for a murder to happen.

So, who should be the next victim? Who did I want to die?

Shotaro looked at me with sympathy.

'Feel free to worry about whatever you want, but I can say this: you don't need to worry about being the next victim. I'm here with you. I'm starting to doubt that's what you'd call lucky, but, anyway. Try to get some sleep. You didn't get much last night, did you?'

That was true enough.

I put the other earphone in my right ear and stretched out on my mattress, eyes closed. With Shotaro in the room, I didn't have to worry about being murdered in the night.

My body wracked by anxiety, I slowly drifted off.

THREE
Severed Head

I

I woke up at seven in the morning. It was the third day of our confinement.

My music had been playing all night. I took my earphones out and shook my head, and it almost felt like the song was oozing from my ear like earwax. I'd been listening to upbeat music to distract me from my anxiety as I fell asleep, but in the morning, it came across as cloying. Saccharine sweet.

I had slept unexpectedly deeply, but I did not feel at all rested.

'Morning!' Shotaro said. It looked like he had been up for a while.

'Yeah. It is. How's the water? Have you checked yet?'

'I have. It's rising at roughly the rate I predicted. The middle floor is going to start flooding just after noon.'

Our time limit was approaching.

'So, our buffer is shrinking.'

'It is what it is. All I did was check the water, though. I can't say if anything happened overnight except time passing us by. So, shall we get breakfast?'

I wasn't hungry, but I didn't want to be alone, so I hurried to straighten my clothes up and left with Shotaro.

No one was in the dining room. I opened a tin of fish, which I'd eaten so much of lately that I could barely recognize the flavour anymore, and ate mechanically.

Hana came in while we were eating.

'Oh, morning,' she said.

'Huh? Oh, hi.' I answered, still bleary with sleep. Hana started picking through the tinned fruit. As she did, she casually asked, 'Hey, is Sayaka still asleep?'

'Probably? I haven't seen her, at least.'

'OK.'

Hana looked gloomy as she opened her tin. She seemed to debate taking it back to her room, but eventually sat at the table and started picking at the fruit.

'Nothing big happened between you two, did it?' I asked.

'Nothing. I mean, this is the normal thing to do, right? No need to stay in the same room. Better for both of us.'

It was what I'd expected. But it did bother me that Sayaka wasn't up and about. She had always been an early riser. It was rare for Hana to be up before her.

Of course, it was probably a mistake to expect people to keep up their normal routines at such a time. Sayaka could simply have been too anxious to get a good night's sleep and be having a lie-in.

But Hana didn't seem ready to brush it off so easily.

After she finished her tin, she sat silent for a while, then said, 'Did you see her last night?'

'Me? No. Did you?' I said and turned to Shotaro.

Of course, he had been with me all night after dinner, so he couldn't have. The last time either of us saw her was when she'd been handing something to Hana.

'Speaking of Sayaka, she gave you something yesterday, right? What was that?'

'Oh, that? I was borrowing a roll of tape.'

She told us the whole story. It had happened while we were still in the dining room.

Sayaka had been eating in her room—108—and had dropped a glass. It shattered all over her floor, so she'd gone down to the middle floor to get a roll of electrician's tape because the sticky tape was good for picking up tiny shards.

Just as she was finishing up, Hana had peeked into her room and asked if she could borrow the tape.

'My undershirt is all bobbly. I don't have a change of clothes, and it feels grotty. I thought the tape she had would be good for pulling them off.'

So, what we'd seen was Hana borrowing the tape to debobble her clothes. That sounded reasonable enough, but Hana wasn't finished.

'But, well, after that... Sayaka was acting funny. I saw her in the corridor before I went to bed. She was looking into lots of different rooms. Like she was searching for something.'

'Really? This was after you borrowed the tape?'

'Yes. Maybe around half nine? I think.'

There wasn't necessarily anything strange about that. Sayaka might have been looking for something she'd misplaced, or something she'd just realized she needed. This was a pretty big place, after all, and it wasn't always easy to find what you were after.

But combined with the fact that, for the first time I could remember, Sayaka wasn't up before Hana, it did make me uneasy. If she was just sleeping in because she'd been up late looking for whatever it was, that was fine, but…

Hana rushed out of the dining room and went to see if Sayaka was in her room.

Not ten seconds later, she ran back in.

'She's not in there!'

'You're sure?'

'I just told you, she isn't! Her room is empty!'

Hana was getting frantic. Her imagination, which had already been going down dark paths, was running wild now.

Shotaro and I stood up and went with Hana to check Sayaka's room.

It was near the stairs down to the middle floor. The door was standing open, but Hana said she had left it that way just now but that it had been closed when she first checked.

Inside, we saw only a mattress and bedclothes in the middle of the floor. Room 108 had been cleaned out.

'Wow, even her stuff is gone,' I mentioned.

Sayaka seemed to have disappeared, rucksack and all.

At first I thought she'd just decided to sleep in yet another room. But if that were the case, wouldn't she have taken her bedding with her?

'Hey, what's going on?' Ryuhei asked from behind us. We turned to him.

I told him Sayaka was gone. He didn't say anything, just stood and swallowed nervously.

'Is everything all right?' Mai came out of her room to join us in the corridor.

Hana had made a lot of noise in coming to get us in the dining room, and the whole building was filling with a foreboding atmosphere. Finally, even the Yazakis came out to see what was happening. The eight of us decided to search the whole building.

The same as we had done two days before, when we had split up to find the missing Yuya.

This time, though, we stayed together and went room by room in order, starting from 101. The last time, no one had ever imagined we'd find Yuya dead, but this time was different. Because as loud and often as we called, Sayaka did not respond.

Was Sayaka in one of these rooms, sleeping so deeply that she couldn't hear all the ruckus? None of us truly believed such a happy ending was awaiting us.

At the furthest end of the upper floor was the storeroom where we'd left Yuya's body. The tension was unbearable as we opened the door. It had already been a crime scene once.

But nothing inside had changed since our last visit two days before, except that Yuya was now giving off a faint scent of decay.

We went down to the middle floor.

This time, we took the opposite route, starting with the highest numbers at the eastern end, opening the metal doors lining the corridor one by one heading west, toward the steel door to the winch room. The lights on that end of the corridor were still out, so we saved it for last.

As we went, everyone had grown silent. At first, we had called Sayaka's name when we opened the doors, but now no one had the strength to do it. There was nothing to say, because we had all grown certain that what we were searching for was something, and not someone.

As we neared the stairs, the sound of machinery grew louder. The generator on the upper floor echoed through the corridors.

And finally, we found Sayaka.

Everyone had been imagining it, I knew. No one thought she was still alive, so we had surely all pictured how she had gone: strangled like Yuya, or perhaps struck on the head with something.

We had been right that she was no longer alive. But the reality of her death was far more gruesome than any of us had imagined.

She was in room 206, across from 207, the tool room.

As soon as Shotaro turned the knob and cracked open the door, we were all struck by the smell of blood, far more powerful than any we had ever experienced.

He pushed the door open wide and flipped the switch on the wall. The room filled with light.

'Whoa… What the hell? What is this?!' I cried out, amid screams and cries from the others.

The sight of that room filled me with nausea. I struggled to suppress the gorge rising in my throat.

The body of a woman lay on the floor. No one who saw it could doubt that she was dead.

Her head was missing.

II

Shotaro went carefully, judging each step as he advanced into the room.

I pressed a sleeve to my mouth and followed him, fighting back fear the whole way.

The headless corpse was on its back in the centre of the room, its legs pointing toward the door.

'It is Sayaka, isn't it?'

'Who else could it be?' Shotaro answered icily.

Of course, the corpse could not possibly be anyone else. It was wearing her jeans and hiking anorak, and the build was the same. And Sayaka was the only member of the group not present. It was a simple process of elimination.

But as I looked at that heart-breaking remnant of a person I had known for so long, I started to wish desperately for it be someone else, a stranger. Thinking of that body as Sayaka was simply too much. Even looking up close, I was filled with doubt. It didn't seem real to me.

I turned around. Everyone except Shotaro and me still stood in the corridor, staring with wide eyes. They were dazed and speechless, mumbling incoherently.

Hana vomited. Others looked sick too, but hadn't eaten breakfast yet, so there was nothing in their stomachs to eject.

Shotaro squatted down and inspected the corpse.

'It looks like she's been stabbed.'

He pointed toward her breast.

I saw the wound he was pointing at, though it was hard to make out through the patch of drying blood blending into the dark brown of her anorak.

'Was that what killed her?'

'There's not much blood around it,' Shotaro muttered to himself. 'Or, perhaps that's normal? If you stab someone with a knife or something, and their heart stops soon after, maybe this is what happens when you pull it out or—' Shotaro broke off as his eyes fell on the ruined neck.

I had somehow been able to bring myself to examine the rest of the body, but the neck was too much. The pale skin simply ended there, giving way to rough flesh that was a dry reddish-black colour, as if it had already started rotting.

He prodded at the base of her neck and leaned in for a closer look.

'Wait, no. She was strangled, too. There's a little bit of a mark left at the base of her neck.'

The remains of her neck had traces of rope burn that the severing of her head had not obliterated.

'So, she was killed the same way as Yuya?'

'I think so. Someone must have sneaked up on her and wrapped a rope or something around her neck. But, what they did afterward is so drastically different, I don't think we can compare it to Yuya's murder.'

The murderer had left Yuya untouched, the rope still around his neck. But this time, they had gone to unimaginable effort working on Sayaka's corpse.

'After strangling her, whoever it was stabbed her in the chest. Maybe they thought they were finishing her off, but it seems like an unnecessary step.'

The murderer had left the rope knotted tightly around Yuya's throat, presumably to be certain he wouldn't regain consciousness. But with Sayaka, they had also stabbed her.

'And then, her head. I think they must have used a saw,' Shotaro said, then looked around the room.

The storeroom was quite large and practically empty, with only a broken bucket in one corner and a bin in another. It was also close enough to the sound of the generator coming from upstairs to hide the sound of sawing, making it a nearly ideal place to kill someone and deal with the body afterward.

There were bloody smears and footprints here and there on the floor, but it looked like the killer had made an effort to clean most of the gore away. On closer inspection, the bin also had bloodstains on its lid.

Shotaro stepped out and came back with a pair of long rubber gloves he'd got from another room. He put them on and lifted the lid of the bin.

'What's this? There's all kinds of stuff left in here...'

The first thing he pulled out was a blood-spattered work apron. Then a pair of rubber gloves. They were the same style as Shotaro's and, of course, were covered in blood, too. Then he brought out a pair of wellingtons. He looked at the soles and verified that the pattern matched the footprints. That was all that was inside. I had been half-afraid that Sayaka's head would be in there, but I was wrong.

Shotaro spread the evidence out on the floor for everyone to see.

'Does anyone recognize any of this?'

'Yeah. The apron, gloves and boots are all from here, the middle floor,' Mai answered. Everyone else agreed.

I also remembered seeing them while we were searching the building. There was no doubt, they were all from this floor.

'This room was really well located for cutting someone's head off, with all this near to hand,' I said.

'I think you're right. I imagine the saw and knife they used were found on this floor, too.' Shotaro responded.

'They're gone, though.'

'Yeah. They're not all that's missing, though. Where's her head?'

Another quick search of the bare room made certain that Sayaka's head was not here.

Of course. We might not know the murderer's reason for decapitating her and leaving her headless body, but it was unbearable to think they had simply done it for fun.

Even if they'd had a reason, though, I doubted the rest of us could ever understand the need for such brutal treatment of her corpse.

Nor could we understand why anyone would kill Sayaka after basically getting away with Yuya's murder. Why take such a risk? And not only that, but to go to all the effort of cutting her head off too? It didn't make any sense. And yet the murderer had done it.

'Where could it be?' I wondered aloud.

'If they don't want us to find it for some reason, I imagine they threw it into the water on the bottom floor, along with the weapons,' Shotaro explained.

'Right. Yeah.'

The flooded bottom floor was the perfect place to dispose of things. There would be no worry of anyone finding them again. The rope, the knife and the saw probably would have been used to weigh down the head and keep it submerged.

The gloves, apron and boots, though, were too bulky and buoyant to get rid of that way, so they had stayed here. We had no way to check for fingerprints or anything, so the murderer had probably not worried about leaving so much evidence behind.

Shotaro started closely inspecting the bloody items again, then found something stuck to the heel of the right wellington.

'Oho, what's this?'

He peeled it away. It was thin and irregular, stained brownish red with blood. It looked to be made of paper.

'What is that? A piece of tissue?'

'No, it's not. It's thicker than that. It's a bit of thick paper towel.'

I looked closer and saw that it had the same dimpled pattern as a kitchen paper towel, but it was thicker. This was a fragment of the kind of paper towel used to wipe off greasy machinery.

The murderer had tried to wipe up the blood on the floor. A piece of one of the paper towels they'd used had got stuck to the sole of the boot.

'Where did the towel come from, though? I don't remember seeing any,' I said.

Shotaro answered, 'I did. On the upper floor, in room 118. There were five packets of two hundred each.'

A few other people agreed. I thought back on my exploration of the upper floor and suddenly remembered. When I'd stepped into room 118, there had been a set of steel shelves to the left of the door with a plastic basket of paper towels on the top shelf.

Judging by the state of the floor, the murderer must have needed a lot of towels. But apart from the piece stuck to the boot, there were none to be seen. So, they must have been thrown away with Sayaka's head.

Shotaro put down the boot and took off his gloves. He turned to us and said, 'I'll take pictures later, but just to be sure, I want everyone to have a good look at the evidence found and the state of the body. When the time comes to identify the criminal, there could be trouble if anyone disagrees about the crime scene.'

So, we were to burn the horrific scene into our memories.

For a moment everyone stood frozen, afraid to step into the room, but at Shotaro's insistence they began to shuffle forward into room 206 one by one, like a line of mourners paying their respects at a funeral, and take their turns at inspecting Sayaka's body and the evidence.

Then, we gathered in the corridor once more, in a ring, with Shotaro at the centre.

'Now, I suggest we visit every person's room together, in turn, and check their belongings. Does anyone object?' he asked.

'No one's going to object. Let's get it over with,' Ryuhei answered before anyone else could open their mouths.

Shotaro pushed ahead with his investigation, not giving anyone time to prepare themselves. No one so much as complained.

Sayaka's death was so brutal and senseless. But, even without understanding what was happening, we began to feel a glimmer of hope.

Unlike with the first murder, this time the murderer had left behind actual physical evidence.

And that murderer was one of the eight of us. Could anyone keep their guilt hidden after committing such a terrible, brazen crime? Were we actually getting close to escaping this underground trap?

III

We walked through the Ark in single file, visiting everyone's room in turn.

Shotaro inspected everyone's bags carefully. We all watched as he opened them and checked everything inside, down to the spare underwear.

I suppose he was thinking there might be bloodstains on a piece of clothing worn during the decapitation. Of course, the murderer might have thrown the bloody item away, but that in itself might be evidence of guilt, if we could see that something was missing.

Sayaka's things had been taken by the killer too, so there was a chance we might find something of hers in someone's bag.

But the quick solution I prayed for did not appear. No one was missing anything they should have had, and no one had anything they shouldn't.

The murderer had not made any basic mistakes.

'Why don't we go and check Sayaka's room again?' Shotaro suggested once we'd looked in everyone else's rooms.

We hadn't found any physical evidence of the crime, so now his idea was to try and find clues about the victim's and the murderer's movements.

We hadn't given Sayaka's room a thorough search on our first visit—merely made sure she wasn't there. Now, we would have a closer look.

We opened the door. Once more, all we saw was an empty room with the mattress and sleeping bag in the centre, but now that we knew the terrible way she'd died, the sight seemed somehow bleak, like staring over the edge of a bottomless cliff.

Shotaro dragged the mattress from its spot. As he did, we saw two small black objects fall to the floor.

'What do we have here?'

He reached down and picked them up. They were pieces of black tape, some four inches long, folded over with the adhesive on the inside.

He opened it up. The tape had been wrapped around several glittering shards of glass.

Shotaro looked around the room again and found more pieces of a broken glass piled in one corner.

'Right, so, Sayaka used the tape to pick up broken glass fragments. Mr Yazaki, do you remember seeing this tape anywhere?'

Yazaki recoiled in shock, as if suddenly he were being accused, but then he understood what Shotaro meant. He took the piece of tape and examined it.

'Ah, yes. I do. This is electrician's insulating tape.'

It was the same tape he'd used when working on the electrical wiring two days before. So, here was proof that Sayaka had done exactly as we'd heard from Hana earlier.

'Hana, you borrowed the roll of tape from her after she used it, right?'

'That's right.' Hana sounded dazed and emotionless.

Shotaro explained Sayaka's movements the night before to the rest of the group in Hana's place.

'But, it seems Sayaka was looking for something yesterday evening, right?' he asked Hana.

She nodded.

'Did anyone else see her last night?' he went on.

'I did. She was wandering the halls, frowning, like something was bothering her,' Mai said.

'I saw her, too. She was looking under the dining room table. I guess now that I think about it, she must have been searching for something,' Ryuhei added.

Mai and Ryuhei had barely been on speaking terms to that point, but it seemed the bizarre murder had dulled the emotions behind their conflict. Now, it was like they were simply two strangers caught in the same situation.

Three people were saying they had seen Sayaka searching for something.

'Does anyone remember what time they saw her?'

'I think it was around ten, maybe?' said Ryuhei. 'I went to the dining room to fill my water bottle before bed. That's when I saw her.'

'I think I saw her around nine thirty,' Hana said.

'I think that was around when I did, too. I didn't pay much attention to the time, though. Sorry,' Mai added.

So, it seemed settled: Sayaka had been searching from around half past nine to ten o'clock.

'Do you have any idea what she was looking for?' I asked, and the three witnesses fidgeted uneasily.

None of them had asked, they said. Mai and Hana had only seen Sayaka at a distance, too far away to talk. And I doubt Ryuhei had felt like talking much, given all that had happened the day before.

'Do you think it had anything to do with the broken glass?' I asked Shotaro.

'I doubt it had any direct relationship,' he said.

Sayaka had broken a glass in her room, used tape to pick up the shards, and then started looking for something. And finally, she had been murdered.

'She was killed on the middle floor…' I said to no one in particular.

'I assume so. At the very least, she was killed near the room where we found her body. Carrying her corpse too far through the corridors would have been much too risky,' Shotaro confirmed.

On reflection, I saw that a victim wandering alone through the Ark was the murderer's best, or maybe only, chance to strike.

When Yuya was killed, we had all been busy rummaging through all the rooms, making a racket in our hunt for a hex key, but this time nearly everyone had been holed up in their own rooms, and the building was silent. Barging into Sayaka's room and killing her there would have been far too risky without any other noise to cover it.

'It was lucky for the murderer that Sayaka was searching for something, wasn't it? All alone down here, far from everyone else. Or, perhaps…' I let the thought go unfinished.

Would the murderer have been happy with any victim at all? Was Sayaka simply unlucky? Could the murderer have been so hungry to kill as all that, down here, in the Ark? Their motive must be something incredibly powerful.

Or perhaps there was some more direct relationship between Sayaka's actions and the murder.

It could have been that whatever Sayaka had been hunting for was connected to the murder. Her wandering through the building might have been a problem for the murderer. That would help explain the timing of the attack.

'The murderer took Sayaka's things, right? That makes me think the motive must be related to something she had.'

'Maybe.' Shotaro shot me a sharp look as he avoided giving a clear answer.

It might have been a bad idea to discuss motive too deeply with the murderer listening. So, I gave up pursuing it any further.

'Anyway, we have a good idea of the victim's movements. I think we're done here. I keep wondering about the paper towels the murderer used to wipe up the blood. They came from 118, the storeroom at the far end of the upper floor, right?' Shotaro said.

The eight of us lined up and followed him to 118.

This room was next to the one where Yuya's corpse still lay. We noticed the change the moment we entered.

The plastic basket that had been on the top steel shelf was now on the floor. There were four packets of two hundred paper towels labelled 'For use on machinery'.

'I suppose it's unlikely I'll get an answer, but does anyone remember taking this basket down?' Shotaro asked.

No one answered. It had been the murderer, of course.

He went on, 'When I looked, there were five packets here. Clearly, the murderer took one.'

Shotaro was the only one who remembered how many there had been, but there was no reason to doubt him. We could all quite easily picture the murderer sneaking in here and taking a packet of towels to the crime scene.

'Right. Next, can any of you see anything else that has changed in this room since yesterday, apart from the basket and missing paper towels?'

Everyone took a careful look around the storeroom.

It was stocked with toilet paper, boxes of tissues, brooms, sponges and other cleaning and sanitary items. As far as I could remember, nothing in particular seemed missing or out of place.

No one else could see anything amiss either. Shotaro nodded.

'I think that will do. The murderer didn't need anything except for the towels from this storeroom.'

That was all there was worth seeing. We decided to go down to the middle floor again to check where the tools used in the crime had come from.

We ended up in room 207, the storeroom for hand tools. Everyone had passed through while we were looking for the hex key, so we were familiar with it.

Shotaro took a worn plastic container from the shelf.

There were several containers holding different tools, and this one was filled with saws. There were coping saws, hacksaws, pruning saws and more.

'There are so many, it's going to be hard to know which one the murderer used. Does anyone notice one that's missing?'

We'd opened the box up during the hex key search, but of course, no one could say exactly which saw had disappeared.

That didn't matter too much, though. The important thing was that the murderer had been able to easily find weapons near the crime scene. Another container was full of all different kinds of knives, from gravers to pocketknives. It was clear the murderer would have had no trouble laying their hands on whatever had been used to stab Sayaka.

After a final glance, Shotaro closed the containers and put them back on the shelf. Then, he looked slowly around the room.

This storeroom was among the most orderly and well stocked in the building. We'd already replaced anything that had fallen from the shelves during the earthquake during the earlier search. There were even some chainsaws and circular saws in a corner, though they were surely far too loud to use in a murder. The shelves also held tins of machine oil and rags.

Shotaro stood in the centre of the room and turned to the rest of us.

'Well, I think we've checked everything we needed to regarding the tools the murderer used. Let's go over what we've seen so far and try to work out the victim's and murderer's movements.'

He started going through each item from the night before, slowly and carefully, one by one.

'First, Sayaka cleared up the broken glass from her floor. Then, she started searching for something. Sometime after ten o'clock, she encountered the murderer. That was most likely here on the middle floor, near the murder scene. There, the murderer wrapped a rope or something similar around her neck and strangled her to death.

'Then, the murderer stabbed something into Sayaka's chest, although we can't be sure when. Given the lack of blood around that wound, it might have been just after death, or later, after they cut her head off.'

'But don't you think the stab wound was just to make sure she was dead, after the killer strangled her?' I asked. 'Why would the murderer stab her after cutting her head off?'

'I don't think so, actually. In Yuya's case, the murderer made sure he was dead by tying the rope tight and leaving it. They could have done the same thing here. But they changed things this time, and going to get the knife to stab her with was much more effort.

'So, we have to assume the murderer had some other reason for the stab wound, and depending on that reason, it's possible they did it after cutting off Sayaka's head.

'I'm sure an expert could tell whether it happened before or after. The real issue is the reason for it. If we knew that, I imagine the order wouldn't really matter.

'At any rate, we know that for some reason the murderer decided to cut off Sayaka's head, then went up to the upper floor and all the way to the furthest storeroom to get paper towels. Then they readied a saw, an apron, gloves and wellingtons, and got to work.

'The work itself would have taken at least twenty minutes, if it went smoothly. When the murderer was done, they wiped down the floor with paper towels. I'm guessing they were very careful about that because they didn't want to leave any bloody footprints in the corridors or anywhere. They'd have taken extra care to check their own clothes and skin for any traces of blood. Then, they put all the protective gear into the bin at the scene.

'After that, they disposed of the severed head, bloody towels and weapons. Right now, we have to assume they were all dropped into the water below.'

We hadn't made a truly exhaustive search of the building so couldn't prove that, but it was by far the most likely place.

'It would be quite easy to get rid of the head on the bottom floor. You could do it from there,' Shotaro said and pointed at the bare rock wall at the back of the storeroom.

The natural rock wall bulged inward, preventing the use of wall panels there. The steel plates of the floor had been cut to follow its shape, but the damp of the rock had rusted away the metal, creating large gaps.

The worst section was large enough to pass a human head through and opened directly onto the flooded bottom floor, making it perfect for disposing of anything you might want to get rid of.

It would also be possible to drop the head into the water covering the stairs leading down from the winch room, of course, but in the future, someone might dive down and find it there. Dropping things through the gap would effectively hide them forever.

I went to that corner and looked down into the bottom floor, my heart pounding in fear.

The black water was almost level with the floor we were standing on. I tried shining my phone light down but couldn't make out anything under the surface. Was Sayaka's head truly somewhere in that darkness below?

Shotaro started speaking again, so I turned around and went back to join the others.

'The murderer went back to Sayaka's room and got her pack, but again, we don't know at what point that happened. They might have done it when they went to get the paper towels, or they might have done it after cutting off her head. Since we still haven't found it, I think we can assume it went down to the same place as her head.

'And then the murderer's work was over. I imagine they just went back to their room and hoped they hadn't left any evidence behind.'

Shotaro fell silent, and the sombre mood drew a sigh from the rest of us.

'Everything the murderer did is simply mystifying,' I complained. 'They killed Sayaka, for some reason. They stabbed her corpse, for some reason. They cut off her head, for some reason. They got rid of her belongings, for some reason. Yuya's murder was almost disappointingly free of puzzles. So, why did Sayaka's murder have to be so bizarre?'

'You're right, but I think you're forgetting one more mystery, Shuichi,' Shotaro replied.

'There's something else?' What could I possibly be forgetting? Weren't all those things enough to puzzle over?

'Yes. And it might be quite an important part of the mystery. Where should I begin? Let's see… Shuichi, why don't you go back over everything the murderer needed, piece by piece.'

I still didn't follow Shotaro, but I did as he said and thought back over everything he'd mentioned.

'All right, so, first, they needed something to use as a murder weapon. A rope or such, right? Then, a knife. A saw. Towels to wipe up the blood. An apron. Wellingtons. Rubber gloves. Is that all?'

'That's what I mentioned earlier, but the murderer likely needed some other things too.

'For example, when they got rid of the head, they probably needed a bag. Something like a bin liner. They wouldn't just carry it around, blood dripping and all. And they would have put the towels into the bag with the head to get rid of them.

'The bag would also be good to hold weights to make sure Sayaka's head and pack would sink. The saw and knife would help, but they probably added something heavy like a hammer to make sure.

'So, now that we've catalogued all the necessities for the crime, how would they have gone about gathering everything?'

'Well, I suppose they just had to search through all the different storerooms, right?'

'Right. They had to go from room to room gathering equipment. And the murderer could have found everything they needed on this floor.'

I fell into thought when he said that. I could see that he was right. The weapons and everything needed for cleaning could all have been found on the middle floor. There were even bin liners and tools to use as weights.

'This was ideal for the murderer,' Shotaro went on, 'because we were all sleeping on the floor above. There was relatively little risk of anyone noticing them as they gathered it all.

'Apart from one thing, that is. The paper towels they used to clean up the blood. For that one item the murderer had to go upstairs and all the way to the furthest storeroom,' Shotaro explained.

'That's right…'

'And that posed a huge risk. Ryuhei, Hana and Mai were all sleeping nearby in 117, 115 and 116. So, the murderer had to be careful not to make any sound when they got the towels. They left the plastic basket on the floor, after all.'

I saw what Shotaro was getting at. Those steel shelves would probably have rattled when they put the basket back.

He went on, saying, 'Contrast that with the tool containers on the middle floor. The murder closed them up and put them back on the shelf. They weren't worried about sound down here like they were up above.

'Well then, why did the murderer do it? Why go upstairs and all the way to the very end of the corridor just for paper towels? That's bizarre.

'I can see why they wanted to wipe up the blood. But they didn't have to go upstairs to do it.'

Shotaro picked up the bundle of rags from the shelf near the tool containers.

I finally understood what puzzle I was missing.

They had what they'd needed to wipe up the blood right here, next to the tools they used. Why didn't they use these rags? Why invite danger by going to get those paper towels?

'Maybe they didn't know the rags were here? No, that's ridiculous...' I said.

'It is. I can't imagine anyone missing them if they came in here.'

The bundle of rags was on a shelf directly across from the door, visible as soon as you opened it. What's more, they were next to the containers of tools where the murderer must have got the saw and knife they'd used. There was no way the murderer wouldn't have noticed them. And anyway, every member of the group had looked through this room before. We had all seen them, including the murderer.

'I think we're all agreed that nothing but the towels was missing, and given what we understand about the crime itself, there's nothing else in that room that would have been needed. So, I think it's clear that the only reason they went was to get the towels. Of course, the murderer did also have to go upstairs to get Sayaka's pack, but that wouldn't have been nearly as risky. Room 108 is near the stairs, and no one is using the room next to it.'

Why did the murderer ignore the rags and put themselves at risk by going to get those paper towels?

'Solving this mystery might be the unexpected key to identifying the murderer,' Shotaro concluded.

He fell silent, and the sound of the generator filled the storeroom.

After a few moments, Yazaki said hesitantly, 'So, then, who—?'

'I don't know who the murderer is,' Shotaro cut his question off.

I could feel the despair spreading through the room. Shotaro had spoken with such confidence and clarity that we'd all begun to hope that he had already seen through the mysteries of these murders.

But in the end, all he'd done was clarify the details of the situation.

'Well then, what do we do now?' Kotaro asked.

'What we have been doing. Just keep thinking about who it could be. It's probably not right to call it a stroke of luck, but whereas Yuya's case didn't feature any real mysteries, this case is practically overloaded with them. And that gives us a chance to put together a logical theory and identify the killer.'

Kotaro didn't back down. 'And then what? I can't believe you're still going on about that, now, after all this. The kind of maniac who'd do something this brutal, you think they'll just sit back and agree to be left behind, just because we figured out their crimes?' He was almost shouting.

'I think it's pretty clear now,' he went on. 'The murderer's not fit to be called human. Otherwise, how could they have gone and cut that girl's head off?

'What do logical theories and explanations mean to someone like that? We can't keep wasting time. Stop sitting around and hoping we find the murderer and things just work out! We have to start looking for a way out! Please, for my family.'

His tone grew more heated with every word, and his wife and son shrank in on themselves, hiding behind him.

I couldn't say he was wrong, either. By searching for the murderer when we could have been looking for a way out, we might be condemning more people to death at the killer's hands for no reason. And I couldn't but think there would be more bodies.

But the fact that no one else spoke up in agreement showed the vast divide between our two groups.

He had a family, while we were a bunch of aimless kids just out of university. Our lives weren't worth as much as his. That's the reasoning we sensed behind his words.

'That's rich, coming from the most suspicious person here,' Hana said.

A shock went through the room. I knew she suspected the Yazakis, but I'd never dreamed she would say it out loud in front of them like that.

Shotaro tried to smooth things over before anyone else said anything more.

'If we don't act reasonably, we'll all end up just as guilty of brutal murder ourselves. That's the one thing we need to remember.'

He pointedly ignored Hana's comment.

The truth was, condemning someone to be left in this place, to drown slowly in the dark, deep underground, might be far crueller than the murders of Yuya and Sayaka. But if someone had to be chosen to stay, choosing the murderer was our only chance of preserving some innocence.

If we couldn't all agree on a decision and ended up stuck in the Ark because of it, then we would all have killed each other. That is what Shotaro was trying to get us to remember.

'I understand your frustration, Mr Yazaki, but I don't know who the murderer is yet.

'One thing I will say, though, is no matter how it looks on the surface, this murderer is no lunatic. Make no mistake. They aren't running wild. I am confident of that much. When the time comes, we'll be able to have a reasonable discussion with whoever it is.

'And, Mr Yazaki, if you can think of a way to get everyone out of here without forcing anyone to stay behind as a sacrifice, tell us. I want to know how as much as anyone. Right now, that's the only question more important than that of the murderer's identity.'

Shotaro was right, but we all knew there was no way out without leaving somebody behind. We had thought long and hard about it already.

And so ended our crime scene investigation. As before, we were free to spend our time however we wanted, and we all scattered, as if fleeing the terrifying aura that emanated from that headless corpse.

IV

It was just after noon.

Although it was our 'free time', Shotaro and I had some work we needed to do—work I wanted to do less than anything I'd ever done in my life, but which no one else was willing to take on. We were going to move Sayaka's corpse.

We had left Yuya where he lay, but we couldn't do that this time. The middle floor was going to be flooded soon.

What would happen to poor headless Sayaka if we left her

there, simply waiting for the dark water to swallow her? I couldn't stop picturing it rising, stained brown-red with rust and earth.

I started out by tying a bandanna over my face. Hana had been sick in the corridor, and I simply could not bear to touch the body with the lingering scent of vomit in my nose.

Standing by the corpse, Shotaro took out his phone.

'I think we should make a record. Just in case.'

He took photos from all angles. I didn't doubt that it was the right thing to do, but I couldn't have borne having those pictures on my own phone.

It would have been better if we'd had some opaque bin liners or plastic sheeting, but all we could find were transparent bags. We wrapped her in layer after layer, covering her whole body.

'Right. Can you take her legs?'

'…Yeah, OK.'

Shotaro slid his arms around her chest, and I took her legs. We lifted Sayaka up and slowly made our way toward the stairs.

The headless body wasn't that heavy, but as we walked sweat started pouring off me. Her corpse now felt to me like something unclean. I could not stand to hold her like that, and irresistible thoughts of corruption filled my head. I wanted to get it over with, more than anything.

We went up the stairs and headed for the furthest end. We were planning to lay her to rest beside Yuya.

When we opened the door to storeroom 120, the smell of rot filled the air. We put Sayaka down beside Yuya's decaying body, and then I could no longer bear it. My strength abandoned me, and I fled the room without even looking back.

Later, back in our room, I said to Shotaro, 'Whoever it is, they must be mad. Who would do something like this, when getting caught would literally be the end of you?' I was curled up on the floor, recovering from the ordeal.

We still had to finish cleaning the blood from the floor and bringing the boots and other evidence up from below, but I'd used my last bit of energy, so I left it to Shotaro.

Once everything was cleared away, Shotaro and I met in front of the steel door on the middle floor.

We stared at the stairwell and watched as the water rose until it came above the level of the floor, spilling over without a sound.

For no real reason, I checked the time on my phone. 2.32 p.m.

The middle floor was finally flooding.

'Well, let's be off, then,' Shotaro said, as if we'd just seen the finale of a fireworks show.

After embracing Sayaka's corpse, I'd begun to feel like my own body was starting to decay.

I knew I should go back to my room and rest. So, I went upstairs, but then I noticed that the machinery room door was standing half open.

Suspicious, I went to peek through it. I saw Hana sitting inside.

'Agh!' She gave a little scream and leapt up in something like a fighting stance when I opened the door.

I understood her nerves, so I didn't go any closer.

Everything had changed from the day before. It was now a serial murder case.

Most of us hadn't believed the murderer would put themselves at greater risk by killing again.

But they had. And the victim had been Hana's closest friend.

Hana stood glaring at me, not saying a word. When she realized I wasn't about to leap on her immediately, she relaxed a bit. But it wasn't until she noticed Shotaro standing behind me that she truly let her guard down.

'Is the middle floor all taken care of?'

'Yeah. We cleaned it up. And moved Sayaka upstairs,' I said.

'I see. Thanks.'

She sat back down. She took off her shoes and cocked her heels on the seat, wrapping her arms around her knees and curling in on herself.

I could see her stockinged toes trembling. She rubbed at them but could not stop the shakes. The terror she had been hiding so far was showing after Sayaka's murder, like an internal haemorrhage finally reaching the skin. Watching her, I could feel my own body starting to tremble, like it was spreading.

The two monitors behind Hana were switched on. She must have come here to watch the camera feeds.

It was still daylight outside. The images weren't clear, but we could see that nothing had changed in the last two days. The withered weeds and fallen trees around the entrance and the buried emergency hatch were still there, but the beautiful sight of the world above seemed to grip my chest, squeezing painfully.

Somehow, staring at the feeds, I began to feel like if we looked long enough, we might see rescuers come to get us out.

We didn't, of course. The only things we saw moving were a few little birds, sparrows or something, fluttering around.

'Hana, have you eaten?'

'I can't. Not now.' Even as she said it, though, she took a packet of gummies from her pocket.

She must have bought them at the convenience store on the way here and kept them, uneaten. Perhaps she thought she could get them down, even if tinned food was impossible. But they seemed to stick in her throat.

Hana was not the only one who hadn't been able to eat since Sayaka's death. I imagined all of us were fasting now. It would probably take quite a while for anyone to get their appetites back after what we'd seen.

'It's so hard to look at this,' Hana said. She was stroking the packet absentmindedly.

The label was decorated with cartoon animals smiling and playing. Whoever had drawn it had surely never imagined someone holding that package while trapped underground, under threat of drowning and surrounded by murder.

I recalled how, in my schooldays, there was a teacher who would call me out for wearing any clothing with cartoon characters or such on it. He terrified me, so I would be careful to choose plain T-shirts on days I had his classes.

'But, listen, about Sayaka… She didn't suffer, did she? I mean, I'm sure she was terrified, but not for very long. Just a minute or so. Her head was cut off after she was dead, right? Right?' Hana's voice was tight with barely restrained stress.

I hesitated before answering, 'Yeah, that's right.'

It was hard to truly believe Sayaka had died peacefully. I imagined her last moments, taken by surprise and strangled.

But then, thinking about how one of us would be forced to face an even more horrific death trapped down here, Sayaka's death didn't seem quite so bad. At the very least, she didn't have to wait in the dark for the water to rise and drown her. You could call that a comfort.

That reminded me of that first night here, when we talked about the worst ways to die.

The thought came to me then. Hadn't the murderer given Yuya and Sayaka a gift of sorts, helping them avoid the fate of being left in that tiny, dark room?

But no, that was a stupid idea. We hadn't decided that either of them would be left behind, only that someone would be. It would have been pointless to speculate on who that might be until the murderer was revealed.

Hana sat and rubbed her stockinged toes while she spoke, 'And what about the water?'

'A few minutes ago, we saw it start to flood the middle floor. You wouldn't want to go down without wellies, at this point,' I said.

'Seriously? Well. I guess it was bound to happen, anyway.' She looked down. 'Four more days?'

'Yeah.'

'And you really don't know who it is?'

Shotaro answered this time. 'Not yet. Narrowing it down to a couple of people isn't much use yet. It's hard to pin anyone down for sure.'

'And is that something you'll be able to do, eventually? We don't have much time.'

'How should I know? I can't make any promises. It might not work out.'

Hana responded to Shotaro's frank answer with only a resentful glare. She might well give up on the Yazaki family and start suspecting Shotaro next. It would make sense, given that he was the next newest acquaintance.

After a moment, she grumbled, 'And if we don't find out who it is before time runs out? What are you going to do about those Yazakis?'

'Do about them?'

'We'll have to convince one of the parents to stay, won't we? Their son is here with them, right? We'll just explain that it's the only way to save the boy. If we get down to the wire, it might be the only way.' As she spoke, her voice took on an increasingly pleading tone.

It was something I'd thought about myself. If we did run out of time, if we never found the real killer, and we had to choose someone to stay behind, it would have to be one of Hayato's parents. Framing it as the only way to save their son's life would certainly be a convincing argument.

Of course, it would also save ours.

Kotaro Yazaki had just held his family up as a shield when he'd urged us to stop focusing on the murderer and start working on another way out.

We could turn that around on him. We'd use our lack of families as a shield to help us survive. It would be like using Hayato as a hostage. We wouldn't even have to threaten them. We would just give them the choice and let it happen.

There were tons of films and comics where a character with no attachments would stand up and sacrifice himself in place of someone with a family or loved ones. I'd seen it over and over. But we weren't in that kind of story.

As I say, the thought had occurred to me, but it didn't seem like something we should be saying out loud. Hana surely knew that. Sayaka's death and the approaching time limit had knocked something in her awry.

I didn't have the energy to try to talk sense into her, though. Which is why I took her question head on.

'It might work that way, but we can't be sure. The Yazakis seem like a happy family, but it's not like we've really got to know them. There's no telling how they'll act when things get truly desperate. What would most parents do? What about yours, Hana? What do you think they'd do?'

Tears suddenly welled in Hana's eyes. 'My father died last year. Didn't I tell you?'

I hadn't known. We hadn't been in contact since graduation.

I'd clearly touched a nerve. From the look on her face, I could see that Hana thought her father, at least, would have stayed behind to die if it meant saving his daughter.

'I'm sorry. Just forget I said anything.'

And what about my own parents? They'd probably start a fight if someone tried to push them into the choice. The time limit would hit us without anything being worked out. My parents had split up, and I hadn't seen either of them since I started working.

Hana's head hung low. I stood silent.

Then we heard footsteps approaching. I turned around and saw that Mai was coming our way.

'What are you all doing in here?' She seemed surprised to find us there, and even more so when she realized the monitors were switched on.

'What's the matter? Did something happen out there?'

'No, nothing. It's all just the same. Nothing's changed at all.' Hana glared at the monitors.

'I see. Of course not. Anyway, I just ran into Mr Yazaki.'

Hana gave a guilty start at the mention of Yazaki's name, as if her words had summoned him.

Mai went on, 'Seems there's something he wants to talk to us about. Says he thinks there have been some misunderstandings. So, he was wondering if we could all get together and talk, later. Does that sound OK to you?'

'Sure,' Shotaro said. 'The dining room again?'

Mai nodded.

What could he want to talk about now? Especially after Hana had openly aired her suspicions of the whole family.

'See you there. Oh, could one of you tell Ryuhei about it?' Mai said with an uncomfortable smile.

V

On the surface, the sun would be going down as we all gathered in the dining room.

The eight of us sat in roughly the same positions as at our

lunch talk the day before. This time, though, there were no tins of food on the table in front of us.

Mr Yazaki began to speak. His tone was dark.

'There's one thing that we haven't told you about ourselves. It has nothing to do with the situation we're in, so I didn't see any need to mention it until now. But, I don't want you to get the wrong idea. I hope you'll keep open minds.'

'We're listening,' Mai said. She was awkwardly filling in for Sayaka, who had previously been the one most open to the Yazakis.

'Right. Well, we told you that we got lost in the mountains hunting mushrooms, I believe. That was a bit of a lie. We did get lost, but we weren't hunting mushrooms. The truth is, we were looking for this place. But we took a wrong turn, then it got dark, and just when we finally thought we were on the right track, we ran into you. Quite a shock that was.'

'You were looking for this place? You were always trying to get here, then?'

'That's right.'

Hana glanced at me. Two days ago, she'd offered up her own theory that the Yazaki family had come here on purpose, and apparently, she had been right.

Mai went on. 'So, does that mean you all knew it was here?'

'I think saying we knew it was here is a bit much. It wasn't exactly like that.'

He was mincing words. The whole thing seemed to be a topic he'd rather not go into. He went on, circling around the point.

'Not long after we got here, you all talked about how this place must have been used by some religious cult. Do you remember? Well, you were spot on. This is all about my wife's younger brother, you see. Truth is, well… He got caught up in some strange religion I don't rightly understand. And then, a while ago, he just disappeared.'

'What kind of strange religion?' Mai asked.

'Like I said, I don't rightly understand. One of those apocalyptic things. The end of the world is nigh, and whatnot. They came here to get ready for it all.

'My wife's brother, Yoji his name is, got in deep. We were worried from the start, of course, but then about two years ago he just… vanished. No one knew anything at all. We couldn't even say it was a crime, so how could we go to the police?

'Then, recently, we started looking at Yoji's computer. It took us a long time to figure out his password, but finally we did and found his journal. There was an entry about this underground building. He wrote that they used it for meditation or some such nonsense.

'It was the first thing we found that seemed like a clue to where he might have gone.'

He slumped forward.

'So, you decided to come take a look at the place he'd written about?'

Mai was doing her best, since no one else seemed interested in asking questions. I was surprised at how little curiosity Shotaro was showing. He just sat and watched the proceedings in silence.

'That's exactly it. At first, I was going to come on my own, but Hiroko and the boy were worried about him, too. And, well, I did think there might be safety in numbers. Hayato's not exactly a child anymore, and he got on well with his uncle. So, the three of us came out. The plan was to just take a quick look around and run off quick as we could if it seemed dangerous. It was a weekend, after all, and the weather was good.

'But, well. We ran into you all. And it didn't seem like something we should go talking about, you see? That's why I made up the mushroom hunting story. After that, it never seemed like a good time to confess, and then you started to suspect things, and, well… At any rate, the truth has nothing to do with what's happening here and now.'

Yazaki was emphatic about that last point.

Overall, I bought the story. I didn't know much about apocalyptic cults, but the very fact that we were in some bizarre underground building called 'the Ark' lent it the ring of truth. It was pretty easy to imagine some weird cult hanging out down here.

Mai asked, 'So, how much did you really know about this place before you came? You said you read about it in his journal.'

'We didn't know anything at all. He called it "the Ark", explained the general location and wrote about how he'd gone down some kind of manhole or something. That's all.'

'You didn't see any pictures?'

'He didn't leave anything like that behind. That's why we got lost. Otherwise, we'd have made it while it was still light out, headed home by dusk, and none of this would have happened to us.'

We could hear the regret and anger in his voice at the end.

I wondered what had come of this cult he was talking about. The inside of the Ark had been left stocked, with fuel for the generator et cetera, as if they'd run off in the middle of the night, taking only what they could grab. Did the cult break up? Or did something even worse happen? I couldn't help thinking of an article I'd read on Wikipedia, about an American cult that had committed mass suicide a few decades ago.

Anyway, the Yazaki family had made it here in the end but found no trace of their missing family member. And they'd had to spend the night, only to get caught up in all of this. That was the long and short of it.

Yazaki turned to us again.

'Do you believe me? Our reasons for coming were nothing nefarious at all,' he said.

'We get it. We just came here looking for something interesting ourselves. I think we're pretty much all equally shady in that regard,' Shotaro said, breaking his silence at last.

Hiroko and Hayato had stayed silent the whole time, letting Kotaro do all the talking. Once he was done, though, they looked up at us expectantly, as if hoping that their story of family tragedy might convince us to accept them.

It seemed, though, that their expressions only irritated Hana and Ryuhei. For all the big production around it, the story didn't help a bit in the search for the murderer. Of course, it was Hana voicing her suspicions that had actually led to this whole talking session, but they seemed to be ignoring that.

Mai, our de facto facilitator, looked deeply uncomfortable. Only Shotaro seemed unfazed.

There didn't seem to be anything else we could do all together like that. So, we agreed that the misunderstanding was resolved and went our separate ways.

I sat in my bed, thinking. It seemed the people who'd been using this place had believed the world was going to end soon. I imagined they'd been caught up in the delusion that through devotion, they alone could survive it.

Maybe they'd been right, in a sense. The Ark truly was approaching its doomsday. We were going to face the final judgment. The irony of it was, unlike the story of Noah in the Bible, this time the flood was rising inside the Ark. There was no salvation to be found on the inside.

All Yazaki's story had done was fill me with a formless dread. If God was going to sit in judgment, I had no faith that I would be spared.

VI

In the evening, my appetite finally started to return. I chose something with as little aroma as I could find, a tin of stewed vegetables, and took it back to my room to eat with Shotaro.

'D'you think we should believe their story?' I asked him.

'The whole thing about the Yazakis coming in search of their missing relative?'

'Right.'

'I think so. There's no proof, but the only thing doubt will do is get between us.'

Shotaro very clearly didn't care much at all.

He had already thought that, whatever the family's reasons for being here, they likely had nothing to do with the murders, and this did nothing to change that. It wasn't as if Yuya and

Sayaka had been caught up in that cult or had had anything to do with the man's disappearance.

When we finished eating, Shotaro seemed uncharacteristically anxious as he sat on his bed, tapping one foot. It looked like he was worrying over something.

'Shotaro, isn't there anything we can do? Anything at all? Or do we really just sit and think?'

When Yuya was killed, there wasn't anything to work on. We could only sit around and fret.

But there were actually puzzles and mysteries in Sayaka's case. Things were different now. There were solutions to chase.

And although Shotaro did look troubled, I didn't get the sense that he was despairing. It felt more like he had got hold of something worth chasing down.

'It's not that there's nothing to do. It's just, I can't be sure...'

Shotaro laced his hands behind his head and lay back on his mattress.

Then, suddenly, he sat back up and said wearily, 'Shuichi, let's lay out all the puzzles in Sayaka's murder, one by one.'

'Um, all right.'

Thinking back on the conversation that morning in the middle floor storeroom, I listed them.

One: What had Sayaka been searching for before the murder?
Two: Who killed Sayaka?
Three: Why did whoever it was kill Sayaka?
Four: Why did the murderer stab Sayaka in the chest?
Five: Why did the murderer cut off Sayaka's head?
Six: Why did the murderer take the risk of going to get paper towels from the upper floor instead of using the rags nearby?

Seven: Why did the murderer get rid of Sayaka's things?
'I think that's all,' I said.
'You're right,' he answered.

Those seven points were the mysteries for which there were no explanations with any serious degree of logical necessity behind them.

Listing them like that, it made me realize that in Yuya's case, there were only two: who killed him, and why. Sayaka's murder was markedly more unusual.

'So, which one should we start thinking about first?'

'Thinking? The truth is, I've got answers for maybe half of the puzzles you just listed, Shuichi.'

Shotaro's voice was matter-of-fact.

'What? You've solved the mysteries?'

'A few of them.'

'But, you still don't know who did it, do you?'

'I don't. If I did, I wouldn't have anything to worry about.'

I was sure I had seen and heard everything that Shotaro had. But I didn't have a solution for a single one of those seven mysteries.

'Which ones have you figured out? I can't get any of them.'

'One, three, five and seven. Those four all have a connection. If you figure out one of them, then they all unravel, one after the other.'

He was saying he knew why the murderer had cut off Sayaka's head?!

'You know why Sayaka was killed? But you don't know the motive for Yuya's murder, right? How can you know the motive for one murder in a series but not another?'

'It's not that odd. It happens. Well, it might be exaggerating to say that I *know* the motive. I can't explain every detail perfectly. But, I think I have the general shape of it. Let me go through it in order:

'The first thing we need to consider is the fifth puzzle. Why did the murderer cut off Sayaka's head? If you know that, the rest just solve themselves.

'Shuichi, why do you think murderers usually cut a victim's head off?'

'Usually? Is cutting someone's head off something that usually happens? Ever? It's only something I read about in old mystery books. There's no way it would ever actually be necessary, would it?'

'Let's talk old mysteries, then. Can you tell me about any you remember?'

Try as I might, though, I couldn't recall anything in particular.

'Well, anyway, the only reason I can think of is to hide the victim's identity. Like, the murderer wants to switch places with a victim. That's not possible these days, though. We've got DNA testing and stuff. Of course, we can't do that down here, but the victim can't be anyone but Sayaka, anyway.

'If the body wasn't Sayaka's, that would mean there was someone else down here with the same build as her, who we didn't know about. And then Sayaka killed her and is hiding somewhere down here where we can't find her. Which is ridiculous.'

'Right. We don't even need to consider the possibility that someone else is hiding down here unbeknownst to us all. The Ark is big, but we'd notice if there were anyone else here. And

Yuya said nothing had changed since his visit before,' Shotaro said. I felt he was just pointing out the obvious.

I went on. 'Any other possibilities? There can't be that many. Oh, wait, like, what if the murderer left some kind of evidence on the victim's head, and they needed to get rid of it?

'But what evidence could there be? Like, if they scuffled during the attack and the murderer left lipstick or something on Sayaka's face? They could just wipe it off. It's not like we have a forensics squad down here. And no one down here is wearing lipstick these days, anyway.'

'It is hard to imagine what kind of evidence like that could help us out down here, and you are right, none of the women have been wearing make-up.'

'What else is there? The murderer wanted the head as a souvenir? Not a chance there.'

Even if the murderer had a kind of corpse-collection fetish and wanted the head for some twisted reason, this was no time for indulging it. There was no place to hide the head in the Ark, and it's not like they could take it home with them.

'One thing that's vital to remember is, cutting off the head was an enormous risk for the murderer. It would have taken fifteen or twenty minutes at the very least. Someone could have come walking by at any time, but they still took the time to cut her head off.

'We've talked over and over again about how dangerous it would be for the murderer if they got caught down here. Which makes it clear that their motive must have been powerful indeed. So, the need to cut off her head must have been enormous.'

'And you have figured out an answer with a high degree of logical necessity?'

'I have. An answer that is the only one possible. And it's not that difficult. It's something I think you could figure out for yourself.'

Shotaro stared at me intently.

When we were kids, he used to give me little challenges like this, but I never, ever managed to find the right answer. It was always just out of mental reach for me. Eventually, I started to just give up as quickly as possible. Like now.

'I don't know. Tell me.'

'Really? Well then, here you go. Why did the murderer have to cut Sayaka's head off? There's actually something else we need to remember when we think about this problem. That is, Sayaka was searching for something before she was murdered. We don't know what that was.

'What's more, that fact is also essential to the murderer's motive. I thought about that a little when Sayaka's body was found.

'There are three possibilities: one, did the murderer want to kill her from the start, and she happened to show up in an opportune place while she was searching? Or, did the murderer just want to kill someone in general, and Sayaka came along while she was searching? Or, did the murderer have to kill her because she was searching for something?

'Of those three, the one closest to the right answer is the third. But I think we need to word it a little differently.

'The murderer cut Sayaka's head off because she was looking for something.'

'Come again?'

Shotaro stared at me like he couldn't believe I still didn't get it.

The truth was, though, that the more he explained, the more mystified I felt. She was searching for something, so the murderer cut her head off. What dreadful thing had she been looking for?

'What was it?'

'Her smartphone.'

'What?!'

'You heard me. Sayaka's phone was a newer one, right? I didn't pay much attention to her using it, but I'm guessing it had face recognition.'

Face recognition! The moment he said it, I felt the clouds lifting from my brain.

'You're right. She used face unlock on her phone,' I said.

'You're sure? Then that must be it. This is what happened.

'There was something, some information or something, on Sayaka's phone that was dangerous for the murderer. I imagine that Sayaka herself didn't know what it was. But it was possible she might realize at any time.

'The murderer, then, was in a hurry to kill Sayaka. Then, yesterday evening, they got their chance.

'Sayaka went looking for something, alone. It was the perfect opportunity. With all these people packed into one place, it's hard to get anyone isolated enough to murder them without getting caught.

'The murderer was able to commit the crime wholly without leaving the middle floor. But, unexpectedly, Sayaka didn't have her smartphone with her. At some point, she'd mislaid it, which was why she was wandering around the place looking for it.

'Which was a problem for the murderer. The original plan was to kill her and get rid of the phone, but now it was off somewhere inside the Ark.

'If someone found it, they could unlock it using her corpse for face recognition.'

'And that's why the murderer cut off her head?'

'That's right,' Shotaro answered with a blank expression.

To keep anyone from unlocking her phone. He was right. It did seem like there was no other possible reason why the murderer had to cut off Sayaka's head.

'So, what about getting rid of her things?'

'I imagine they just wanted to conceal the fact that Sayaka had lost her smartphone and had been searching for it that evening. If her phone and her head were the only things missing, then we might connect the two and figure out that the victim had data on her phone that the murderer didn't want the group to see.

'They didn't want us to make that connection. So, it was worth the risk of going up to her room to get rid of her backpack.'

Sayaka's room was near the stairs, so there wasn't that much danger of being seen.

And, just like Shotaro had said, I could now see the second mystery starting to unravel, too.

But I also knew why he didn't seem too pleased with himself. He still didn't have the answer to the most important question:

who killed her? That was the essential thing. If we knew that, then what would their reason for cutting off Sayaka's head matter?

'I wonder what was in Sayaka's phone that the murderer was so worried about.'

'Yes. That's the question. That's exactly why I said I couldn't account for everything about the motive. What was so important to hide that they killed Sayaka and decapitated her?'

'I mean, I can make a few guesses. Assuming it's something that they thought it vital to conceal right now, it must be related to the first murder.'

'You think Sayaka had evidence related to Yuya's murder in her phone?'

'I can't think of anything else.'

'But it seemed clear she didn't realize it herself, right? How could that be?'

It was hard to believe that Sayaka had been walking around carrying evidence of a murder without knowing it, especially while all of us were frantically trying to identify the murderer.

'I know. But, Sayaka took lots of pictures, didn't she? Maybe she had one that could identify the murderer.'

'I get it. Like, she just took a load of pictures without realizing that one of them showed some crucial evidence. Damn, if that's true, we were so close...'

Shotaro's face darkened.

'That's right. If only I'd asked her to show me her pictures. I might have figured out who the murderer was right then. I regret it so much.'

Sayaka had just been wandering around taking random snapshots, though. Who would ever have dreamed one of them could show vital evidence?

'Anyway. Sitting and thinking about what the murderer wanted to hide won't get us anywhere. We just don't know enough about what the murderer did that might be revealed, or how the murderer realized Sayaka had the evidence. The murderer is one step ahead of us. But there is one thing we could do now.'

'There is? What?' I asked.

'Find Sayaka's phone. It must still be around here somewhere. We can't get do anything else until we have it.'

The murderer cut off Sayaka's head because of that phone. And it was just lying around somewhere waiting for us to pick it up.

'Now, I wanted to ask you, do you think anyone knows Sayaka's unlock code? Do you?'

'No, are you serious? I doubt even Hana would know.'

We wouldn't be able to get into Sayaka's phone without the code, since face unlock was out of the question. But no one gave out their unlock code, did they? Most people didn't even tell family members.

'You're right. Too bad.'

Come to think of it, we hadn't checked Yuya's phone, either. It was still in his pocket. On his corpse.

His was too old a model to have facial recognition, and the fingerprint sensor was broken, so he'd used a really long code. Like, six digits.

Yuya had been killed suddenly, soon after the earthquake, so there wasn't likely to be anything incriminating on his phone.

That was why we hadn't thought to check it out before, and presumably also why the murderer didn't bother with it either. We couldn't access it without the code, anyway.

'I suppose we could just try guessing. It can't do any harm. Oh, but some people set it up so if you enter the wrong code a few times, it erases the phone. Yuya said he did that.'

'It's better than doing nothing, but we shouldn't get our hopes up. So, let's see…'

Shotaro sat cross-legged on his mattress and folded his arms in thought. Then, he gave me a look that set my alarm bells ringing.

'There's one more thing that we might try, for better or worse, but it is truly wretched.'

'What?' I couldn't remember ever hearing anyone actually say the word 'wretched' before.

'We could go down to the bottom floor and get Sayaka's head.'

'That… That is actually wretched.' It was a shockingly simple, yet unimaginably difficult method. 'How would we manage the dive?' I asked.

'No idea, but I thought you'd know better than I. You've got a diving licence, haven't you?'

'Oh, yes, there is that.'

We had all taken diving licences back at university. But I'd only gone diving a few times since then, so I wasn't what you could call an old hand at it.

'There was some diving equipment on the middle floor, wasn't there? The tanks had air in them, at least. But I don't think there were any harnesses to strap them on,' Shotaro reminded me.

'That's right.'

I'd checked them along with Sayaka.

'What about rigging a backpack to carry a tank? Could you use that instead of a harness to dive?'

'I wouldn't call it impossible, but…' I trailed off and thought it over.

The vital thing was to securely fix the tank to your back so it would not shift or fall off. My pack wouldn't hold a tank, but perhaps we could knot together some ropes or rubber tubes too.

I went on. 'It would be difficult, but maybe we could use Yuya's daypack? That might fit a tank. Then we could wrap rope around it from the outside to hold it tight. That'd make a simple harness. It might not be very comfortable, though. We'll also need a light, but one of us must have a waterproof phone that could do the trick.'

The bottom floor was littered with exposed beams and iron bars, and I might have to open doors underwater. I couldn't go down there without light. And we'd have to fix it to the tank harness so I could use both hands.

'I see. But the dive itself isn't impossible, is that right?'

Shotaro seemed set on the idea.

'No, but hold on,' I cautioned him. 'Don't go thinking it'll be easy. When you dive, you usually wear a vest used to control buoyancy, called a BCD. But this time we've only got a harness, tank and regulator. I guess that'll work if I'm just moving along the floor, but it's going to be tough adjusting the weights and everything…'

Weights were essential. We'd have to find something just heavy enough to keep me underwater and fasten it to my body.

'I'm not sure I'll be able to move easily enough to search properly either. I might just about be able to walk around, but if the slightest thing happens and I have an accident, I'm dead. And the water's cold, right? Like, ten degrees or something? No wet suit or dry suit, just clothing. It's going to be tough. And that tank was only about a third full. That won't give me much time,' I added.

If Sayaka's head had been dropped through that hole in the tool room, I should be able to reach it. But if it was further in, I might run out of air and have to come back early. Thinking about possible obstacles I might have to navigate, I couldn't help worrying about that single, nearly empty tank.

'Sure. Of course, you're right.' Shotaro nodded as if still convinced it would work out, but every potential problem I'd raised was a matter of life and death.

If it was absolutely necessary, I could make the dive. But... The truth was, just imagining the sight of Sayaka's face down there under the pitch black water took all the life out of me. Then there was the act itself. Swimming through the cold water to find her pale severed head, holding it to my body with one hand and clawing at the water with the other as I struggled back to the surface... Setting aside the physical difficulty of it, the whole thing was so filled with grim, stoic bravery that I couldn't believe myself capable of it.

And even if we found her head, would we be able to unlock her phone with it? Would it still recognize that head as Sayaka?

'I am also worried about the head's condition,' said Shotaro, as if he'd read my thoughts. 'There's a chance the murderer damaged the face so much it won't work.'

'It's likely they did so, in fact, if they thought it at all possible we might retrieve the head from down below. And, if their only goal had been to prevent us using her face to unlock the phone, that would have been enough.

'But the murderer surely also wanted to distract us, so we wouldn't figure out there was something important on Sayaka's phone. That was another reason for decapitating her, and for getting rid of her backpack.'

'Ah, there is that.'

Slicing up Sayaka's face beyond recognition would have been enough to hide the evidence, so there must have been another reason for taking the extra step of decapitation... Like simply shocking everyone into inactivity.

'But do you really think they did it that way? Mutilating her face strikes me as somehow worse than cutting off her head.'

'I agree. I suppose it's a matter of opinion which is worse, but I can imagine the murderer choosing to cut off her head because they couldn't bring themselves to mutilate her face. And if that's true, then Sayaka's face should be unmarked.'

Which meant that taking the very real risk of going down to get her head might pay off.

'So, should we do it? Some of the others might be better divers than I am.'

Surely someone else in the club was more into diving than me.

'No, I'd rather not mention our thoughts about Sayaka's phone to anyone else for now. If anyone goes, it'll be you.'

'I see. There's no one else you can ask.'

Because, after all, we might unwittingly ask the murderer to retrieve her head, in which case they would just pretend they didn't find it.

'I don't want to make you do the dive, Shuichi. It's a very dangerous plan, and our lives don't depend on it yet. But there might come a time when we have no other choice. So, first, let's find her phone,' he said firmly.

'Yeah. Good idea.'

There was no point talking about the dive until we had her phone. And if we did track it down, there was a chance we might miraculously unlock it and find the evidence without needing to venture into the flooded bottom floor.

Shotaro slapped his leg and stood up on his dusty mattress.

'Right, then, let's go and look for that phone. I'm not holding out much hope, but there's no use wasting time.'

If the murderer beat us to it, they'd get rid of it for sure. And the middle floor was flooding more every minute.

I followed Shotaro out of the room.

We slipped into wellingtons and went downstairs to the middle floor.

The water had already risen six or seven centimetres above the floor. In another day, it would be above our boots.

We splashed down the darkened corridor and stopped in front of the steel door to the winch room. We were planning to search each room in order.

'This is going to take a while. We should split up.'

'...Right.'

We each took a side of the corridor and started going through the rooms, checking to see if Sayaka might have forgotten her phone on a shelf or something.

Under the flickering fluorescents, the water looked dirty. All the dust, dead flies, cockroaches and mouse corpses that had accumulated in the Ark's forgotten corners now floated and swirled about my feet. I tried to push the clumps under the shelves but the backflow just washed them back out again to lap against my boots.

Walking around alone like that, I kept imagining someone coming up behind me, looping a rope around my neck, pulling it tight…

Considered rationally, it was hard to believe that the murderer would strike again so soon. And, with all the water, I would immediately hear anyone approaching. Even so, I made sure not to get too far from Shotaro, so he would be within earshot if I shouted.

When we'd finished with the middle floor, we took off our wellingtons and went upstairs to carry on the search.

We didn't find Sayaka's phone.

'Where on earth could she have dropped it?'

We could only look in the most obvious spots. There simply wasn't enough time to check every gap in the shelves or open every container. And it was hard to imagine Sayaka putting her phone somewhere like that, anyway.

But then, Sayaka herself had apparently looked for quite a long time the night before. It must be somewhere out of the way.

Or, maybe, the murderer had found it first. And now it was gone forever.

'Well, I think that's enough for today,' Shotaro said and thumped me on the shoulder.

We went back to our room and got ready for bed. Shotaro started to fiddle about with Yuya's pack but he must have been exhausted because he put it aside and went to sleep almost immediately.

I just couldn't to get to sleep, though.

I saw Sayaka's corpse and her severed head resting at the bottom of the dark water every time I closed my eyes. And the frustration of not finding her phone weighed on my chest.

It didn't feel right to sleep at a time like this. But, there was nothing else to do.

I put my earphones in. I couldn't stand to listen to the same music I'd used to help settle myself the night before, though. I could only think about how the songwriter, the producer, the singer and everyone involved must surely be enjoying themselves somewhere far, far better than where I was.

I scrolled through my song list and found one by an American musician who had committed suicide at the age of nineteen. I put it on repeat and closed my eyes. The eerie psychedelic folk sound filled my mind.

After an hour or so, I finally fell asleep.

VII

I woke up and checked my phone for the time. It was ten in the morning.

It had been an odd night, and I could barely tell if I'd been sleeping or waking. I couldn't say whether the disturbing images of the things I had seen and done the day before that kept flashing through my mind were dreams or simply intrusive memories. But since now it was suddenly morning—if you could call this morning—I must have slept.

I looked over, but Shotaro was not there.

Toilet, or breakfast? Or perhaps gone to check the rising water level? If this had been a normal trip, it was late enough that I couldn't have complained about being left behind in the hotel room, but under the circumstances, it made me feel lonely.

And hungry. I had barely eaten the day before.

I went to the dining room and found Shotaro there. He was just finishing up his breakfast.

'Ah, you're up. I was thinking about getting back to the search. Be careful, all right?'

Shotaro left. It was like we were trading places.

I sat alone and ate the same tinned fish I had the day before.

There was no real difference between day and night in the Ark, but it was somehow comforting to see the time displayed on my smartphone. It felt less terrifying to be on my own during the daytime.

After I ate, I went back out into the corridor.

I wandered the upper floor for a while, wondering if I should help Shotaro with the search.

I didn't find him, but I got hints of activity in a few of the rooms. It seemed everyone was up.

Then I realized that I could hear the sound of voices coming up from the middle floor.

I couldn't make out what they were saying, but it had the feel of the quick, direct exchanges you hear at construction sites.

Before long, I recognized the voices. It was the Yazaki family.

I wondered what they were doing. I had an ominous feeling. The way they had been acting, it wouldn't surprise me if they were trying something untoward.

I decided to take a look and headed toward the stairs.

As I got closer, I saw a figure standing at the top of the steps, about to go down.

'Is that you, Mai?'

'Whoa!' She had just been stepping down to the first step. She spun around in surprise, still gripping the handrail. But she relaxed when she saw it was me.

'Shuichi? It sounds like they're doing something down there. I thought I'd go and see what.'

'Right, me too. It's the Yazakis, I think.'

Mai and I stuck close together as we went down the narrow stairs.

The water level was already much higher than I'd imagined. We put on wellingtons and stepped into it, but the waves kicked up at each step washed over their tops and the boots soon filled with water.

We had no choice but to go barefoot. We took off the boots and rolled our trousers up to the knees, then stepped back down into the cold water.

We heard the Yazaki family's voices coming from the winch room.

It was dark down there. I turned on my phone light. The fluorescents at the other end of the corridor were still holding out, so we weren't walking in the pitch black, but going barefoot made me nervous about where I was stepping.

Mai leaned close to me, the light bearer. The two of us slowly progressed down the corridor.

Finally, we reached the steel door and saw the three of them.

Hiroko and Hayato had their trousers rolled up like Mai and me. Hayato must have stumbled at some point, because he was soaked head to toe. Kotaro was wearing the lone set of fishing waders.

The three were holding a long metal pole extending into the depths of the room. It looked like they were working hard, with sweat pouring down their faces.

Hiroko was the first to notice us.

'Do you need something?' she asked.

'No, sorry. We heard voices and wondered what was going on,' I answered. Hiroko just snorted and went back to her work, ignoring us.

Dripping wet, Hayato shot us an angry glance. It seemed they were unhappy that we had seen their project.

The Yazakis didn't explain, but we could see what they were up to at a glance. They were trying to use the long pole to turn the winch from outside the room, connecting it to the handle like the coupling rod on a steam locomotive's wheels.

'Hayato, try pushing harder. A little further back.'

'I... am,' Hayato answered in a strained, miserable voice.

'Right, then let's change the angle. Mother, come over here...'

The three of them held the rod and moved one step to the right. Then, they all bent in to push at the rod and turn the handle.

'Waaah!'

They all lost their balance and fell backward into the water with a splash.

What I'd taken for a pole had broken apart and bent. I saw now that it was actually a bundle of three thin aluminium pipes held together with wire. The wire had come undone, and the pipes had come apart, bending and collapsing as they did.

It was an effort obviously doomed to failure. The makeshift pole was too weak to withstand the force. Even with a pipe that was strong and long enough, it would have taken enormous strength to work the winch and pull down the rock from so far away.

But they were taking it seriously. They had taken on Shotaro's challenge of finding a way to get out of the Ark without leaving anyone behind, and they had to try.

Looking again at the winch room, I could not help but feel it was hopeless.

I had pondered it myself. For example, what if we tied a rope to the boulder and pulled it down from outside the room? But no, the rope would get caught on the edge of the steel door. And there was no way to firmly attach a rope to the stone above us.

Or what about setting up some kind of support under the rock? Someone could run the winch in the small room, and the rock would fall onto the support. The person could crawl under the support and get out. Then we could collapse the support from outside the room, which would allow the rock to fall all the way into the small room and allow us to escape through the exit above. That would solve all the problems.

But we had no way to build a support that could take all the weight of the rock. The wooden chairs and desks down here were all rotted away, and we didn't have the tools to build something from the steel shelves. They weren't strong enough, anyway.

The most interesting idea I'd come up with was to make a support out of logs, then drop the rock on top. Then, we could collapse the log pile by dousing them in fuel and setting them on fire. But, of course, we had no wood, and with the middle floor now flooding, it wouldn't burn, anyway.

In the end, the only hope remaining was this ridiculous idea that the Yazakis were now trying.

And they were giving everything they had.

Watching them struggling so hard, I had to accept that their misery was something more than ours. I was terrified that I wouldn't be able to escape this buried building, but their terror was that when the time for escape came, one of their own would be left behind.

They'd totally embraced Kotaro's announcement of the day before that escape took precedence over finding the murderer. But there was no way out without a sacrifice. That fact had not changed.

The three fallen Yazakis pushed themselves up, dripping wet and miserable.

Kotaro dragged the pipes up from the floor and waded into the tiny room, kicking angrily at the water.

'Damn! Does this bloody winch actually turn? If we can't get that rock to fall, I don't know what we'll do.'

He put his hand on the winch handle as he spoke.

'Oh...'

I heard Mai gasp next to me.

There was a metallic shriek as the boulder above shifted against the steel.

Yazaki stopped turning the handle, but he didn't take his hand from it.

He stood like that, still as a rock, for a few moments. I could see that he was at his wits' end from the way he glared at the rock above.

I thought to myself, *He's going to turn it again, isn't he?*

In the moment, I felt a faint spark of dark hope. Would he just pull the rock down right here and now? There was a chance, tiny, but not zero, that the falling rock might catch between the iron door and the floor on the way down, giving him a route out. Was he thinking of wagering his life on that chance? If he was, then he might decide to take the gamble of being left behind while letting the rest of us out.

I could see Kotaro grip the handle tighter and start to turn it.

There was another metallic shriek. The boulder began to descend.

'Dad! Stop it!'

'No no no nooo!'

Hiroko and Hayato began screaming.

When I heard the sound of their voices, I forgot all about my dark hope. Mai and I added our own protest to theirs.

'Stop!'

'Please, don't! You'll just trap yourself!'

He stopped.

It seemed he'd just wanted to check the resistance in the first place, and hadn't realized how far he'd gone. The sound of our voices brought him around, and he jerked his hand from the winch.

Hiroko beckoned him out of the room. Kotaro walked unsteadily over to us and ducked through the door.

'Someone has to turn that handle, or we're not getting out,' he said in a dazed voice, only repeating what we already knew.

The three Yazakis gathered up the pipes again from where they'd sunk beneath the water. They looked near tears. They retreated to the corridor with the stiff, stumbling legs of defeated soldiers.

When they passed us, each looked our way and nodded in greeting. Still, I sensed a touch of animosity in their eyes.

I just watched them pass, but Mai couldn't resist speaking out.

'Mr Yazaki, I truly do understand your fear, but we can't go and do anything crazy. We still have time—'

'But no one has any clue who the murderer is, do they?' Kotaro shouted her down. His family pulled him away and they went up to the stairs.

Mai and I looked at each other.

Then Mai turned to the winch room. She put her head through the doorway and peered up at the rock.

'How is it?'

'I think it's come down a bit. Shuichi, could you take a look?'

I traded places with her. I leaned in further and touched the surface of the stone.

Like she said, Yazaki had pulled the rock slightly down into the room. But it was wedged solid. I couldn't get a wiggle out of it by hand.

'It has shifted a little, but I don't think it'll be coming down on its own. It would be great if it did, though.'

'Yeah, but I don't see that happening.'

I'd hoped that Yazaki's little stunt might have dislodged the boulder so that it would fall under its own weight, but it was still stuck fast. It would take more power to get it down.

The knowledge filled me with an odd mix of both relief and disappointment.

The sight of Yazaki turning the winch handle had gripped me with fear, like watching a car about to crash. If he'd pulled down the rock, we'd have been saved. But I'd forgotten all of that in the moment and told him to stop.

And the crash had not come. We had not been freed.

Mai must have been feeling relieved too. A faint smile played across her face.

'Shall we go back?' she said, and gently took my arm.

We went back to the stairs. I saw where Kotaro Yazaki had dropped the waders he'd been wearing. The family had left sodden footprints up the stairs.

We climbed up a few steps and used our bare hands to sluice water from our legs and feet.

'Should have brought a towel,' Mai muttered absently. She probably just wanted to talk about something, anything, except what was going on around us.

Just as we were sliding our wet feet into our hiking shoes, a shadow blocked the light coming through the door at the top of the stairs.

Mai and I both looked up at the same time. Ryuhei stood in the doorway, looking down on us.

'What are you two up to?'

His voice was unexpectedly calm, but with a shrill undertone of barely suppressed emotion.

Mai answered, her voice cold, 'I came to see what was happening down here. I ran into Shuichi on the way.'

It was simply the truth. Yet, Mai and I had been quite close while we put on our shoes. Right then, with so much mistrust between the two of them, it must have looked particularly suspicious.

Ryuhei's face was lost in shadow, silhouetted against the fluorescent lights behind him.

'You just ran into him?'

'That's what I said. You heard the Yazakis banging around down here, didn't you? Shuichi and I both wondered what they were up to and came to check. Is there something wrong with that?'

Ryuhei seemed to be hunting for a response before finally saying, in a voice barely above a whisper, 'Don't go playing dumb with me.'

Mai said nothing.

After a moment, he tried another tack.

'What did the Yazakis get up to, then? And why were they so wet? They were fiddling with the winch, weren't they?'

'If you already know that much, then you know about as much as we do. The Yazakis were trying to figure out a way to get the stone down. And you're the one playing dumb. You heard us yelling, didn't you? And you must have felt the shaking when the rock moved, right? It's not like you didn't know something was happening. Mr Yazaki came really close. You had to know what was going on. Right? Didn't you?'

'What are you getting at?'

'I'm saying you knew what they were doing. You heard us screaming, but did you come to see what was happening? No. Why not?'

Ryuhei couldn't answer.

I finally got what Mai was trying to say.

Surely all the sounds from the middle floor would have been enough for him to figure out the Yazaki family was trying to get the rock to fall. He had to have known they were up to something dangerous, at least.

And he had ignored it. Why? If one of the Yazaki family ended up trapped, then the rest of us could escape. Could he honestly deny that the thought had occurred to him?

'What's with your tone? Did I do something wrong? No one else went to see, either, did they? Just you two.'

'You're the one who came barging in here with your questions. And I'm not blaming you for anything. I'm just saying that Shuichi and I both happened to be worried about the Yazakis and came to see what was going on. That's all.'

Mai dropped her gaze, ending the conversation, and retied the laces of her shoes.

Ryuhei snorted and turned to leave, but stopped for one last comment.

'And what about the rock? Any changes?'

'Nothing much. Just a little shift,' Mai answered, and Ryuhei walked off.

Even with our shoes on, Mai and I stayed sitting there, in no mood to go up.

We sat side by side in the narrow stairwell. Cold water seeped into the bottoms of our trousers. We stared down on the dark, flooded corridor, like two people taking in a view.

'Shuichi, there's something I wanted to ask you,' Mai said. Her voice was a whisper.

'What?'

'If we get out of here alive, what happens to us then? Do we just go back to normal life? Can you imagine yourself going to back to work and everything like none of this happened?'

I hadn't really thought about it until she asked. I mean, maybe a bit, but there were more important things to worry about.

'Isn't it enough to get home alive? After that, I'm sure things will work themselves out. People have accidents in the mountains or at sea all the time. They might have to deal with some trauma, but most people end up getting on with their lives, I'm sure.'

I tried to leave it at that, but this wasn't just another accident. We were trapped with a murderer.

Mai hung her head.

'I was just thinking. Just now, when Mr Yazaki was turning the winch, he almost trapped himself in, right? Like, if that ended up saving the rest of us... What would people say? They wouldn't blame us, right? Would people say we left him to die, do you think? But then, if we catch the murderer and force him to stay behind, and then people found out? Everyone would blame us, wouldn't they?'

'Do you think so? I wonder...' I thought it over.

If we returned alive, I imagined it would be pretty big news. And when it came out that we'd left someone behind, even a murderer, to escape, there would certainly be a lot of suspicions, however unfair. I could hear the questions now.

Did you agree with the idea of sacrificing the murderer? Didn't someone force you to do it? Wasn't this basically a lynching? Were you absolutely certain that person was a murderer? Could you have condemned an innocent person?

And the suspicions might not even be unfair. There was no guarantee that we weren't about to force an innocent person to run the winch.

'So, maybe it would have been all right to just let Mr Yazaki have his accident. It's not like it would be the worst thing humans have done or anything. And, if he had brought the stone down, it wouldn't have been our fault. There was nothing we could have done to stop it. Not really.'

'Yeah. I guess you're right.'

It was true that part of me had secretly hoped that Yazaki would trap himself and let the rest of us escape. But when he actually started to turn the handle, I couldn't stand back and not try to keep him safe. That was also true.

'Do you think the Yazakis have given up? Our only choice really is to find the murderer.'

'It is. I don't know what people will say, but…'

For us, it was the only way we could deal with that final decision.

Still, it seemed Mai was struggling to make it all fit together.

'That means we'll be getting the worst one of us to sacrifice himself for the rest of us. But then, if we figure out who it is, and that person agrees of his own free will to give his life for the group, is he really the worst of us?'

'Who knows...'

If that happened, then the murderer would choose to stay behind and seven people would live. And the rest of us would not be saving anyone.

'Or, let's say it doesn't go like that, and the murderer wants to live. So, we force him to turn the winch. Isn't that the same as killing him? And that'll make us all killers, too, right?'

'Yes. I suppose that is right.'

The seven of us would be killing the murderer. The fact that we'd be doing it to save our own lives didn't change the fact that it was taking another human being's life.

But that human being had already murdered two people. It was right for them to die. Still, something bothered me. Did that equation truly balance out?

Mai laughed weakly.

'I know it's just arguing for the sake of arguing. I mean, if the murderer gets out and gets caught, he'll just end up being hanged, right? If we don't use that life to save ourselves, he'll still just end up another corpse. But then I just thought someone who didn't want to be a killer could volunteer to turn the winch themselves.'

She was talking more than she ever had before. She must have been struggling without anyone else she could discuss things with down here.

'Mai, you aren't thinking of volunteering, are you?'

'Not a chance. I can't see any sense in my dying if we can't figure out who the murderer is. I know there's no perfect way to figure out who will be the sacrifice. Of course there isn't. Shuichi, do you ever think about what normal people would do at a time like this?'

'What do you mean, normal?' What could normal possibly have to do with this bizarre situation?

'No, I don't mean, like, down here. Have you heard about how unmarried police officers volunteer for dangerous jobs and such?'

'Oh, yeah, I think I've heard that.'

I hadn't just heard about it. I'd been thinking about it myself. If this were a story, some loner would step up to volunteer in place of someone with family. The idea had come to me when I was talking to Hana.

'I think the idea is that fewer people will suffer that way, if anything happens to the volunteer. But then, that's saying that the lives of people who aren't loved are worth less than the lives of people who are.' I could hear the loneliness in Mai's voice as she said that. 'It's like in the films. Someone is about to be killed, and they start talking about their spouse or their family, begging to be spared. So, if they didn't have anyone, no family, no partner, does that mean it'd be all right to kill them?

'If we all have the same rights, when it's time to choose someone to sacrifice, is it the one who's least loved that gets picked?

'It's like some kind of death game from a manga. You know, they have these games where people who aren't smart or strong enough get eliminated and die. Isn't it just as cruel to decide that people who aren't as loved have to die?

'Then there are those public safety campaigns with slogans like "To keep your loved ones safe bla bla bla" you see all the time. But then you have to think, doesn't that assume that everyone in the world has loved ones?'

Her words were like a knife to the heart.

If I died down here in the Ark, how would my family react? I imagined they'd be shocked that I'd died in a place like this. Maybe they'd feel a little guilty. But, little by little, they'd forget me.

If everyone down here had a family or was in a relationship apart from me, how would it go when we had to choose someone to leave behind? Maybe it would be like Mai said—a death game that the least loved person would lose. The one who nobody will miss should be the one to die. They might all agree with that. Perhaps even I would agree, too, and then I'd volunteer to operate the winch.

'It's not up to anyone else to decide whose death causes more unhappiness: the one who dies and leaves a loved one behind, or the one who dies unloved,' Mai said, and laid her left hand over my right.

My voice trembled when I replied, 'And who's the unloved one here? You? Me?'

'I wonder. I don't know.'

'But you got married. Not like me.'

'My marriage is no different to being single. You've heard me talk about that enough.'

Mai leaned against me.

'I don't believe you really thought it would be better for Yazaki to trap himself in that room, did you, Shuichi?'

'No. And neither did you.'

She laughed quietly.

These past few days, Mai's face had been make-up free, of course. Her skin was getting rough. Even so, I found it beautiful, like a weathered stone statue.

We hadn't changed clothes or bathed in days, so we both reeked. Our faces were close enough to get a full dose, and we grinned at each other.

I kissed Mai's dry, cracked lips.

It was just a few moments. Then, she said quietly, like someone making an embarrassing confession, 'I want to get back alive. No matter what.'

'Of course.'

It took time for the intoxication of that moment to recede. When it did, we stood and went upstairs.

We stepped out into the corridor and turned to each other.

'See you.'

'Yeah.'

We whispered our goodbyes to each other, then headed to our rooms.

VIII

When I got back to my room, Shotaro was out. I wondered if he was looking for Sayaka's phone again.

Should I go and help him? I was still walking on air after the last few minutes with Mai. I ran back over that one bright moment when we kissed as I stretched out on my mattress.

It was hard to believe that such happiness could exist in this underground trap. If we were out on the surface, it was a happiness I would have rejected on moral grounds.

My head was filled with clouds, and I closed my eyes. I relaxed and left my body to drift on the aimless flow of time.

It must have been about an hour later that the door suddenly opened. I leapt up in shock.

Shotaro was standing in the doorway.

'Shuichi! Were you asleep?'

'Hey, Shotaro…'

I felt a bite of guilt. I wasn't quite ready to talk about what had happened with Mai yet.

Shotaro didn't pay any mind to my unease. He swept into the room and took my arm.

'Sorry, but I need you to come with me right now. There's something I want you to see.'

'What is it?'

'I found Sayaka's phone.'

'You did? Where?!'

He didn't answer. He just dragged me up and out of the room. We went down the stairs.

On the middle floor, I once more had to roll up my trouser legs and wade into the water.

'It's this way,' Shotaro said and pointed down the corridor, away from the steel door of the winch room.

We splashed along until he stopped outside room 215.

'Here?'

'Right.'

I had searched this room yesterday.

Shotaro opened the door and pointed at a blue toolbox made of tin on the bottom shelf. It was filled with electrician's tools and its lid rose to an angled arch. It was now almost completely underwater.

When my eyes came to rest on the lid, I couldn't hold back a shout.

'What?! It was there all along?'

There the phone sat atop the arched lid, the water lapping at its blue denim case.

Shotaro picked up the phone.

'Come to think of it, it makes sense. The electrical tape that Sayaka used came from this box. When she came to get the tape, she must have set her phone down when she closed the box and forgot it.'

'And it's been here the whole time?'

'Right. And see, the case is almost the same colour as the box.'

I looked back and forth between the phone and the box. The denim phone cover and the painted toolbox were both a dull indigo blue.

'So, she forgot her phone here and just overlooked it when she came to search for it…'

'She must have. Just like that time when you made all that ruckus over losing your wallet and ended up finding out it was in your bag all along. Remember?'

'Oh, yeah, that did happen.'

I once overlooked my black wallet in my black bag and convinced myself I'd lost it somewhere. It must be a common occurrence.

Shotaro turned the phone over and pointed at a small brown stain.

'This is a spot of chilli con carne sauce. Sayaka's last meal. There's a similar spot on the lid of the box. See?'

I looked at the lid, and sure enough, there was a matching spot.

'She must have put the phone here before the sauce dried. That gives us a clear idea of Sayaka's movements before her murder. Which are pretty much as we'd thought, but now there's evidence backing that up.'

So, the night before last, this is what Sayaka must have done:

When she was eating her dinner of chilli in her room, she accidentally smashed a glass. To make sure she got all the shards and splinters, she came to this storeroom to get a roll of tape. When she did, she forgot her phone here.

After clearing up all of the splinters, Sayaka noticed her phone was missing. She had no idea where she'd left it, so she went searching through the whole building. That was when the murderer caught and killed her.

I asked the vital question.

'So, is the phone dead or alive?'

'Not sure. It does nothing when I push the power button. The battery might be flat, but I'd guess the water got into it. It doesn't look like it has any waterproofing.'

I was getting the feeling he was angry with me.

I had been the one to search this room the day before. If I'd been less careless, I'd have found the phone, and then it wouldn't have got wet.

'I never dreamed it would be in a place like this. If I'd looked more carefully—'

'No use crying over it now. She even overlooked it herself, which is why she kept wandering around so long. I was careless, too. I should have realized it might be here earlier than I did. It's the first place I should have checked.'

'So, what now? There's a chance a water damaged phone can work again once it's dried out.'

'Yes, there is hope, but it might take a day or two to dry out. And, even if it works, it doesn't change the fact that it's going to be hard to find whatever she had on it. At this point, I don't think we should worry much about the data. The mere fact that we have the phone is important enough. And the place where we found it.'

Shotaro put the phone in his pocket.

What on earth was he talking about it? I asked him to explain, but he wouldn't. Just said he wasn't ready to talk about it.

So, we left the storeroom and went back upstairs.

Shotaro went around announcing to everyone that he'd found Sayaka's phone. He showed it along with photos he'd taken of the scene, and everyone was satisfied that Sayaka had left it on top of the toolbox herself. He left it there, though, and didn't discuss his ideas about the reason for her decapitation.

In other words, the murderer was now definitely aware we had the phone, but that was all right because it wouldn't make any difference to them.

'I need everyone to know that we found the phone on top of that toolbox. Otherwise, I might miss my chance to identify the murderer.'

That is all Shotaro would tell me. He kept hold of Sayaka's phone.

IX

The whole next day, nothing at all happened.

Most people stayed holed up in their rooms to pass the time. At no point did all eight of us gather in one place.

I ran into Mai a few times, when I was on the way to the toilet or to get tins of food, but we just exchanged smiles. Nothing more. The case was still in progress. We needed to avoid attracting attention.

We didn't have any more interactions with the Yazaki family after the incident of the previous day, but I did happen to overhear their conversation once, when they came to the dining room to get some tins.

They weren't talking about the situation in the Ark at all. They were talking about the dog they'd left behind.

It was a Shiba Inu named Saburo, apparently. I remembered them talking about him at the big group lunch we'd had. They'd bought him for Hayato's birthday the year he entered middle school. Kotaro had sold off a coin collection he'd had since his youth and used the money to buy the boy a dog.

I felt like the dog must have become a common bond for the whole family. They'd probably shared the same stories over and over. How Saburo would go to sleep atop his cushion but without fail slide off onto the floor. How he liked bananas, and any time they put a bunch on the table, he would jump up on a chair and sit, his front paws on the table, waiting for his share. For the family, trapped in this terrible place as they were, the stories were brief moments of escape, like pockets of air in a flooded cave.

Then Kotaro went off on his own, wandering here and there around the Ark. He was probably searching for some overlooked evidence that would help identify the murderer.

Even though the sun didn't reach us here, we all seemed to stick to the breakfast, lunch, dinner cycle. But as our time underground dragged on, the cycle began to blur.

I checked the time on my phone. It was already past nine at night. The time of day hardly mattered anymore compared to the fact that we only had some forty hours left on our time limit. We would have to decide who would stay behind before then.

Like most everyone else, Shotaro and I stayed in our room.

As the time limit approached, I could feel myself struggling to focus. I would open my pack to get something, then realize I'd forgotten what I wanted. I was beginning to recall unhappy memories I hadn't thought about in years, like how when I was a child, I gave my mother a papier-mâché animal I'd made and she crushed it. Or how embarrassed I was in high school, when another student found the secret blog I had been keeping and let the whole school know. Every new recollection made me groan in misery. As calm as I tried to remain, the fear ate away at my spirit. It was like there was a bug in the software running my brain.

Shotaro gave me a sympathetic look.

He had been deep in thought the whole day.

I knew what he was thinking about. He was, of course, building a theory about the murderer.

'Hey, Shotaro?'

'What is it?'

He wasn't upset, but neither was he relaxed.

'Have you figured anything out?'

I had been asking the same questions all day. I didn't talk about any particular suspicions I might have.

And it wasn't just me. Everyone was trying to avoid pointing the finger at anyone else, apart from Hana, of course, with her comments about the Yazakis.

Given the fate that lay in store for the murderer, it wasn't something anyone felt they could casually speculate about. Not to mention that if you made accusations without any evidence, the suspicion would just turn back on you.

Shotaro scratched his head.

'I guess, to a certain extent, I understand. I think I'm close to being able to name the murderer. But I don't have the last piece. The question is if I'll be able to find it before time runs out.'

Looking at him, I didn't doubt that he knew something. He'd found a vital clue somewhere.

'If you tell me what you understand "to a certain extent", I could help you think about it.'

'Not just now. It's not a problem where your expertise will help.'

It seemed he didn't want to open up until he could narrow it down to only one possible suspect.

But was this a problem he could solve just by thinking about it? If he didn't have enough evidence, shouldn't we somehow force the murderer to act? Or, at the very least, hope that they did on their own?

'There won't be any more murders, will there? Surely they are done with that.'

'I don't think there will be. Everyone is much more on guard than before. And the middle floor is almost flooded. I don't think there's anywhere else they could kill without being noticed. And if you're wondering what we should be doing, Shuichi...'

Shotaro stifled a yawn and looked over at me.

'If you can, sleep. We might not get another chance with the time limit creeping up on us.'

He was right, of course. I was exhausted, anyway. I couldn't find the power to even move, like a car with a broken drive belt.

I turned away from Shotaro, who was still thinking, and fell asleep.

But our predictions were wrong. Just a few hours later, there was a third murder that defied all expectation.

FOUR
Knife and Nail Clippers

I

I woke to screams.

'Dad! Dad, whyyy!'

The uncomprehending cries went on and on.

The voice was Hayato's. It sounded like the cries were coming from the half-flooded floor below.

I checked the time on my phone. It was 2.32 a.m. I'd slept for just about five hours.

Shotaro sat on his mattress in exactly the same spot he had five hours before. It didn't look like he'd slept much, if at all.

'What is going on?' I asked pointlessly, and stood up.

Something had happened. Something terrible, obviously. Could it be the thing we had been so sure wouldn't?

Shotaro and I got up and went to the top of the stairs.

The water flooding the middle floor had risen about 70 centimetres.

We immediately noticed changes. The waders were no longer at the top of the stairs, but lying in the water at one side of the corridor.

There were two pairs of shoes lined up on the step above

the water. Hiroko's and Hayato's. We could hear their wails of grief from the depths of the corridor below.

We went down and I followed Shotaro as he pushed through the water. I rolled my trousers up as high as I could, but the water came up over my thighs and splashed up hip high with every step.

They were in room 207, the storeroom where the murderer had got their knife and saw for the second murder.

The door was standing open. White fluorescent light flooded out. From outside we could hear mournful sobbing mingling with the sound of water lapping at the walls.

We looked inside. It was obvious at once what had happened.

Hiroko and Hayato were crouching awkwardly in front of the steel shelf to the right. They were trying to pull up something from the bottom shelf, below the water's surface.

We couldn't see well past their backs, but it appeared to be Mr Yazaki's corpse.

'What happened?'

The two spun around at Shotaro's question, glaring at us, like they were trying to protect his body.

'What happened? Has Mr Yazaki been murdered?'

They two seemed to wilt and Hiroko said only, 'Yes.'

Mr Yazaki's upper body was flopping out from the bottom shelf. He was dressed in a vest and black leggings. It was hard to see through the rippling water, but the chest of his vest was torn. We could make out stab wounds.

One diving tank was rolling around on the floor, as if it had fallen off the shelf. The regulator was attached.

There was a pair of garden shears with long wooden handles floating in the water near the far wall. I wondered if they had caused those stab wounds.

I struggled to make sense of the sight. What had the victim been doing here? Had he been diving in his underthings when the murderer killed him?

Hiroko and Hayato began to tug at Kotaro's corpse once more, but his leg caught on one of the uprights. The body twisted unnaturally, like no living person would, and they had to back away at the sight of it. They both collapsed against the shelf, moaning in grief.

'Let us carry him,' Shotaro offered. They didn't answer. He stepped forward anyway and reached below the water to take Kotaro by the shoulders. They didn't try to stop him.

'Shuichi, take his legs.'

Just like I had three days before, when we had moved Sayaka, I embraced a corpse. We slid him through the water face up. The bereaved pair splashed through the water behind us.

Hana, Mai and Ryuhei were gathered at the top of the stairs.

They had surely guessed at the third murder when they heard Hayato's cries. And yet, when we carried Kotaro out, they seemed surprised.

'What's happening?' Hana moaned. We didn't answer.

Mai looked at soaking-wet Hiroko and Hayato and said, 'We should get you some sleeping bags or something. You'll catch a chill.'

'Good idea, thank you,' Shotaro answered. She went to get the sleeping bags. We lifted the body and climbed slowly up the stairs.

We laid Kotaro Yazaki in the upper floor corridor for the time being.

II

The surviving seven of us gathered in the dining room.

The two Yazakis sat wrapped in the sleeping bags Mai had brought. Shotaro and I carefully wiped dry our legs with some towels. The water's chill had seeped into our bodies, and we could not wipe that away so easily.

Shotaro looked to the Yazakis bundled up like a couple of caterpillars and asked, 'What happened? What was Mr Yazaki doing? Can you tell us?'

They didn't respond.

'You understand that we still have to find the murderer, don't you? We're running out of time.'

Hayato turned a hate-filled gaze on the rest of us. The murderer had to be in this room right now.

We waited patiently. Finally, Hiroko managed to find words.

'Our Kotaro was trying to catch the murderer down there.'

'In that storeroom?'

'Right.'

I couldn't fit the pieces together. Yazaki was in his underclothes with a diving tank. That was all to catch the killer?

'He went looking through the whole building yesterday. He was hoping to help catch the murderer. He thought there had to be some evidence somewhere. And he found it. The knife. The one used to stab that girl... Sayaka, was it?'

A shock ran through the room.

We had never found the knife used to leave the wound in Sayaka's chest. We'd assumed the murderer had got rid of it with her head, by dropping them into the flooded bottom floor.

'The knife was in that storeroom?'

'It was stuck under a shelf at the back of the room. It was hidden where the steel of the shelf was bent down, with the tip wedged into a seam.'

'I see.'

That would certainly have been hard to find. We hadn't actually looked that hard, since we'd thought it had been dropped down below.

'So, Kotaro wanted to set up an ambush there. Since the murderer hadn't got rid of the knife, they must be going to come back for it at some point, he thought. Then, he could get the drop on them, you know. Catch them.'

I couldn't imagine why the murderer would hide the knife instead of getting rid of it. But, given that they had done so, it did seem logical to assume they would come back to get it at some point.

'If he caught the person in the act of coming to get the knife they'd hidden, that would be hard proof, right?'

'And that's why he had the diving equipment?'

'Yes.'

Things were becoming clearer by the moment.

He'd wanted to set up an ambush in the storeroom to catch the killer unawares when they came to get the knife.

Until very recently, it would have been impossible. There weren't any good hiding places in the storeroom, so the killer would have noticed him the second they stepped into the room, before they took the knife, and simply made some excuse for their presence.

But with the rising water, there was now a way to do it.

'So, Mr Yazaki took the diving tank and hid under the bottom shelf, under the water. His plan was to wait until the murderer took the knife, then he would jump out and catch them in the act. Is that right?'

'Right.'

That would certainly be the killer's blind spot. They wouldn't have expected anyone to be hiding under the water. There was no harness for the diving tank, but that wouldn't be a problem for Yazaki if he was just lying in wait under the shelf. He would just have to stay hidden until the moment the murderer took the knife.

Breathing through the regulator underwater would release bubbles, but the shelf would help hide those. He had probably exhaled toward the wall to make sure the murderer didn't notice.

'Last night, around seven, Kotaro went to the storeroom. He told us to stay in our room. If someone saw us acting funny, the murderer might figure out something was going on.'

'And he was in his underclothes because he doesn't have a change of clothes?'

'That's right. He didn't want all his things to get wet.'

That did explain why he was on the middle floor in his vest and leggings.

Yazaki hadn't worn the waders. Of course he hadn't. They had remained at the top of the stairs after the Yazakis' failed attempts with the winch. If they weren't there, the murderer would have noticed.

'Kotaro was going to stay above water until the murderer came down the stairs. Then, he'd go under and wait for them to come into the room.'

Sure. The tank hadn't been full, and the water was cold. He wouldn't want to spend the whole time under the water. He would have been able to hear the splashing when the murderer came down, or maybe even tell by the way the water moved. When he was sure, he'd have gone under.

It wasn't a great plan. There was no guarantee that the murderer would come. But given that our escape was on the line, Yazaki must have been willing to try anything he could.

But the murderer had showed up, just like he'd thought.

'We waited and waited. He said he wouldn't come back until he was at the end of his strength. But after seven hours, I went to see.'

And she'd found him dead.

The murderer must have spotted him before he could ambush them. Maybe he'd made a noise, or the bubbles had given him away.

Then Yazaki, trapped beneath the bottom shelf, had been speared like a fish with those garden shears. The long handles meant the murderer wouldn't even need to get their arms wet.

Yazaki had been waiting in the cold water in his underclothes. He probably hadn't been able to move as quickly as he'd planned and had been killed without managing to lift a finger. I doubted there had even been a sound. The murderer had been lucky.

Shotaro continued to question Hiroko, whose gaze wandered around the room.

'Did the murderer get away with the proof? The knife? Did you check?'

'We didn't look.'

Naturally, Hiroko and Hayato had paid no mind to anything in that room except Kotaro's body. But the question seemed to jar something in Hiroko's memory.

'There's no doubt that the knife was there, though. Our Kotaro had a picture on his phone. But the phone... Come to think of it, I think the murderer might have his phone...'

'Your husband's phone is gone? And you think the murderer took it?'

'Yes. Our Kotaro had planned to use it to record a video as evidence.'

She said that his smartphone had been able to record underwater. He was planning to capture the murderer retrieving the knife on video as incontrovertible proof.

'Shuichi, I have to ask, did you see a phone anywhere in the storeroom?' Shotaro asked.

'No. I didn't look that closely, but I don't think there was a phone anywhere.'

There was no way the murderer would have left the phone at the scene.

Hiroko had nothing else to offer. Shotaro stood up.

'Let's check the scene one more time. All we had time to do before was move the body.'

He took me by the shoulder.

Once more, we had to go into that cold water.

The two Yazakis came with us. Their faces were slack and blank, like they'd been anaesthetized, and their steps were faltering. They must have been drained, emotionally and physically. But it was their husband and father who had been killed. How could we tell them not to come?

III

We went downstairs and through the corridor. It was more like swimming than walking. Hana, Mai and Ryuhei waited at the top of the stairs like they had earlier.

When we stepped inside, we immediately saw a set of diving goggles on the shelf. We hadn't noticed them before in the stress of the moment, but of course Kotaro would have needed them to see under the water.

There was also a scrap of cardboard about the size of a postcard floating on the surface. Shotaro paddled the water to bring it over and picked it up.

'Kotaro was going to use that to hide his phone screen,' Hiroko explained.

It was a clever idea. The screen would glow while he was filming, so he'd want to hide it to keep the murderer from noticing. Press the cardboard over the screen, and it would hide the glow. But look as we might, we couldn't find the phone itself.

Shotaro peeked under the shelf at the back of the room.

'I'll be. There it is.'

He reached down and took out something wrapped in a bit of bin liner.

The inside of the liner was stained brownish red. He opened it up, and we saw a thin bladed knife about twelve centimetres long.

It was clearly the knife that had made the stab wound in Sayaka's chest. For whatever reason, the murderer had left it here. Again.

The two surviving Yazakis gazed at the knife as if it were a symbol of the dead man's honour and nodded reverently.

'It is certainly reasonable to assume that the murderer came here to get the knife, but then why did they leave it here in the end?' Shotaro mused.

'They must have panicked, right? I mean, they thought they would be alone here, but then they saw that someone was waiting under the water.'

I was painfully aware of the two grieving people listening as I spoke.

'I suppose so. It does seem the murderer was less cool headed this time than the other two. This murder seems unplanned, almost like a reflex. Which might mean the murderer wasn't as careful about cleaning up afterward. Shuichi, let's try to move this,' Shotaro said, and he put a hand on the steel shelves under which Kotaro had hidden.

We transferred the tools to another set of shelves. When the shelves in question were all clear, we each took one side and pulled the whole set away from the wall.

It was hard going. It was up tight against the shelves to either side, which made it difficult to get a good grip, especially with all the cold water.

The frame shifted and there was a high-pitched squealing. The shelves began to slide out. When the floor came into view, Hayato let out a gasp.

The large black smartphone that Kotaro had used was lying up against the wall.

Hayato snatched it up, unmindful of the water. The screen was off. We were shocked that the phone was still there. The murderer hadn't taken it.

He pressed the power button, and the lock screen appeared. 'Mum, what's his PIN?'

Hiroko shook her head. 'I don't know.'

The frustration was unbearable. If Kotaro had been recording, what was on his phone? Did he manage to get any footage of the murderer?

Shotaro asked me, 'Shuichi, what happens if you press the power button while recording? When the screen goes off?'

'Uh, I guess the recording stops immediately, right? And it saves the video up to that point, I think.'

'That's what I was thinking. We can try it out later.'

So, Kotaro had hidden his phone under the shelves. He must have done it when the murderer attacked him. Even if the murderer saw it, there was nothing they could have done.

We had just seen how difficult it was to move the shelves. Two people had struggled to shift them, making an incredible amount of noise as they did so. And it would have been even more difficult for the murderer to move them, with Kotaro's dead body underneath. There was no way they would have tried anything so risky.

It's not like they could have used a pole or something to drag the phone out, either. They would have had to get down on the floor to do it, which would have soaked them head to toe. If the body were discovered right away, anyone soaking wet would be the prime suspect.

The murderer hadn't had time to prepare, unlike with Sayaka's murderer. It was a spontaneous crime.

In other words, even if there was some crucial evidence on Kotaro's phone, the murderer had no way to get it. They had to leave it there under the shelves.

Hiroko and Hayato stared unblinking at the phone.

Shotaro went on.

'I doubt there is any conclusive evidence on there. Mr Yazaki was recording underwater. To get a clear glimpse of the murderer's face, he would have had to raise the lens above the surface, and he must have been killed before he could do that. Otherwise, I don't think the phone would have ended up where it did.

'Even if it doesn't show the murderer's face, though, there's a good chance it did record something important. The time alone might tell us something vital. We need to access the data. But you don't know the PIN, do you, Mrs Yazaki?'

Hiroko shook her head.

'Did Mr Yazaki use any other kind of unlock? Fingerprint or face recognition?'

'I suppose he probably used the fingerprint thing...' Her answer was hesitant. She didn't seem very clued in about electronic devices.

So, could we use the corpse's fingerprint to unlock the phone? The murderer hadn't been able to get rid of the physical thing that could unlock the phone this time, unlike with Sayaka. This crime was so much sloppier.

But when we had carried Mr Yazaki up the stairs, his skin had been wrinkled as a prune from its hours in the water. I doubted the sensor would recognize his print like that. And how long would it take for his body to dry out enough?

'You don't have any guesses what the PIN might be? His birthday, or your numberplate? Something simple like that?'

'It might be, but...' Hiroko's voice tailed off in despair. She seemed to have given up even thinking about it. She answered questions, but her eyes never left her son's face. It was like she was drifting ever further away.

Hayato stowed his father's phone in his jacket pocket.

And so ended our crime scene investigation. We pushed through the water back toward the stairs.

We announced our discoveries of the knife and phone to the three waiting above.

The Yazakis towelled themselves off and immediately wrapped the sleeping bags around themselves again.

Shotaro and I were well drenched by the waves kicked up when we moved the shelves and were shivering from the chill, but our investigation was not finished. We had to check one more item the murderer had left. The waders still lay where they had been dropped near the stairs.

Shotaro rolled his sleeves up.

'Obviously, the murderer didn't put these on to go to the storeroom planning on killing anyone. There just wasn't any other way to go down without getting wet.

'Then, suddenly, they found themselves committing murder without any preparation. The two previous crimes showed supreme composure, but this might be the first time they lost their head. Not only was Mr Yazaki hiding down there, but someone could have come along and caught them at any time. And with the water up to their knees, it's not as if they could easily slip away and hide somewhere.

'The very best they could hope for was to get away as quickly as possible. And that's what they must have done. The knife was left behind, after all. Once they'd made it up the stairs, that would have been the most dangerous place of all. So, they quickly took these waders off and dropped them at the bottom of the stairs.'

Shotaro scooped the waders up in his arms.

When he did, something that had been wrapped inside almost fell out into the water below.

'Whoops!'

He pounced on it with both hands.

'What is this?'

Shotaro gingerly placed the little bundle in the palm of his hand and held it out for us all to see.

It was a resealable vinyl bag wrapped around a pair of fingernail clippers.

'Hey… Aren't those Yuya's?' I asked.

'Yes, I believe so,' he said.

Shotaro and I weren't the only ones to recognize the set. We all immediately recalled where we'd seen them.

They had been in Yuya's daypack. He had packed all his grooming items in their own little resealable bags, just like this one. We had gone through his pack item by item, and I'm sure we all recalled the occasion.

'What are they doing here?' Hana asked, glaring at Shotaro and me. I began to feel nervous.

These must have been left by the murderer. Which would make Shotaro and me the new prime suspects, wouldn't it?

Shotaro had taken custody of Yuya's daypack and was keeping it in our room. I couldn't think of any explanation for how the clippers had got here, but I could feel how they now cast suspicion on us.

Shotaro didn't seem bothered at all, though.

'These were in Yuya's daypack, as you all remember. The murderer, for some reason, took them from our room.

'But anyone could have done that. Shuichi or I could, of course, but it wouldn't have been difficult for any of you to do so, either. Shuichi and I spend a lot of time out of our room. Someone could have snuck in while we were eating and taken the clippers from the bag, for example.

'It wouldn't even have been that risky. Even if one of us had walked in on them, they could have just said they wanted to clip their nails. We might have thought they were a bit rude, but it wouldn't have been incriminating at all.'

I didn't make a peep. I was worried I might make it sound like the two new suspects were desperately pleading their case.

No one argued, though. Anyone could have casually taken the clippers from Yuya's daypack. There was no disputing that.

Ryuhei glared almost angrily at the bundle on Shotaro's palm. 'What would the murderer have wanted the clippers for?'

'Who knows? That's the problem. At the very least, they had nothing to do with the murder. I hate to keep repeating myself, but this murder was unplanned.'

What could they have possibly been planning to do with nail clippers? The murderer had most likely gone to retrieve the knife, and if that was true, then they had failed because Kotaro was there.

But the clippers were out of the bag. The killer had brought the clippers, so must have somehow needed them to get the knife. They had then taken them out of the bag, so it seemed natural to assume they'd been used. But the killer hadn't got the knife, so what were the clippers used for? Or could the killer have had some other goal; one we hadn't discovered yet?

Shotaro placed the bag and clippers on the stairs. He picked up the waders and shook the water from them, then put them beside the two items. Finally, he looked around the corridor to make sure nothing else had been left behind.

'All right. I think we can finally get up on dry land.'

The seven of us climbed the stairs, taking our discoveries with us.

IV

The knife and clippers lay next to each other on the dining room table.

After the discovery, we had all gathered around Mr Yazaki's body where it lay in the corridor.

He was still soaking wet. I could see into his gaping mouth and noticed that he had gold fillings in his left back molar.

Shotaro spoke to Hiroko and Hayato as they stared down at the lifeless remains of their beloved.

'I really want to check the data on Mr Yazaki's phone. I hope you understand.'

'Right,' Hiroko answered in a hollow voice.

'Could you do it? Try whatever codes you can think of? And when the body… improves… I'd like to ask you to try the fingerprint sensor. That's not something we can do.'

'Yes. I will try.' Hiroko sounded now like she was trying to drive us away. She thrust her hands under his arms and began pulling the body down the corridor.

'Where are you going?'

Shotaro tried to stop her. She looked up, still holding the body, and said, 'To our room. We'll do it there.'

'We want to be there when you unlock it.'

The two of them, surrounded by the five of us, cowered like they were bracing for attack.

I understood that being forced to do such a miserable task under our observation would be agonizing. Anyone in their situation would have wanted to get away from the rest of us as quickly as possible.

But could we really trust them with that evidence, which might determine all our fates? Should we take the corpse and the phone from the bereaved and deal with them ourselves?

'Please, let us go to our room,' Hiroko eventually replied, in a tone of utter misery.

With that, they dragged Mr Yazaki's body to the room all three of them had shared. The body left a streak of water behind.

'Are you sure we can leave it to them? Those two are completely devastated. I doubt they're in any state to make rational decisions,' I said.

Shotaro responded, 'I'm not sure at all. But it would be worse to put too much pressure on them. Because this situation won't just end when we figure out who the murderer is. The whole hunt for the murderer is just a means to an end. Our true goal is getting out of here, and for that we need the Yazakis to be as calm and relaxed as possible.'

The two of us headed for room 120. The storeroom where Yuya and Sayaka were laid to rest.

We had one final, tiny little job left to do, before it was too late. We opened the door, covering our noses to block the smell of decay, and avoided looking at the two corpses on the floor. We grabbed a two-metre length of PVC pipe and rushed from the room.

We needed it for a drying pole. The soaking wet waders had to be dried. The murderer would wear them to go into the winch room to turn the handle and free us.

When we were alone, I asked Shotaro about something that had been bothering me.

'When do you think those clippers were taken?'

'No idea. When was the last time you saw them?'

'When we searched through everyone's things after Sayaka was killed. I didn't even think about them apart from that.'

'I see. I checked the daypack that evening. We had talked about using it to carry one of the diving tanks, and that had made me think about it. The clippers were still there when I did.'

Which meant they had been stolen after that.

'And yesterday, we went to get some tins of food around eight in the evening, right? We didn't leave the room after that.

'Which means the murderer must have stolen the clippers either the morning of two days ago, when we were out of the room, or yesterday around eight in the evening. I guess it's not that big a deal, anyway. I doubt that knowing when they were taken would help us narrow down the list and close in on the murderer.'

Surely no one would have paid much attention to someone sneaking into our room. Even if someone remembered seeing it happen, it wouldn't definitively prove the person they saw was the murderer.

So, how could we find proof? We decided to go back over the events of the previous evening.

According to Hiroko and Hayato, Mr Yazaki had gone down to his stake-out in the storeroom around seven in the evening.

We didn't know what time the murderer had arrived, but at some point, the murderer had picked up the clippers, put on the waders and headed for the tool storeroom.

Yazaki had noticed the murderer coming, gone underwater and hidden in the shelves. Then, presumably, he started recording. He'd hidden the glow of the screen with a piece of cardboard.

Eventually, the murderer came into the room.

Yazaki must have been doing everything he could to avoid being noticed, but something had obviously given him away. A noise, a bubble, maybe the screen of the phone bled through. The murderer had noticed something.

They had picked up the long-handled garden shears and stabbed Yazaki in the chest.

I was sure that, in the final moments, Yazaki had noticed the attack coming. But he couldn't fight back. His body must have been numbed by the chill water, and fear would have made it even harder to move.

Kotaro Yazaki's murder had been easy. Even his death throes had been silenced by the water. It had all been so lucky for the killer.

The murderer would have been upset and wanted to get away as quickly as possible. They left the victim's phone behind as well as the knife they'd come to get in the first place.

The murderer rushed out of the storeroom, went back to the stairs, stepped up out of the water and dropped the waders along with the clippers and the bag. Then they climbed the stairs and hurried back to their room, trying to avoid prying eyes. That must have been how it happened.

But there were things that bothered us.

'The clippers and bag weren't exactly incriminating, were they? We don't even have any idea how the murderer would have used them,' I said.

'That's right. It would only have seemed a little suspicious, at most, if we found out someone had taken them.'

'Then why leave them at the scene like that? If the killer wanted to get rid of them, they could have left them in any number of places without anyone noticing. Leaving the clippers with the waders just screams that it was the murderer who took them from Yuya's daypack.'

'That's exactly right. I guess it just shows how panicked they were. We can't assume the murderer was acting rationally at that point.'

The murderer must have wanted to get rid of anything connected to the crime as quickly as possible.

'But why did they take Yuya's clippers at all? If they needed a set, there were nail clippers in the machinery room desk drawer, right? Why not use those?'

We'd seen those clippers the evening of the day we'd arrived, when we'd checked the map of the Ark.

'Well, I don't think we can be sure that all of us knew about those clippers,' he answered.

'Oh, right.'

On the other hand, we could be sure that everyone in the group knew about Yuya's set.

'There's something else I'm wondering… Can we be absolutely sure that the person who killed Kotaro is the same one responsible for the others?'

'You're saying that maybe Yuya and Sayaka were killed by one person, and Kotaro's murderer was someone else?'

'Yeah.'

It seemed ridiculous at first thought, but we had to at least consider the possibility.

It appeared that the murderer had returned to the storeroom to retrieve the knife that they'd used to stab Sayaka. If that were true, then it was clear that it was all the work of one person.

But the murderer hadn't retrieved the knife in the end, so it might be that whoever killed Yazaki didn't even know it was there. On the other hand, maybe the murderer had simply forgotten it in their panic, but we also didn't know at what point, exactly, Yazaki had been spotted.

'It seems safe to assume that whoever it was, they killed Yazaki before even touching the knife, right? In which case, Yazaki had no proof they were the murderer at all. They just went into the storeroom. There are any number of excuses for that. They could have needed a tool, or something.'

'That's right, but maybe they just couldn't manage to pull off a lie that big.'

'Let's think about it. The murderer walked into the storeroom, where they were hiding a secret, thinking they were alone. And suddenly there was Kotaro, underwater, completely unexpected. The murderer might well have believed that he'd seen through their crimes completely and was there to ambush and subdue them. Knife or not, they probably felt they had to kill him.

'Now, imagine you're someone with nothing at all to do with the crimes. You go into the storeroom and find Yazaki hiding under the water. Would you be able to keep quiet?'

'Not a chance. I'd freak out and probably scream my head off.'

'As would most of us, I imagine. I certainly would. If anyone except the murderer went into that storeroom and found Yazaki, I'm sure they'd have thought he was the murderer and their turn was next. They'd have called for help, for sure.

'But, since that's not what happened, and whoever it was picked up a pair of garden shears and stabbed him to death, the only reasonable conclusion is, the murderer just added another crime to their list.'

'Yeah, I guess so,' I conceded.

The only thing that made sense was that the same culprit was behind the third murder as Yuya's and Sayaka's.

The second murder had been committed to hide data on Sayaka's phone, so the killer had to be the same person who killed Yuya. So it was safe to say that all the crimes were by the same murderer.

Now, we had a good idea of the motives for the second and third murders. The murderer was trying to avoid getting caught. But we still had no idea why, while we were caught in this trap, they had killed Yuya.

Shotaro slid the pipe into the left leg of the waders and stood them up like a scarecrow near a vent in the corridor.

'I think that'll do.'

'Will they dry out in time, do you think? Before the end?'

'No idea. Whoever uses them will just have to bear a bit of damp, I fear.'

We had about thirty-two hours left until someone would have to turn the winch.

And in one corner of the upper floor, near the stairs, the torture tools lay waiting in case they were needed.

V

The two of us headed back to our room.

Shotaro took Sayaka's phone from the pack where he was keeping it.

He had packed the charging port with tissue paper in hopes that he could draw the moisture out of it and bring it back to life.

His attempts the day before had failed. After another day's wait, he once more connected the charging cable and pushed the button.

We waited almost a minute, but the screen stayed black.

It might still have been wet inside, or it might have shorted out so badly it was dead. And even if it started up, we didn't know Sayaka's unlock code. It looked like we would have to give up on whatever was on her phone.

We decided to gather all the evidence we'd found in one place. We took Sayaka's phone and Yuya's pack and went to the dining room.

Hana, Mai and Ryuhei were there already.

It was like a scene out of a hospital waiting room. Everyone looked like they were dreading news of a fatal illness, pacing nervously between the tables or slumping down into one of the chairs, occasionally going to the toilet or their room just for a moment of release from the terrible tension.

No one stayed away for long, though. They came right back to the dining room, as if waiting for their name to be called.

Our situation was nearing its end. We all knew it. We couldn't keep avoiding each other much longer.

When Shotaro and I came in with our burdens, Hana snapped at us. 'Where have you been?'

'Just hanging up the waders to dry.'

'Oh, for...'

She broke off, seemingly exasperated.

'Has anything happened with the Yazakis?' I asked her.

'Not yet.'

We had not heard anything from Hiroko and Hayato since they shut themselves away with Kotaro's body.

Hana slumped over the table and said out loud, to no one in particular, 'Will the fingerprint sensor really work with a dead man? They call stuff like that biometrics, don't they? Bio is, like, living things. Not dead things. Right?'

'I think it'll work. Phone fingerprint scanners use electrical resistance to read the ridges on the skin, so there's no reason it wouldn't work on a dead person. I read somewhere online about how someone copied a fingerprint using gelatine and fooled a fingerprint scanner.

'Oh, but I have heard that the latest phones use ultrasonic waves to detect blood flow. In which case, a dead man's fingerprint wouldn't work,' Shotaro answered.

'Is Yazaki's phone that new?'

'It didn't look it, actually. Maybe two or three years old.'

'I guess that's all right, then,' Hana said. She raised her head and looked straight at me.

Shotaro and I put the evidence on the long table and sat down nearby.

It was Ryuhei's turn to speak.

'How many digits is the code?' He was walking around nervously.

Shotaro answered, 'When I caught a glimpse of his screen, it looked like it was six digits.'

I hadn't noticed that myself.

If it had only been four digits, we could have just tried to brute force it with random guesses. It probably wouldn't have taken a full day. We would make it by the time limit. With six digits, though, it would be essentially impossible unless we knew some numbers related to the family.

'Mr Yazaki's body must still be soaked,' Mai muttered. No one had anything to say to that.

Fingers wrinkled after a long bath would have dried out by now, but there was a good chance that Yazaki had been underwater for hours. And the absence of the processes of life might also influence the time his body took to dry out.

All anyone could think about was the data left on Yazaki's phone.

It was the only way we could see to identify the killer. They had murdered three people without being seen.

Shotaro still wouldn't, or couldn't, say anything about the murderer's identity.

I knew he had ideas. I could also see that he wasn't planning on sharing them until he could confirm what was on the phone. If the video showed the murderer's face, we wouldn't need any kind of logic or theory. There could be no better solution than clear evidence that eliminated all the messy arguments.

We all took pains not to let our gazes meet for fear of setting someone off.

Who was the murderer? The unspoken question grew to fill the dining room almost to bursting.

So far, we had all felt some taboo against laying blame on anyone by name, but now it felt like the slightest provocation could set people to hurling accusations at each other. Only the hope of unlocking the smartphone was allowing us to maintain our composure.

I looked from person to person in the dining room, but no one struck me as a likely suspect. No one stood out as particularly nervous that their crimes might be revealed.

Which was understandable. The murderer wasn't the only one with their life on the line.

If we discovered the murderer, we would then have to make this argument: since they would be headed for the gallows anyway, why not give their life to save ours? And we had no idea how they would respond. Would we have to torture them? If they continued to resist even then, we might all end up dying down here.

In a sense, the murderer held all our fates in their hands. We were all caught in the same dilemma.

Our spirits were being crushed by fear and futility. This was how soldiers must feel when being sent off to war on the orders of a mad despot, I thought.

We had been hunting a killer for a full five days, ever since we'd been trapped here after the earthquake and Yuya's murder.

In that time, two more people had been killed. The fact was that more of us would have survived if we'd just drawn straws to decide the sacrifice right after we found Yuya. But that was really just wishful thinking with the gift of hindsight. Because, as it had actually happened, after it was clear that there wasn't a single piece of meaningful evidence pointing to Yuya's killer, hadn't we all been secretly hoping for another murder?

Had we been right to do as we did? Surely not right, no. We simply hadn't been able to choose any other path. I saw no reason for us to blame ourselves. But even so, the real choice was still to come.

Even before we knew the killer, I couldn't stop thinking about what came next.

Who, if they were identified as the killer, would be likely to agree to operate the winch? And who did I want it to be?

I personally had clear answers to both those questions.

But I could not let anything slip. I had to hide those names.

Because I knew I wasn't the only one thinking about those questions. Even as their gazes wandered aimlessly, they all had to be doing the same.

By accident, my eyes met Ryuhei's. We stared at each other for a few seconds.

I could see from his expression that, even with Yazaki's murder and our time running out, his animosity toward me had not faded at all.

He must surely have seen the same in my own face.

VI

We had twenty-four hours left.

I stood to go to the toilet. On my way, I passed the Yazakis' room.

I wanted to see what was happening. So much time had passed, and still we had learned nothing from Hiroko and Hayato.

Were they wracking their brains and struggling to unlock the phone? Or were they not even trying to open it and check the data?

Kotaro's death would have been an enormous shock. It had probably taken them hours just to function again after that.

And now they were locked in a room with the body of their husband and father. Unable even to look away. Would they be picking up his hand to try the sensor, time and again, asking themselves each time, 'Has he dried out enough? Will it work?' And if it didn't, would they be entering every possible combination of six digits they could think of? Were they doing what we needed them to do?

I doubted that Hiroko and Hayato were capable of rational decisions. Surely it would be better for us to take the phone and body from them to unlock it ourselves. But, if we did that, how could we guess the numbers—

A sound from inside the room caught my attention.

It was Hiroko speaking. Her voice was filled with grief, but she spoke with firmness and conviction, saying, 'If this doesn't go well, then I'll work the winch. You get out of here with those people and go home.'

Hayato was weeping when he answered.

'No! I won't do it! I'd rather die here with you!'

Her son's answer raised only a moan of grief in reply.

That was the end of their conversation, but I could hear them both weeping still. It seemed there was no progress on unlocking the phone.

Was there still time? Even if there wasn't, I couldn't think of anything to say to them. I left, trying to walk as quietly as possible.

VII

I went back to the dining room and sat in one of the decrepit chairs.

I couldn't find it in me to share what I'd heard with the others. I'm sure I didn't need to. They could imagine what the mother and son were going through. We would just have to wait a bit longer for them to calm down.

But could we afford to wait? The shock of Kotaro's murder might not start to fade before the time limit was on us.

And time continued to flow past.

Though there was still no clear definition between day and night, morning and evening, there had never been a point where the passing of time felt so clear and oppressive. The whole building had become one enormous water clock.

I heard footsteps in the corridor. Someone pushed open the dining room door slowly, cautiously, as if doing so might unleash a vicious beast.

Hiroko stepped in. She was alone. Hayato must have stayed back in the room.

Her expression was stiff. I saw no tracks of tears on her cheeks.

'On the subject of Kotaro's phone. We haven't got the fingerprint sensor to work yet. Please wait just a bit more,' she in an emotionless, dead voice. I had the feeling that she was hoping to return to her son and husband as quickly as possible.

The five of us looked at each other.

'What do you mean? Is the sensor broken?' Hana asked, though of course Hiroko would have no way of knowing.

Mai interjected, 'Fingerprint sensors can be tetchy. Sometimes you have to reregister a finger to get it to work.'

I'd had the same experience with my own phone.

That might mean the only way to unlock the phone was to guess the six digit code, which was as good as hopeless.

From then on, Hiroko came to the dining room with regular updates on their progress.

Which, since they were basically repeats of her initial report, meant no progress at all. We offered inane suggestions like giving the sensor a good wipe, to which she would nod meekly and return to her room.

It got too much for me, so I went to the machinery room and sat staring at the two monitors. There had been no change in the scenery outside. I could see that it would soon be sunset.

As if inspired by my movement, the others came to check things as well, like co-workers all gathering around for a smoking break.

We were all searching for release, but all we got was a kind of craving, the pressing need of an addict. The need to get outside chafed at us. As painful as it was, though, we could not stop looking at the monitors, clinging to the memory of the outside world.

Even after the sun set, we stayed in the machinery room. A nearly full moon lit the surface above. Even through the dark, blurry video from the outdated cameras, we could almost smell the scent of plants in the clean, cool air. The idea of wrenching open the iron door, throwing off the hatch and bathing in that air burned in my heart.

We had just over fourteen hours left.

Our problems wouldn't all be solved once we found the murderer. We'd have to convince them, or torture them, into doing what we needed. Was there enough time for that?

VIII

The five of us went on waiting in the dining room.

'This is really bad, isn't it?' Ryuhei said. 'They're not telling us anything anymore. If we can't check the data now, what's the use in waiting? I reckon they're hiding something else from us, too. Or maybe the plan is to stay in there and hope we decide to sacrifice one of ourselves. They're just going to hide out until then, that's what I say.'

He went on to insist that Hiroko and Hayato must have already barred the door.

He was convinced they'd never come out, no matter how we pounded on the door, so the five of us would have to pick someone from among us to operate the winch. Then, when they heard the rock drop and knew the door was open, they'd come popping out, wouldn't they?

I didn't see that happening, based on what I'd heard through the door earlier, but anyone could change their minds with enough time.

Ryuhei went stomping out of the dining room.

We followed him. We couldn't be certain he was wrong, after all.

Our footsteps echoed through the corridor as we all went to the Yazakis' room. Ryuhei pounded on the door with a heavy fist.

'Hey! What are you up to in there?'

It was clear from his tone that he'd convinced himself of his theory that they had decided to bar themselves in.

The door opened after a hesitant moment. Hiroko peeked out. She looked frightened.

The room was dark. Half the fluorescent lights were burnt out.

Kotaro's body lay on the floor behind her. He was face up, his head pointing toward us. There were three mattresses up against the walls. The aluminium pipes they had used were scattered around, and Hayato was sitting on the floor by the body, holding the phone.

Shotaro spoke in an odd tone, like he was both trying to reassure and threaten them at the same time.

'Hiroko, Hayato. Please. Time is getting very short. We wanted to check Mr Yazaki's phone, but it would seem that isn't going very well. It would be best for everyone if we had some evidence, but if we don't, we need to think about other options. Even if we don't find the murderer, we need to decide who is staying behind.'

'Even if we don't find the murderer?' Hiroko repeated quietly. 'In that case, we should have chosen right away. That way, maybe Kotaro would still be alive, wouldn't he?'

'That is true. If we'd taken the chance of an innocent person being sacrificed, then perhaps fewer people might have died. But still, if we don't choose now, we're all going to die. We have to make the most of the time we have left.'

They didn't react at all to Shotaro's words. Maybe they couldn't imagine what 'making the most' of the time might actually mean. Whatever we did, Kotaro Yazaki was gone. He would not be coming back.

They looked utterly drained, but I also got the feeling they were trying to hold back their hatred. Hatred born of the conviction that, at this very moment, one of the five of us who had stormed into their room had killed Kotaro.

Looking on as the conversation between his mother and the rest of us stalled, Hayato took his dead father's hand and, one by one, touched the fingertips to the sensor.

The movement of his hands spoke of frustration. He was doing something he'd tried over and over already, knowing it was a waste of time. It had the feel of a show of pique, or perhaps he was trying to make a point to us.

Ryuhei watched him and noticed how the fingertips barely even touched the sensor. He pushed Hiroko out of the way and strode into the room.

'What the hell are you doing? Give it here.'

Ryuhei grabbed the phone from Hayato's hand and, pinching Kotaro's fingers gingerly, like something filthy, touched them one after the other to the phone.

Yazaki's body was looking even more dead than the last time I'd seen it. His skin had turned a mottled white and purple, what I thought they called 'livor mortis'. Hiroko and Hayato were there beside it, watching the changes happen.

'This is a waste,' Ryuhei said in disgust. He used Kotaro's clothing to wipe the phone, then went through all ten of the fingers again, touching them to the sensor one after the other.

Hayato was left on all fours after Ryuhei took the phone.

I couldn't see his face. He stayed there on his hands and knees, groaning like an animal. He inhaled a gasping, squealing breath.

He grasped one of the pipes from the floor and stood up. He screamed, his eyes wet with tears. Then, he raised the pipe and, without hesitation, brought it down on Ryuhei's head.

'Ow! What the hell are you doing?!'

Ryuhei grabbed at Hayato, but the flailing pipe in the boy's hands struck Ryuhei directly in the stomach. He lost his balance and tumbled over Kotaro's corpse.

The silent corpse's expression seemed to twist. The sight of it gave Hayato pause, holding back his attack.

Hiroko had collapsed near the door, her hands pressed to her cheeks. I stepped over her legs to get into the room and try to stop Hayato.

In response, Hayato gave a full-throated scream and attacked me next.

The pipe hammered into my left wrist, and I grasped the injured spot with my right hand.

I tried to grab hold of him, but Ryuhei and the corpse got in my way.

I fell over.

The pipe came down again.

'Stop! Stop it!'

'What are you doing?'

Mai and Hana were crying out in the corridor.

But, before any serious damage could be done, Shotaro stopped Hayato short with perhaps the only effective argument.

'Hayato! Stop it now! If Shuichi is the murderer, what do you think happens next? If he can't operate the winch because of you, who will take his place?'

The pipe dropped onto my shoulder.

Hayato had given up his attack. He stumbled deeper into the room and collapsed face down onto a mattress. He started shivering and sobbing.

Ryuhei slowly pushed himself up from the body.

'God damn. That hurts,' he groaned. He shook his head as if trying to clear it. It didn't look like he was badly injured.

I pushed myself up with one hand. My wrist was still painful, but it wasn't anything serious.

Hiroko still sat stunned near the door, and in a voice just barely audible, said, 'Forgive him.'

The first signs of violence had arrived. We hadn't even begun to talk about who would be sacrificed, and even so, Hayato had attacked us with something near to murderous intent.

I could understand how the boy might feel we had insulted his father's body. It was also perfectly understandable for him, the youngest of us all, to have reached the very limits of his mental reserves. None of us had any desire to blame the teenager, who still lay at the back of room weeping and moaning.

But the outburst had sparked a fresh kind of terror. When we finally decided who would stay behind, it might set off even worse violence. And then, in the end, maybe no one would be willing to turn the winch. It felt like we'd just had a preview of what was to come.

For the moment, we just waited for Hayato to calm down. When his sobs had eased, Shotaro began to speak.

'Right, everyone, can we all just talk reasonably for a moment? We don't have any more time to waste. We have a decision that needs to be made. I've got a few ideas. I was saving them until I was sure there wasn't any clear evidence. Now, would you listen?'

'Um, sorry, just a moment. Before you go on, there's something I just thought of,' Mai interrupted just as Shotaro was getting started. 'Isn't there one more thing we haven't tried? Maybe it wasn't his fingertip that Mr Yazaki used to unlock his phone.'

'Oh! That could be it!' Shotaro seemed to catch on right away, but I was still in the dark.

'I have a friend who registered a spot below his knuckle instead of his fingertip. Because fingertips sometimes don't work when they're wet or dirty. Is it possible Mr Yazaki did something similar?' Mai went on.

That made sense.

You could register patterns other than your fingerprint into the sensor. Mr Yazaki had been an electrician. It would have made sense for him to register a knuckle or joint or something so he could unlock his phone when his fingertips were dirty.

Hiroko had been sitting by her son, rubbing his back, but she stood and picked up the smartphone from where it had fallen.

She went to her dead husband's body and took his right hand. Then, as Mai had proposed, she touched the phone's sensor to a spot on his thumb below the first joint.

'Oh…' Hiroko gasped quietly.

Everyone gathered around and looked.

The smartphone was showing the home screen. The phone was unlocked.

'Well? Is there a video?' Shotaro prompted.

'Wait a moment. Let's see…' Hiroko was finding it difficult to work the phone under the pressure of Shotaro's urging. She kept tapping the wrong apps until, finally, the gallery opened.

'This must be it…'

She scrolled until, at the very bottom, she found a solid black thumbnail.

Was that Mr Yazaki's final recording? She tapped it. The screen turned black, and we heard what sounded like underwater noises.

At first, the image was fuzzy with low light ISO noise. The only way I could tell that the video had recorded at all was a barely perceptible tremble in the scene. Soon, the burbling sound died down. It seemed Mr Yazaki had steadied himself against the bottom steel shelf underwater.

The pitch black went on for a few more seconds.

Then, the upper right of the screen started to show a blur of white light.

It was the murderer coming in! The white spot was the torch they were holding.

A few seconds later, just when I was thinking the screen had frozen, the screen got brighter. The murderer had switched on the ceiling lights.

It took a bit of time for the camera to focus. When it did, it showed two legs in waders advancing into the room.

Everyone gasped. The murderer strode toward the back shelf.

The video followed. It looked like Mr Yazaki's hands must have been trembling from the way it shook.

The murderer suddenly stopped in the centre of the room. The legs turned a bit, like the body above was rotating.

They turned toward the camera. The wader-covered legs stood still.

Could we be watching the moment when the murderer spotted Mr Yazaki? Soon, the legs went toward the back left of the storeroom. Then, they turned and advanced toward the camera.

'Ah!' Hiroko put her hand to her mouth.

There was no doubt. The murderer was coming to attack Kotaro Yazaki.

The video jerked violently. It looked like Mr Yazaki was trying to get out from under the shelves.

As we all knew, he didn't make it. We saw the blades of the shears spearing into the water.

The phone fell from his hands. It spun in the water, and the last thing it showed was Mr Yazaki's final breath foaming up through the water.

The video ended and the screen went black.

We all looked at each other, our expressions confused and dissatisfied, like we'd just watched a horror film with an ending we couldn't work out.

'Does this tell us who it was?' Hana asked doubtfully.

From what I could tell, there hadn't been anything that would pin down the murderer's identity. All we saw were legs inside waders.

Would we all take turns wearing the waders and recreating the murderer's walk? Would whoever had the same walk be our killer? That surely would never work. The video was shaky and shot underwater. The waders were bulky and came up to the wearer's chest. They would look the same on anyone, anyway. Maybe we could have figured it out with the latest video analysis software or something, but just talking it out would get us nowhere. We'd probably end up throwing blame around and everything would break down.

'Hiroko, what time was that video taken?' Shotaro asked.

Hiroko seemed to come awake. She clutched at the phone that had been close to slipping from her slack fingers. Seeing her husband's murder in real time must have been a terrible shock.

'It says 10.48 p.m.'

'I see. That was about four hours before we discovered the body. Can I?' Shotaro looked to check that she'd not made a mistake, and then went on.

'This video is not enough to identify the murderer. I assume the murderer must have known that. However, it is still worth watching. I think that it supports what I was about to say.

'Unless there are any objections, I'd like us all to go back to the dining room. All right? This is going to be an unhappy conversation. I think we should have it somewhere a little more open. And the evidence we've gathered is all there, too.'

Hiroko nodded, not taking her eyes from her husband's body.

'Are we going to talk about who the murderer is?' she asked.

Shotaro's answer was clear and direct.

'Yes.'

Hiroko sighed deeply. She took her son's arm and leaned against him. Hayato did not resist.

Shotaro took the lead and left the room. The rest of us filed after him, like a funeral procession.

Soon, one of the seven of us would be sentenced to death. A funeral procession, indeed.

FIVE
Choice

I

We all stood in a circle next to one of the long dining room tables.

Only seven of us survived. We looked at each other's faces in turn, probing for signs. We were all dead-eyed with tension and exhaustion. But even now, at the end, no one betrayed any sign of guilt.

After checking the evidence lined up on the table, Shotaro spoke.

'As you all know, we are going to have to decide who will stay behind so the rest of us can leave. We only have about twelve more hours.

'However, for the time being, I'd like you all to forget that as you listen. It might seem impossible, but I need you all to set everything else aside, at least until you decide if my reasoning is correct or not. If you don't, it might well end up with us condemning an innocent person to death.

'I will also completely ignore personal relationships in narrowing down the suspects. For example, I will avoid arguments such as: Kotaro Yazaki's murder was a terrible shock to his wife and son, so neither can be the murderer. Everyone, including myself, is equally viable as a suspect. We need to accept that basic starting assumption to ensure objectivity and make sure there's no lingering ill will or suspicions when we decide.

'On that understanding, I want to make sure everyone accepts now that I'm approaching this with sound reasoning before we move on to the matter at hand. What do you all say?'

Shotaro looked from suspect to suspect. Each nodded in turn.

Was he really about to identify the murderer? The room was filled with an uneasy doubt, as if we only half believed it could even be possible. But, time was running out. If Shotaro was confident enough to declare that he had deduced the murderer's identity through sound reasoning, then escape was within our grasp.

II

When Shotaro began to speak, he maintained a totally dispassionate tone.

'Very well then, let us begin. First, I would like to go over Yuya's murder.

'About one hundred and forty hours ago, while we were all waiting for morning here underground, there was an earthquake. That set the barricade boulder rolling, which blocked the exit, trapping us here. At the same time, water began flowing in and flooding the building, and we realized that we would not be able to escape without sacrificing someone to stay behind.

'Soon after we learned all that, Yuya was killed. He was strangled with a rope in the storeroom at the furthest end of upper floor. It happened while we were all looking for a hex key to remove the support rods under the boulder.

'The method was simple, and there weren't any big puzzles that might serve as leads. The only confusing thing was, why would anyone commit a murder just after we had learned we were trapped here?

'The murderer was putting themselves in a terribly dangerous position. If they were identified, they must surely have known they would be the one forced to stay behind.

'At the same time, the rest of us, the innocent, struggled with how to deal with the fact of the murder. On the one hand, it was a terrible crime. But there was also the undeniable urge to wonder what we would have done if Yuya hadn't been killed. The decision about the sacrifice could have turned into a bloody fight. But, for better or worse, that was put on hold.

'I have no idea what the killer's motive was, but I'm not so sure you can use motive to identify a murderer. Given the timing, I think we must assume that the discovery of our terrible situation led directly to the murder. However, that situation was the same for every suspect.

'So, the major problem raised by the first murder was, what could we use to identify the murderer? Apart from that of the motive, and the identity of the murderer, there were no real questions raised by Yuya's killing.

'There hadn't been a single piece of meaningful evidence left at the scene. The murderer had essentially committed the perfect crime with their first murder. That is when I got the feeling that we were all hoping for a second.

'Of course, it's not true that there was no evidence. There must have been something that we just didn't notice.

'And my missing that evidence is my greatest regret. If I had thought of it, we might have been able to prevent the second and third murders. And now, the only way to figure out what that evidence was, is to ask the murderer directly.'

Apart from the murderer and myself, no one else could have any idea what Shotaro was talking about. However, the suggestion that somehow, we had overlooked a way to prevent the other murders filled the room with a darker atmosphere.

'What are you talking about? What evidence?' asked Hiroko harshly, through pursed lips. 'You've not mentioned a word of it until now.'

'By the time I realized it even existed, it was already out of reach. It would have been meaningless to tell anyone at that point. But for now, let us talk about the second and third murders. If you listen closely, I think you might be able to guess what the evidence was. And this is where the real hunt began.'

III

'The second incident happened on the second night of our confinement. Sayaka was killed and her head cut off. Now, I want everyone to think back on what happened in the hours before the crime.'

Shotaro went through a timetable of that night, almost like he was reading a report.

'At around eight that evening, Sayaka came to the dining room to get a tin of chilli con carne, which she then ate in her room. Up until the day before her death, Sayaka had stayed with Hana, but after a discussion, the two had decided to sleep apart. Is that right?'

'Yeah. What of it?' Hana answered angrily.

Shotaro paid her no mind.

'While she was eating alone in her room, she dropped a glass, and it shattered. To clear up the scattered shards of glass, she went down to room 215 to get a roll of electrician's tape from the toolbox there. She used the tape to pick up the glass shards.

'Around when she finished, Hana came to check on her. She thought that the tape Sayaka was using would be good to remove the bobbles from her clothing, so she borrowed it and went back to her room. That is what you told us then, Hana. Is that correct?'

'…Right.'

Hana's voice was dull now, like she was unsure what Shotaro was getting at.

I had seen her borrow the tape, so I had no reason to doubt the story.

'When she was finished clearing up, Sayaka began searching for something. Several people saw her wandering the building from around nine thirty to around ten. That is correct, yes?'

Ryuhei, Mai and Hana—the witnesses—nodded when asked.

'At the time, no one knew what she was searching for. However, we later found her smartphone left on the toolbox on the middle floor. Matching chilli stains on the phone case and box showed she must have left it there absentmindedly when she retrieved the tape.'

Shotaro had been the one to find it. At the time, he had announced the discovery to everyone, so this was all familiar information.

However, he was careful not to leave anything out of his explanation.

'So, we can assume she was looking for her smartphone, which just happened to have a similar colour to the toolbox.

'Sayaka noticed her phone was missing after cleaning up the glass, so she must have gone straight to the storeroom to check. Everyone goes to the last place they were when looking for something. But the indigo blue case was camouflaged against the box, so she didn't spot it.

'When she didn't find it there, she must have started searching anywhere she could think of. She probably started doubting her own memory, as well, and looked in places it couldn't have been.

'I think we've all had similar experiences of spending far too long looking for things that should be easy to find.'

'Yeah, I know that feeling. It happens sometimes,' Hana said. She seemed more at ease, perhaps because of the relatability of what Sayaka had been going through.

Everyone knows what it's like to be on that kind of fruitless search. I certainly did. And down here, we were all constantly distracted by the mortal danger hanging over us, so it was easy to lose things.

'Indeed. I doubt anyone has any objections to that particular conclusion.

'Now, back to the events. Sayaka was last seen around ten, but she kept searching. Then, when she was down on the middle floor, she was strangled to death.

'The murderer stabbed Sayaka in the chest with a knife. They went to get some paper towels from the storeroom on the upper floor and cut off her head. Her head, most likely, ended up underwater down on the flooded bottom floor.

'The murderer took Sayaka's bag from her room and got rid of it. I don't know when exactly that happened, but I can be sure the murderer did it. Finally, the murderer left.

'So, I think that covers the major points of the second murder.

'In drastic contrast to Yuya's murder, the second was absolutely packed with questions and puzzles. The most bizarre was the fact of Sayaka's decapitation. Now, let me explain the reason behind that.'

Why had the murderer gone to the trouble of cutting a corpse's head off? I had heard Shotaro's answer that evening.

Sayaka had something on her smartphone that the murderer didn't want the group to see. So, they killed her to keep it secret.

Her phone had still been missing at the time of the murder. For all the murderer knew, we might find it at any time.

If they had left Sayaka's body as it was, there was a danger that someone could use her face to unlock the phone and discover whatever they wanted to hide. And that is why the murderer had cut off her head. Shotaro explained all that to the group, just as he had done for me.

The group, finally aware of its significance, all stared as one at Sayaka's phone.

Hiroko was the only one to speak. 'Just now, when you were talking about evidence you missed, is that what you meant? Is there evidence inside that phone?'

'It seems so. It's the only explanation I can find.'

'You said it was broken.'

'That's right. It was half underwater when I found it. Even if it weren't broken, we probably couldn't have unlocked it. We couldn't use face unlock, so we'd just have to guess the code. I think you know how difficult that is.

'So, the murderer succeeded. We have no way of accessing that data. Now, the only way to find out what it is would be to ask the murderer.

'However, in all the work they did to hide that one piece of evidence, they left another. If we can pin that down, we can narrow the suspect list a bit.

'Shuichi, there are some mysteries about Sayaka's murder that remain unsolved. Do you remember?'

'Huh? Oh, yeah.'

The day Sayaka was murdered, I had listed seven mysteries about the crime. We had solved four of them then, and the rest went unsolved.

'First, is who killed her. Of course. Then, there was the question of why they stabbed her. Oh, and then, why did they go to the upper floor to get towels from the far storeroom. I think it was just those three?'

'Right.'

After Sayaka was already dead, the murderer had stabbed her in the chest with a knife for seemingly no reason.

Then, despite the fact that there were cloth rags in a storeroom on the middle floor, the murderer had gone all the way upstairs and to the storeroom at the far end of the corridor to get paper towels. We still had no rational explanation for why they did those two things.

'The issue of the knife that Shuichi just mentioned touches directly on the motive for murder. The knife is vital in explaining why exactly the murderer would go so far as to kill in this extreme situation. But, we mustn't discuss motive before we identify the murderer.

'Let me start with the paper towels. Why did the murderer not use the rags on the middle floor to clean up after cutting off Sayaka's head, and instead go upstairs to get paper towels?

'The trip to room 118 would have involved real risk. There were people sleeping nearby. If someone had spotted the murderer sneaking out of the room with the towels, they would have been the prime suspect when the headless body was found. You all saw the evidence that the murderer took care not to make unnecessary noise when getting the towels.

'The basket which had held the packet of towels had been left on the floor rather than replaced on the shelf. The toolbox and containers on the middle floor had been neatly cleared away, so it would seem the murderer had been too nervous about making noise to put the basket back on the metal shelf.

'So, even aware of the risk involved, they went to get paper towels. Why?

'It's hard to believe the murderer didn't know about the rags on the middle floor. They were stored next to the tools that they used in the murder.

'For some reason, the murderer felt those paper towels were essential.

'But when it comes to wiping up blood, rags are as good as paper shop towels. Either would do. The murderer must have had some intent other than just wiping up blood in mind.

'What did they use the towels for? Well, let's think about what paper towels can do that rags can't. Can anyone tell me what the two main differences between paper and cloth are?'

Shotaro stood looking around like a teacher asking the class a question, but no one said anything.

I gave in to the tension and said the first thing that popped into my head.

'Um, well, are paper towels easier to burn?'

'That might be true, but there was no evidence of fire involved in this murder. And we haven't seen any way to start a fire down here. No, it's something simpler.'

'Well, paper towels are lighter than rags. Thinner. And they tear easier.'

'That's correct. Exactly it.'

I had hit on the right answer.

But it was an accident. I still didn't see what he was getting at. What was good about the paper towels being lighter, thinner and more destructible for the murderer?

'Something about the towels being easier to tear made them necessary for the murderer. I think what that was will become clear if we carefully go through the situation when the murderer cut off Sayaka's head.

'After Sayaka was dead, how long would it take for the murderer to hole up in room 206 and cut off her head? They would have to put on wellingtons, then an apron and gloves, cut off the head with a saw and clean up. I think it would take fifteen to twenty minutes at the very least. And for someone who isn't used to it, and wanted to do it carefully, it would probably take closer to an hour.

'And during that time, the one thing the murderer had to be most careful about was being seen.

'I doubt they would have been worried about being heard. The location was near the machinery room. The generator would cover most of the noise.

'The problem would be light. Does anyone think the murderer could cut off someone's head using just the light on their phone?'

Everyone shook their heads hesitantly. No one thought so.

Phone lights were tricky. They were just about enough to light the task, but nothing else. The murderer could easily have ended up missing a bloodstain on their clothes. And there wasn't anything to use as a phone stand, so they'd have had to lean their phone against the wall. It would not be easy at all.

'Right. And that's exactly what the murderer was thinking. They would have to turn on the fluorescents while they were cutting off Sayaka's head.

'That required some further consideration. Apart from the iron doors at the exit and stairs, all the doors in the Ark are quite crude, right? And they don't have proper frames, so whenever the lights are on inside, they shine out into the corridor.

'Which in itself might not be so bad, but it was a problem for the murderer because the lights in the corridor in that part of the middle floor were all out.

'That meant any light leaking from the room would be clearly visible. If someone happened to come downstairs, they would immediately notice the lights on in that room.'

'That is true...'

Now that he said it, of course the murderer would be worried about light spilling under the door while they were at work. It was obvious, and yet none of us had thought of it.

'If anyone noticed that light, it would be deadly dangerous for the murderer. They were somewhere no one had any reason to be. If anyone saw that light, they would surely come to investigate, and there would be nowhere to run.

'So, the killer would have to make sure that no light leaked around the door, in case anyone came down to the middle floor.

'To turn it around, as long as they stopped the light from leaking, it was extremely unlikely they would be found. There wasn't anything particularly important in that room, so there was no reason to think anyone would come there specifically.

'Anyway, the murderer had to seal up the spaces around the door. And that is why they went up to the storeroom on the upper floor to get the paper towels.'

'Because they needed something thin and easy to tear.'

'Exactly. The rags were too thick to fit into the cracks around the door. The paper towels, though, were perfect for blocking any light leaks. And, when the work was done, they could use them to wipe up the blood and get rid of the rest with the head.'

As Shotaro explained it all, I could hear a ripple of whispers go round the room, like the hiss of a leaking tyre: 'Yeah', 'Makes sense'... It seemed they were accepting his theory.

It was all to keep light from leaking through cracks around the door. There certainly didn't seem to be any other rational explanation for the murderer's trip to the upper floor.

People started looking at Shotaro with new tension and even awe. His declaration that he had a convincing theory of the murderer's identity was starting to seem well founded.

He went on.

'Now, we know why the paper towels were needed. That explanation also holds vital meaning in terms of identifying the murderer. The reason being, there is a much, much simpler and safer way to seal up the cracks around a door.

'Shuichi, if you wanted to seal the cracks around the door in your own apartment, what would you do?'

I was starting to get a sense of where Shotaro's reasoning was taking us.

'I'd use tape. Electrician's tape or something like that.'

'Right. That would, I think, be the logical choice for anyone wanting to seal door cracks to keep light from leaking out. Stuffing a bunch of cracks with paper towels is much more work than just taping over them.

'And it's not like the murderer didn't have that option. There are all kinds of tape on the middle floor. Not everyone knows this clearly, but in room 205, next to the tool room, there is a cardboard carton on the back left shelf, third from the bottom, that is full of electrician's tape, duct tape and more.'

Shotaro and I had found it when we were looking for the hex key.

'Taping up the door is clearly a better way to stop light from leaking out. But the murderer did not do it. They went upstairs to the furthest storeroom to get paper towels.

'I can't think of any other reason for that trip, either. I checked that out.

'And so, the murderer must have had some particular reason that they could not use tape to seal up the door.

'Who is someone with a reason preventing them from using tape? Following that question helped me narrow down the suspect list to two people.'

Shotaro broke off. He seemed to be urging us to prepare ourselves.

We were finally ready to begin dividing the innocent from the guilty.

'Now, let me just head everyone off and say, I am removing Shuichi and myself from the suspect list. We were the ones who found the box of tape when looking for the hex key after the earthquake.

'So, Shuichi and I knew about the tape and would not have needed to go upstairs to get paper towels. I think the Yazakis can attest to that.'

Shotaro looked at Hiroko.

She hesitated a moment, but eventually answered honestly.

'Yes. Those two certainly did know about the tape.'

We had brought a roll for Mr Yazaki when he cut the wires. He'd had a roll in the toolbox he found already, so he hadn't needed ours. But it was enough to prove our innocence.

With Shotaro and me free of suspicion, he went on.

'Hana is also clear of suspicion. She had a roll of tape she'd borrowed from Sayaka to remove the bobbles from her clothes. If she were the murderer, she'd certainly have used it to seal the room, so she would have had no need to go get the paper towels either.'

'That's right,' Hana said, probably before the reason had settled in. She was staring wide eyed.

Shotaro nodded slightly, and this time he turned to indicate Hiroko.

'The Yazaki family were also aware of the tape we'd found on the middle floor after we brought a roll to Kotaro, though he didn't end up using it. I'm not sure they knew where it was, of course. There's no way to prove that one way or the other, so it's not useful as evidence. However, if any of them were the murderer, they'd never have needed to cut off Sayaka's head.

'Why is that? Let's run a mental simulation.

'If one of them had wanted to seal the door, what would they have done? Surely the first thought would have been the roll of insulating tape in the toolbox in room 215. Kotaro had used it the day before, so any of them could have used to it to seal the door. And they wouldn't have worried about being seen getting it.

'Of course, Sayaka had taken the tape from the box to clean up the shards of glass in her room, so it wasn't there anymore.

They didn't know that, though, so they would have gone to check.

'And Sayaka's phone was on the lid of the toolbox. Even with the colour of the case blending in with the toolbox, they would definitely have noticed the phone when they opened the lid.

'So, if any member of the Yazaki family had wanted to seal the door, they would have certainly found Sayaka's phone.

'And, having found her phone, they would no longer have had any reason to cut off her head. Given that the reason for cutting off her head was to prevent the unlocking of her phone, if they had the phone, they could have just dropped it into the water on the bottom floor. No need for the decapitation. So, we can exclude the Yazaki family as suspects.

'Now, shall I answer the possible objections in advance?'

Ryuhei, his face pale, had opened his mouth to speak. Shotaro raised one hand to stop him and went on.

'This is all based on the assumption that the Yazaki family did not know that Sayaka had taken the tape from the toolbox. If they did know, a member of the Yazakis might actually have gone to get the paper towels from the upper floor.

'So, when could they have learned about Sayaka taking the tape? Let's think about it.

'First, is there any chance that they saw Sayaka walking through the corridors holding the tape?

'None at all. Sayaka took the glass and tin of food to her room around eight in the evening and handed the tape to Hana around nine. The only time they could have seen Sayaka was during that hour. However, the Yazakis were holed up in room

103 the whole evening. I can attest to that. Shuichi and I were in the dining room for that hour. If any member of the Yazaki family had come out and walked down the corridor during that time, we would have noticed, wouldn't we?'

'That's right. We didn't know that the tape had been taken,' Hiroko answered.

Shotaro was right. That evening, he and I had eaten and then tried to repair the hob in the dining room. Mr Yazaki had come to get tins of food just before seven that evening, but after that none of the Yazakis had left their room.

'Another possibility is that the murderer learned from Sayaka about the tape before killing her. That's not particularly realistic, though.

'The murderer seems to have sneaked up behind Sayaka and strangled her. It doesn't strike me as likely that they would have tried to engage her in conversation first. She might have shouted for help.

'Remember, there were limited opportunities for the murder. There would never be a better chance than when Sayaka was wandering around alone searching for something. There's no way they would have risked missing that chance by talking to her.'

Sayaka had a clear voice that carried. The murderer would have taken pains to ensure she didn't say a word. Even if they did end up in a conversation, I couldn't imagine Sayaka bringing up the idea of the tape with a hypothetical killer from the Yazaki family.

So, I, Shotaro, Hana, Hiroko and Hayato were all off the suspect list. Just like Shotaro had said, that left two people.

Our united front was collapsing. We had initially been standing in a circle beside the long table, but now five of us stood surrounding Ryuhei and Mai.

Ryuhei was trembling. He shouted, 'No way! This is crazy! Are you going to accuse someone of murder over some paper towels? What if this is some trap the murderer set for me and Mai? What then, huh?'

Shotaro was unmoved.

'Luckily… Or, I suppose from your perspective, unluckily, that possibility is out of the question. I don't think it at all possible that the murderer would act so irrationally just to throw suspicion on someone else.

'The fact is the trip upstairs and the decapitation were terrible risks for the murderer to take.

'More than that, even. If the murderer intentionally used paper towels just to throw suspicion on Ryuhei and Mai, they would have had to know everything: that Sayaka had taken the tape from the toolbox, that the phone was on the box, everything. Otherwise, it wouldn't work.

'That in itself is hard to imagine, but let's say it's true. That would mean the murderer went to the trouble of cutting off Sayaka's head despite knowing where the phone was.

'Decapitating someone not to hide incriminating data, but just to frame one of you two? I can't believe it. No matter how much care they took, there was always a risk of being found. And what a roundabout way to go about framing someone.

'Do any of you really believe that the killer planned every detail of Sayaka's murder just to manipulate my reasoning now?'

Everyone, including Ryuhei and even I, answered only with silence.

The decapitation, the trip to get paper towels, it was all nothing more or less than self-preservation. I couldn't argue with it.

But I was shaken by the fact that Ryuhei and Mai were the only two remaining suspects.

It's not that I hadn't considered the possibility of one of them being the killer. On the contrary, the idea had been weighing on me. Mai and Ryuhei. Which was the murderer? The answer to that would have a huge influence on all of our futures.

Shotaro pressed Ryuhei further.

'Is there anything else you want to say, Ryuhei?'

'No, I guess not.'

'Right. I'd appreciate it, then, if you would please listen to the end.'

Ryuhei gritted his teeth and glared at Shotaro.

Shotaro ignored him and turned to Mai.

'Well, how about you, Mai? I'd like to hear if you have any objections at this point.'

'No. None. I think your reasoning is amazing. It seems perfect so far,' Mai answered calmly.

Ryuhei shot her a pleading glance, perhaps wanting her to join his resistance. But she didn't even look his way. It was as if she was announcing aloud her refusal to cooperate with her husband, even in the most extreme situation.

IV

With the two suspects surrounded, Shotaro began the final judgment.

'I've explained how the details of the second murder allowed me to narrow the suspect list down to two. But that was as far as it could take me. There was nothing decisive pointing to either suspect.

'But, just over twenty-five hours ago, there was a third murder. Kotaro Yazaki was killed. It might have been a senseless, unnecessary murder, but it has given me the last piece. I am now able to say which of the two suspects was the killer.

'First, I want you all to think back the events leading up to Kotaro's death.'

Once more, Shotaro went back over a timetable of the evening of the murder.

'Mr Yazaki took the diving equipment down to the middle floor tool room, where he hid under the shelves. According to Hiroko, that was around seven in the evening. Is that right?'

'Yes...' Hiroko murmured. She and Hayato refused to look at the two suspects.

'His plan was to lay an ambush for the murderer. Mr Yazaki had searched through the Ark for some overlooked piece of evidence and found a bloody knife hidden under a shelf.

'I can't say for certain why the murderer hid it there. But Mr Yazaki assumed that, since they'd hidden it, they would be coming back to get it. So, he wanted to use the diving equipment to hide underwater and capture the murderer when they did.

'It seems he was correct. At 10.48 p.m., the murderer came into the room. As planned, Mr Yazaki hid under the water and recorded a video on his phone.

'Before they could retrieve the knife, though, the murderer realized someone was hiding under the shelves. So, they picked up the garden shears, stabbed Mr Yazaki under the water and hurried away without getting the knife.

'The body was found later, around half past two in the morning, by Hiroko and Hayato.

'Much of the above is based on testimony from those two, but I don't see any reason to doubt them. Clearly, Mr Yazaki was killed by the same murderer. That's the really important part.

'At first glance, there was no direct evidence pointing at the murderer this time, either. The video Mr Yazaki took did not show the murderer's face.

'However, there was indirect evidence. The murderer had left Yuya's nail clippers and a plastic bag with the waders they had used.

'Those had come from Yuya's daypack. The murderer had taken them without us noticing.

'Why did the murderer take the nail clippers? It's hard to believe they were needed to retrieve the knife. I struggle to imagine why they would take the clippers with them on a trip downstairs at all.

'But now, with the suspect list whittled down to just these two, the fact of the clippers being taken is even more bizarre. Why? Because there are other nail clippers here in the Ark. And Ryuhei and Mai both knew about them.

'There are some in the machinery room desk drawer. Mai and Ryuhei both saw them the first night we came here. Isn't that right?'

I remembered it myself. When Yuya, Hana and Sayaka went out trying to get phone reception, the two of them had been with us.

When he was sure that Mai and Ryuhei weren't going to deny it, Shotaro continued.

'If they just needed clippers, those would have done. There was no need to sneak into our room and take Yuya's.

'In which case, I could only think of one possible reason for the murderer to take the clippers with them downstairs. To get rid of them.'

'Get rid of them?!' I repeated after him, my voice sounding hysterical even to myself.

'That's right. The murderer took the nail clippers to throw them away. And since they had taken the clippers from Yuya's daypack in secret, disposing of them somewhere on the upper floor would lead to unwanted questions if they were ever found.

'In which case, dropping them somewhere on the middle floor would be best, right? It's flooded down there, so the killer wouldn't have to worry about them being discovered. It would be the simplest and surest way.

'But then they were surprised by Mr Yazaki hiding under the water, and they were forced into an unexpected murder. They forgot about dropping the clippers in the panic. And that's why they ended up with the waders. The murderer had only brought the clippers along to get rid of them in the first place.

'I assume that's what happened. At any rate, the murderer did not take the clippers to use them, that's for sure.'

'Then why take the clippers from the daypack in the first place?' I asked.

'Given that I can see no reason why they might have needed the clippers, the only conclusion is that they needed something else,' Shotaro said, and reaching over to the table, picked up the resealable bag.

'They needed the bag?' I asked.

'Right. This is what the murderer was after. I'll go even further. Only one of the two suspects needed it, and that person is our murderer.

'Can anyone think of a reason that the murderer might have needed this bag on the middle floor?

'It wasn't to hold the knife. The bag is too small for that. And for that purpose they could have used bin liners, or even the folded-up shopping bag from Yuya's pack. But the murderer didn't need a bag like that. It had to be a resealable bag.

'And there is only one conceivable reason to need such a bag down on the middle floor. It's not difficult to imagine, either. I think anyone could guess it.'

That was easy for Shotaro to say, but none of the rest of us offered an answer. Could no one actually think of the reason, or were they afraid that saying it out loud might invite accusations of guilt?

I myself was stumped. Shotaro, seeing right through my expression, said to me, 'Think back on the video that Mr Yazaki recorded. Do you remember? The murderer came into the storeroom using a light. What light was that?'

'Oh! Right! I get it. A smartphone!'

'Right.'

Yazaki's video had shown the murderer come into the room using the LED light on their phone.

'The murderer used their phone to light their way, but did they carry it exposed in their hand? Surely not.

'They were wading through water that was splashing up nearly to their waist. They could easily have dropped the phone. And life without a usable phone down here would be so much worse. So, the murderer would have wanted to prepare for that risk.

'And that is why they used one of Yuya's resealable bags. A bin liner or shopping bag wouldn't have served for a smartphone guard. They're too large and would have made it impossible to use the phone. The nail clippers were just a useless tagalong.'

I seemed to recall hearing somewhere about people putting their phones in resealable bags like that to use them in the bath.

Shotaro's voice had a decisive note when he went on.

'The murderer took the bag for their phone. They worried that keeping it might seem incriminating, so they left the bag and the clippers it had held at the scene. Does anyone have any problems with this conclusion?'

No one spoke up. Ryuhei looked like he might have an objection but seemed to be struggling to put it into words.

And finally, Shotaro was ready to get to the heart of things.

'Now, if we accept all of that, it is easy to pin down the murderer's identity. They required a resealable bag to protect their smartphone. Which means their smartphone is not waterproof. Ryuhei, Mai, please show us your phones.'

For the first time, the pair at the centre of our circle looked at each other.

The two of them, as if in perfect sync, reached solemnly into their pockets. They took out their phones.

I didn't need to look. I knew. Just after the earthquake, in the winch room down on the middle floor, we'd gone to check the rising water levels. Ryuhei had dropped his phone into the water. It had been fine afterwards.

Later, Mai and I had gone down to the flooding middle floor. When we were walking down the darkened corridor, I had offered to light the way with my phone. Mai had snuggled up against me and didn't even try to take out her own. She'd been worried about dropping it into the water, hadn't she?

Shotaro took both phones and turned them off. He opened the SIM slot. You could tell a waterproofed phone by a rubber gasket to seal it against water.

He passed the phones to everyone.

When we had all checked, Shotaro announced his judgment.

'The waterproof phone is Ryuhei's. Mai's does not have any waterproofing.'

I felt dizzy, like I'd just given too much blood. My vision went dark. I couldn't see my own feet.

'No. It can't be. This is a frame job.' I was surprised that Ryuhei was the first to object.

Shotaro brushed him aside.

'Let me say, just as with the second murder, there's no conceivable way someone faked this evidence. It's unrealistic to think someone would leave that resealable bag with the waders just to incriminate someone who didn't have a waterproofed phone. And the murder was spontaneous. The murderer hadn't planned for it to happen.

'Well, Mai. We have identified the murderer. If you have anything to say, I'd like to hear it,' Shotaro prompted.

Mai looked down at her feet as she answered,

'No. Nothing. You're right. I killed Yuya, Sayaka and Mr Yazaki.'

V

Ryuhei was freed of suspicion, and Mai stood alone in the centre of the circle.

Everyone glared at her with trembling eyes.

Mai's actions had gone so far beyond our understanding, it was like we'd caught a crash-landed alien. But even without understanding, we closed in around Mai as if to keep her from escaping.

It felt like being faced with a monster beyond the reach of human speech. Only Shotaro remained unchanged as he spoke, his voice calm.

'Mai, there's a lot we need to discuss, but before all that, I want to clarify one thing. The motive. I'd like you to tell us yourself.'

Mai raised her eyebrows slightly.

'If you know, I'd prefer if you did it. I think you're better at explaining things clearly. I'm not very good at speaking,' she said.

'Well then. I'll say what I think. If I get anything wrong, please correct me.'

The motive was the final mystery.

Now that I knew Mai was the murderer, a thought was blooming, like a terrible premonition.

Was I right? Shotaro seemed half-hearted as he began to speak.

'The motive puzzle really only applies to the first murder. We already know that the second and third were done to keep from being caught. Of course, there was probably more to them than that.

'But Yuya's murder was truly incomprehensible. Ten people were trapped underground by an unpredicted earthquake. One person would have to be chosen as sacrifice for the rest to escape. And under those circumstances, someone committed a murder.

'It was, clearly, not a murder of vengeance. It was not done for money. And above all, why do it at that time? There must have been some reason that she had to kill then. What could that be? Mai grasped the trap we were in before anyone else and decided to kill.

'I think this must be the only possible reason. When we found Yuya's corpse, we all immediately decided to start looking for the murderer and force them to stay behind, didn't we? And I think the goal of the murder was to create exactly that situation.

'In other words, she committed murder to set everyone on the path to forcing the murderer into the worst imaginable fate and at the same time, was hoping she could frame someone she hated for it. That was Mai's plan.'

Frame someone she hated? And who would that be?

Ryuhei had begun trembling, like Shotaro's words had pierced him through. He stared at his wife as if unable to believe it was the same Mai he had known.

Ryuhei had just been trying to cover for Mai. As bad as their relationship had got, no one would find it easy to accept that the person they married could be a murderer.

But now it was proven. And beyond that, her end goal had been to sentence Ryuhei himself to a horrific, inescapable death.

Mai said nothing. It seemed she had no complaints about what Shotaro was saying.

He went on.

'So, then, how could she go about framing Ryuhei? She would have to plant fake evidence.

'That would be the knife she stabbed into Sayaka's chest.

'With Yuya's murder, she hadn't had time to create any false evidence, because she had to leave the scene of the crime immediately after killing him. We suffered from the lack of evidence left in the first murder ourselves, but it turns out that Mai, the murderer herself, did as well.

'And that is why she also stabbed a knife into Sayaka's chest after killing her, and then hid it under the shelf. She was going to plant it in Ryuhei's things when the time was right.

'Under normal circumstances, such a childish plan could never get anyone convicted for murder. But things here are different. We have a time limit. We have to choose someone to stay behind.

'So, let's imagine that time is starting to run out with no clues revealed, and suddenly we discover a bloody knife in someone's things. What would we have done?

'We might well have decided immediately that whoever held the knife was guilty, denounced him, ganged up on him and forced him to operate the winch.'

Shotaro's deductions were possibly all that stood between us and chaos. If he hadn't been able to work out the identity of the murderer, we might well have been torturing Ryuhei at that very moment.

'That plan would only work at the very last minute. She had to wait until we were near panic and had lost hold of our better judgment.

'That is why she hid the weapon. She had to wait for a good opportunity. But Mr Yazaki found it before that time came.

'And so, Mai ended up killing him.

'Mai, I don't have anything else to add about motive. Would you like to make a statement?'

'No.'

'I see. There is something I wanted to ask. What actually was the evidence left on Sayaka's phone?'

For the first time, Mai seemed to struggle to respond. Finally, she said, 'Well, the truth is, Sayaka had a picture that showed the rope I used to strangle Yuya. The evening of the day we came here, Sayaka went around taking pictures, right?

'She didn't realize that one of her pictures showed the rope, though. It was in a room that I had searched when we were looking for the hex key, and no one else had been in there. So, if anyone ever went through her pictures carefully, I thought they might realize that I was the only one who could have found the rope.'

'Ah, I see.'

Shotaro didn't seem all that interested, though, despite being the one who asked.

No one else much cared, either. Now that we knew who the murderer was, there was something else we had to take care of that was weighing on all our minds.

Shotaro started intently at Mai, still in the centre of our circle.

'Well, I think it's time we talked about the job of staying behind.'

VI

We stared at Mai like a captured lion in a cage.

No one spoke to her. We could not read her thoughts from her expression.

'She's got to die,' Hayato blurted out.

Hiroko rushed to cover her son's mouth.

'That's right,' Mai answered Hayato in a gentle voice, like she would to a nursery school child.

A shock ran through my brain, like the path of a bullet. I was struggling to bring myself to face the truth, that Mai was a murderer.

I reflected on the fanciful thoughts I'd had just a few hours ago.

While we were waiting for Mr Yazaki's phone to be unlocked, I had wondered, who did I want to be the murderer? And who would accept being left behind if they were the murderer?

I had wanted, I had prayed, for it to be Ryuhei that stayed behind as the murderer. And Mai had wanted that, too. And, in trying to make that hope a reality, she'd made these terrible mistakes. Had this been what I had actually wanted? I felt myself falling into delusion, that I had made these murders happen because of my own desires.

No one knew how to deal with Mai, now.

Should we try to convince her with words? Or would we try to torture her?

Now that we had the murderer here, in front of us, though, we seemed to have lost all our nerve. All we could do was hope that she would somehow say, of her own free will, that she would sacrifice herself for us.

It was Shotaro who broke the silence.

'Mai, you committed these crimes with forethought. You must have known this might happen. What were you planning to do if it did?'

She shrugged and said, 'I didn't work out a plan just to imagine it failing.'

I still couldn't tell what was actually going on behind her eyes.

She was a cold-blooded, vicious murderer. But forcing her to stay behind was no different than killing her ourselves. Did we have the courage to go through with it? We each had to be asking ourselves the same question.

Finally, Hiroko put an arm around her son's shoulder, and said to Mai, 'Please. Save us. This boy is only fifteen years old.'

Hana joined her.

'Mai… Please. Can't you do this? You're the only one who can.'

Then came Ryuhei, his voice gentler than I had ever heard it. 'I'm begging you, Mai. Help.'

Mai stared, mystified, at the three people pleading with her.

Shotaro added his argument, sounding like a teacher lecturing a disobedient student, 'Mai, I believe that you are as capable as anyone of remaining reasonable under extreme circumstances.'

It was an odd sight.

The Yazakis had lost a family member to brutal murder. Ryuhei had been the target of a frame job that would have sentenced him to a horrible death. And these people were pleading with the culprit for salvation.

They were choosing their words carefully. They didn't want to anger her, and more than anything, did not want to touch on the fact that their pleas would lead her to her death. Even when we looked back on this moment after escaping to the surface, no one would want to think that they had been responsible for someone dying.

I could not say anything. There was something repulsive about the sight of them begging Mai like that.

It might be that by trying to get away with being the only one not only asking her to die, I was actually much more of a coward than they. But if I said it, too, that would mean all of us were openly hoping for Mai's death.

And would that be right? I thought back on the conversation I'd had with Mai, on those flooded stairs, about a death game for the least loved. And here was Mai, everyone hoping for her death, clearly unloved by all, with our lives thrown at her feet. Who could believe she would save us? Was I the only one who couldn't plead for her to die?

Was Mai truly the killer? I couldn't fault Shotaro's deductions. But in my eyes, the brutality of the crimes simply didn't fit the Mai I knew.

It almost felt like she was waiting for me to speak.

But, as if giving up, she finally smiled gently and said, 'Sure. I honestly knew it would come to this. Fine. I'll pull the rock down. It's the best solution, isn't it?'

Who, if they were the murderer, could be convinced to stay behind without needing to be forced?

Clearly, that would be Mai. Which is what I had thought all along. And I had been right.

VII

We had around nine hours left.

We gave that time to Mai. Everyone helped her get ready. Ready for her final hours after pulling the rock down.

Yuya's power bank, resealable bags and such, all went to Mai. Shotaro gave her the paperbacks he'd brought. Everyone gave her anything they thought might be useful.

Hana handed her that half-eaten packet of gummies and said, her voice shaking, 'Would you like these? You can have them.'

'Thanks. That would be nice.'

Mai glanced at the package label and took the offered gummies.

She would live out her final moments with these gifts. Waiting in that cave-like room for the chill water to rise and drown her. How long would it take? Might she possibly suffocate before she drowned?

Shotaro went to check the water level of the middle floor. When he came back, he said it looked like the water was rising faster than before, although not so much that we'd have to bring the time limit forward.

He didn't tell Mai that.

Mai was waiting for the time to come, charging her smartphone and the power bank.

From here, she looked relaxed. She sat on one of the dining room chairs, flipping through the paperback travelogue Shotaro had given her.

Everyone watched her from a distance. Like they were afraid of getting too close, afraid she might attack them.

It also seemed like the rest of the group were trying to keep me away from her. They made sure the two of us had no chance of being alone together. They must have been worried I might talk her out of it.

I had the feeling Mai was waiting for me in those remaining hours. I didn't know what to say to her, though. It felt to me that if I added my voice to the others, if I said anything at all, it would be the same as accepting her fate. As abandoning her to die.

When we had about two hours left, Shotaro spoke quietly to Mai.

'Mai, it's about time.'

'Right.'

Mai got up from the long table.

She had looked so calm, but now she appeared to be trembling in fear. She shouldered her tiny backpack and walked down the corridor, taking each step slowly and deliberately.

Before she went down the stairs, she said she wanted to go to the machinery room.

She turned on the monitors and looked at the scenery outside.

The feeds from the exits showed, of course, that nothing had changed on the surface.

Mai looked for a few seconds.

'Right then, let's get going,' she said with what sounded like satisfaction. 'We shouldn't leave it too long.'

We went to the stairwell.

The water on the middle floor had risen to about the height of my navel.

Mai put on the waders as we watched. She went down the stairs until the water rose to her knees, then turned back.

'I'm fine from here. Don't worry. I'll do what needs to be done,' she told us as we looked on.

We all averted our eyes. There would be no final farewells called out to her. I felt a vague sense of guilt. There was no mistaking that she had taken the lives of three people. There was also no mistaking that she was now willing to give her life for us.

I recalled the thing she had said to me on the stairs that night, like an embarrassed confession, 'I want to get back alive.

No matter what.' What she had actually been trying to say was, only if it meant her life after would be with me.

Suddenly, an idea bloomed in my mind that I could not shake off.

What would happen if I said I would stay behind with Mai? What would she say?

The idea of living the rest of my life without knowing the answer to that question seemed unbearable.

And if she would have me, what would it be like to spend the remaining hours of my life with her in that room?

I was sure that nothing in the rest of my existence up above would compare to those hours.

I would never have another chance to say it. And there was no other way to avoid being complicit in Mai's death. Staying with her was the only way for me to escape that sin.

My gaze met Mai's as she stood at the bottom of the stairs.

My whole body felt hot. The conflict ran through me.

It was the thought of the view through those cameras just a few minutes before that stopped me.

I would soon be out on the surface. Could anything be worth more than that?

Finally, I spoke to Mai.

'Well, goodbye.'

She nodded, as if she'd expected it, and answered, 'Right. I'm off.'

Mai turned her back on us all and waded down the corridor into darkness.

EPILOGUE

After watching Mai leave, the six of us went back up the corridor to wait in front of the steel door for her to turn the winch.

We kept as quiet as we could. It was almost like we didn't want her to notice us leaving.

Finally, from the other side of the door, we heard the sound of stone grating against metal as the boulder began to slide.

Mai was trading her life for ours.

It seemed to be going well. Even through the steel door, we could feel the boulder moving little by little.

Any minute now. Mai would lose all chance of turning back.

Even when we were out, we wouldn't be able to help her. We would have to think about how to get past the landslide and off the mountain. And that whole time, the water would be rising, and Mai would be dying.

On the other side of the door, the sound stopped.

And suddenly, the phone in my pocket stared vibrating.

I checked the screen. It was the walkie-talkie app. Mai's phone was requesting a connection.

I had thought I'd never get to talk to her again. It was like getting a call from a ghost. I felt a slight chill.

I had to answer. Everyone watched me as I tapped the 'Connect' button on my screen.

'Shuichi, can you hear me?'

'Yeah, it's me.'

The connection was poor, coming up through all the steel between us. But I could make out Mai's voice.

'Oh, good. I think the rock should come all the way through with just a little more pulling. There was something I wanted to tell you before the very end.'

What could it be, after everything that had happened?

Everyone was staring at me in confusion. I let them know that Mai wanted to talk and ducked into room 102.

What could be left to say after that final parting?

When I told her I was alone, she went on, saying, 'The thing is, Shotaro made one mistake in his deduction. I wanted you to know the truth.'

'A mistake? Shotaro made a mistake?'

What had he missed in his reasoning? And if he had been wrong, why hadn't Mai said anything?

I had a terrifying thought that I couldn't keep silent.

'You can't mean… Mai, are you innocent?'

'No, not that. I killed them all. No mistake there. The mistake was about my motive.'

'Your… motive? You didn't want to frame Ryuhei for everything?'

'No, I didn't.'

'Um. Well, why did you do it? This is ridiculous. You could have done something else and not had to die—'

'No, no, you've got it all wrong. It's so complicated. I guess I should just say it straight out. I'm not the one who's going to die down here. You all are.'

I jerked the phone from my ear by reflex.

Mai wasn't going to die here. We were.

That's what she had said. I hadn't misheard it.

She sounded so calm. Not like someone who'd lost her mind in fear. Not like someone making up a desperate lie. Like someone who was simply stating a fact.

'How are we going to die, and you not?'

'Right, I suppose I should explain. So, you know those video feeds in the machinery room? The ones hooked into the monitors? The monitors are labelled "Entrance" and "Emergency Exit".'

'Yeah…'

'You went to check them after the earthquake, while everyone was searching for the hex key, right? That's when you realized there had been a landslide on the surface. There was nothing out of the ordinary on the entrance monitor, but the emergency exit had been completely buried.'

'…Right.'

'And then we all knew that even if anyone got out onto the surface, we couldn't get help in time, so whoever stayed behind would have to die. But what if, before you realized all that, someone had switched the feeds on those monitors? So, the entrance monitor was actually showing the emergency exit, and the emergency exit monitor was showing the entrance?'

A wave of dizziness swept over me and the world spun. I squatted low, afraid of falling over.

'You mean… It's not the emergency exit that was buried in the landslide, but the entrance?'

'Right. Even when I pull this rock down, you won't be able to get out. The hatch is buried under a landslide.

'The only way out of here is using diving equipment to leave through the flooded bottom floor and out of the unburied emergency exit.

'I saw the monitors before anyone else, and I realized it right away. That's why I switched the feeds. Because there were only a couple of masks and tanks. If everyone knew, we'd have got into a fight to the death over them.

'Even if the bridge wasn't down, the earthquake could have blocked the trail down. Even if someone escaped with the diving tanks right away, there was no telling if they could have brought help for the rest of us in time. We didn't even know how much time we had at that point. Anyway, I had to do it.'

Mai had checked the monitors before I had. Switching the feeds would have been easy. It was just changing two cables.

And in doing so, Mai had kept to herself the fact that escape would require the diving equipment. And she'd also let everyone convince themselves that they would have to sacrifice the murderer to escape.

'Those monitors had both just showed meadows on the surface, so you couldn't tell them apart, could you? And it was already near dark when we came, so we'd never actually seen the places in the light. No one even looked at the monitors during the day until the earthquake, either.

'So, I didn't have to worry about anyone noticing that I'd switched the feeds.

'Except for Yuya. He'd been here before, so he'd probably had a good look around the two hatches. I thought that if he checked the monitors, he was the only one who might notice the switch.'

'That's why you killed Yuya?'

'Yeah, mostly. There was one other reason, though. If there weren't a murderer, we'd have ended up deciding the person to leave behind by drawing lots, wouldn't we?

'And that might not have worked out for me. If I lost, it wouldn't be me on the other side when the rock fell, meaning the only one able to get out. But, I couldn't say that, could I?

'That's why I had to kill someone. If I got everyone hunting for a murderer, we wouldn't drop the rock until we found one. It would buy me time.

'I needed that time, too, because I couldn't use the diving tanks as they were.'

I'd discussed that with Shotaro when we were talking about diving to retrieve Sayaka's head from the bottom floor. The diving equipment did not include a harness to hold the tanks, so no one could dive without some kind of replacement.

Mai had had the same problem. She would have had to make a harness herself to escape.

'So, what about Sayaka? Why did you kill her? It was to hide the first crime, wasn't—'

'What? No. That whole story about a picture on her phone showing where the rope came from was all made up. How could anyone prove I was the only one who went in or out of that room? And I couldn't have checked her phone, anyway, could I?

'But it is true that there are photos in her phone I absolutely didn't want anyone to see.

'You remember after the whole potato crisp thing when we all gathered in the dining room to talk? Sayaka said that Yuya had sent her pictures of this place when he'd come before. And that there were pictures of the entrance and emergency exit hatches in there.

'Sayaka hadn't noticed, but I'd be in trouble if she compared those photos to the monitors. There might be clues to show the switch, like the location of the trees or something.'

So Mai had felt that keeping anyone from noticing her trick with the video feeds was more important than hiding her guilt.

That reminded me of how, back when the Yazaki family revealed that they had some connection to the cult that had used the Ark, Mai had been oddly insistent in asking how much they knew about the building. That must have been because she was worried they might cotton on to what she'd done with the monitors.

'Then there's the knife. I wasn't planning on framing anyone with that. That was going to be my proof that I was the murderer.

'If no one managed to figure it out, everyone would start panicking and things would get chaotic, I figured. If that happened, no one might get out at all.

'I thought that if things really got out of control, I would confess to being the murderer. It wouldn't work without proof, though, right? Even if I volunteered to operate the winch, I imagined you and Ryuhei would try to stop me.

'That's why I hid the knife. Just in case, you know. I could say there was proof behind that shelf.

'It looks like it didn't matter, though, in the end. Mr Yazaki found it first.'

There was something about that I didn't understand.

'But, if that's the case, then why did you go to the storeroom where you killed Yazaki?'

If she was just wanting to prove she was the murderer, all she needed to do was tell us where the weapon was. There was no need to retrieve it.

'It was for the harness. I used rope and a bunch of things to make sure it would hold the tank fast. But I wanted to get some wire to make it stronger. When I went to the storeroom to get some, though, I found him waiting.

'It's not like I actually touched the knife or anything, so there was still no evidence I was the murderer. But I had to kill him.

'He was using an oxygen tank. If I didn't kill him, he might use up air I needed to escape. The tank didn't have much left in the first place.'

I had had trouble fitting these murders with the Mai I knew. But now I could see how it all worked in her mind. It was no longer a mystery. This Ark had given Mai permission to kill.

She had decided that she could kill any one of us. Because, in her mind, we were already dead.

Strangling Yuya and Sayaka, stabbing Mr Yazaki, it was fine. They were dead anyway. In fact, those quick deaths might almost be a blessing. Compared to the fate awaiting the six of us…

Among us all, Mai alone had received this revelation.

Her calm voice still came through the phone.

'It was hard to make the harness, you know. I had to keep it secret from everyone. I wove rope into a net in my room, and I had to hide it whenever it sounded like someone was coming. And I had to make it good and strong to make sure it wouldn't break.

'When I was done, I hid it on the middle floor. Just after I found Mr Yazaki in the storeroom. The flooding made it easy.'

'And you know what else, Shuichi?'

Mai went quiet, like she was waiting for a reply. Like she was making sure I was listening.

I forced one out. 'What?'

'The truth is, I made two. One for you. Cause there were two tanks and regulators. I thought maybe you'd say you wanted to stay behind with me, and then we could both use one to escape. But, it didn't work out that way. It's too bad, but there it is.'

Of course. She had been waiting for me. If I'd gone with Mai at the stairs... I'd have been saved.

But how could I ever do that? The urge to scream that denial fought in my heart with the desire to beg, to say 'Please, let me come now.' I knew, though, that both were equally meaningless.

This time, I did fall to the floor. I was near to fainting.

Over the phone, I heard her throw my own words back at me.

'Well, goodbye.'

She cut the connection.

I lay on the floor, breathless, my brain spinning like someone falling from a sheer cliff.

Trapped forever, I could only wait for the water to rise. I would die.

I heard the crash of the boulder falling through to the middle floor.

There was a shaking, nearly as great as the earthquake. But it was all happening in the distance.

I could hear voices in the corridor. Everyone rushed through the door, heading for the exit.

It was pointless. The hatch would never open.

In that instant, the world around me went pitch black.

The time limit was up. The generator had stopped.

And a few seconds later, I heard the sound of five people crying out in despair.

AVAILABLE AND COMING SOON FROM PUSHKIN VERTIGO

Jonathan Ames
You Were Never Really Here
A Man Named Doll
The Wheel of Doll

Simone Campos
Nothing Can Hurt You Now

Zijin Chen
Bad Kids

Maxine Mei-Fung Chung
The Eighth Girl

Candas Jane Dorsey
The Adventures of Isabel
What's the Matter with Mary Jane?

Margot Douaihy
Scorched Grace

Joey Hartstone
The Local

Seraina Kobler
Deep Dark Blue

Elizabeth Little
Pretty as a Picture

Jack Lutz
London in Black

Steven Maxwell
All Was Lost

Callum McSorley
Squeaky Clean

Louise Mey
The Second Woman

John Kåre Raake
The Ice

RV Raman
A Will to Kill
Grave Intentions
Praying Mantis

Paula Rodríguez
Urgent Matters

Nilanjana Roy
Black River

John Vercher
Three-Fifths
After the Lights Go Out

Emma Viskic
Resurrection Bay
And Fire Came Down
Darkness for Light
Those Who Perish

Yulia Yakovleva
Punishment of a Hunter
Death of the Red Rider